MURDER OF A DOCTOR

A gripping mystery based in the Midlands

TONY BASSETT

Published by The Book Folks

London, 2022

© Tony Bassett

This book is a work of fiction. Names, characters, businesses, organizations, places and events are either the product of the author's imagination or are used fictitiously. Any resemblance to actual persons, living or dead, events or locales is entirely coincidental.

All rights reserved. No part of this publication may be reproduced, stored in retrieval system, copied in any form or by any means, electronic, mechanical, photocopying, recording or otherwise transmitted without written permission from the publisher.

ISBN 978-1-80462-005-2

www.thebookfolks.com

Murder of a Doctor is the third standalone title in a series of mysteries set in the Midlands. Details about the other books can be found at the back of this one.

Chapter 1

Scott Deeley drew back the heavy oak door of his mother's thatched cottage and peered out. The lane was shrouded in a silvery mist which masked the sun's rays and threatened another cold, autumn morning. Sadly, for him, it would prove to be his last.

Scott, who was dressed in a light-blue sweatshirt and matching tracksuit bottoms for his morning run, knelt down briefly in the gloom of the antiquated hallway to slip on his running shoes.

He flicked through the opened envelopes still on the hall table from the previous day. They were mainly final bills he'd been expecting after the sale of his seaside house. One letter was a reminder to re-tax his thirteen-year-old Morgan Plus Four. He had managed to make space for his prized sports car in his mother's cluttered, ramshackle garage.

Another letter was from a tenant, complaining about a damp problem. He would attend to them all later in the day, he thought.

Scott paused as he stood by the door, listening for any sound to suggest his aged mother was awake. At first, the house was silent, apart from the steady ticking of the mantel clock, echoing round the cottage. Then he detected a creaking noise from her bedroom. A sign that she was stirring.

'Are you all right, Mother?' he yelled while ensuring his door keys were safely tucked inside the running belt he wore beneath his shirt.

'Yes, dear,' she called back.

'I'm just going for a run. I'll be back in about an hour to sort you out.'

'All right, dear. Don't worry about me.'

He examined himself in the ornate hallway mirror. A small, clump of his greying hair was out of place. Once this had been rearranged with a sweep of his right hand, he slipped out of the cottage door, quietly closing it behind him, and strode to the front gate.

The dawn air was filled with birdsong and his senses were regaled by the delicate fragrance of the pale, yellow honeysuckle that climbed round the porch and the red and white rose bushes on parade beside the stone path.

Scott turned left out of the cottage gate and bounded along the narrow lane like a greyhound sprung from its trap. He passed St Michael's Church and the Old Bakery, a house belonging to friends of his mother's who now ran a thriving bed-and-breakfast business. Then he turned left again into the main street.

It had just turned eight o'clock. Two paperboys with bags round their necks were arriving back at the newsagent's after their rounds. Next door, some early risers were tucking into their fried breakfasts at the only cafe in the village. As he approached, a man in dark clothing came out and collected a bicycle that had been propped up against a side wall.

While maintaining his constant rhythm, Scott broke into a smile as he saw a mother duck leading her newly hatched offspring on an early morning swim at the edge of the village pond. Then he turned left for a third time and set off towards the woods at Foxwell Heath. If he had looked back, he would have noticed the cyclist had left the cafe and was travelling in the same direction.

As the sun finally emerged through the haze, his mind was filled with thoughts of his mother's impending eighty-fourth birthday on 28 October. What could he buy her? A book was out of the question as her eyesight was rapidly fading. She struggled to manoeuvre her way round her home because of the pain in her legs, and spent most of the day watching television.

Perhaps a gift for the home? Yes, that was the answer. A vase, an ornament, an antique lamp – something of that order, he thought. He would drive into Queensbridge later that day. There was a gift shop called Keepsakes opposite the supermarket in the high street. He would browse for a suitable gift and a birthday card.

A scraping sound disturbed the peaceful morning. Without reducing his pace, he glanced back. A man with a bicycle a hundred metres behind had stopped on the pavement and dismounted. He seemed to be having a problem with his back wheel.

Within a few minutes, Scott was moving at a steady pace towards the west, running along a footpath at the edge of a ploughed field. He gazed across the rich, brown earth of the farmer's land, where new crops had been sown, and then, as he sprinted past a public footpath sign, he entered the wood.

The terrain was at once cooler and more shaded. On he ran along his familiar route close to the fields, following a makeshift path. He passed dozens of trees before coming to a woodland glade where, for some reason, several oak and birch trees had been cut down and removed. Here, there were signs of a disused campsite – the charred remains of a fire along with black plastic sheeting and blackened utensils, which had been discarded haphazardly among the ash and cinders.

After a while, he lost sight of the field and, on his right, beyond the continuous line of trees, he could glimpse the main road, known as Heath Road, which ran parallel to the woodland path.

Scott was an observant man with a keen mind. He noticed a white Ford Transit van with its two nearside tyres parked on the pavement, close to the trees and bushes. A petrol station stood immediately across the road. The fine mist was clouding his vision, but he could just distinguish a man in a white baseball cap who was sitting in the driver's seat. He appeared to glare at Scott as he sprinted past.

Eventually, the runner found himself approaching the village of Foxwell Green, which lay two and a half miles from his home in Sinton Bank. He circled the grassy village green, peering through the windows of the Cricketers Arms public house as he went. Then he jogged down a lane leading to the church and dashed past the village shop before returning to the main road and re-entering the woods.

He had managed a steady pace for five minutes when he noticed a man ahead of him behaving oddly. The stranger, wearing dark clothing, was using a stick to poke about in a pile of dead leaves. He had a bundle of black sacks with him and a spade. Perhaps he was gathering leaf mould, Scott thought. The man turned to acknowledge him.

'Hello!'

'Good morning!' Scott yelled back as he sprinted past.

When his homeward journey brought him close to the roadside again, he noticed a grey Mini Hatch pull in. Its driver, an elderly, grey-haired man, parked his vehicle partly on the pavement and turned the engine off. Then the motorist sat and watched as Scott swept by. The white van was still parked opposite the filling station, but now the cab was empty.

Soon he found himself running close to the open field again. Just as he neared the abandoned campsite for the second time that day, he spotted a man whose sudden appearance filled him with dread. Could it be the same man who'd once threatened to kill him?

As he drew closer, his worst fears were confirmed. It was the last person on earth he wanted to see… and, fatefully, it was.

Chapter 2

Howard Cooper was following the main woodland path out of the woods when his inquisitive golden retriever veered off to the right and manoeuvred her way through some dense undergrowth. She stopped still beside some bracken, barking excitedly.

He became annoyed. 'Bella! Bella!' he called out loudly.

The barking caught the attention of two women twenty metres away who were walking towards him. Their own small dog, a black and tan cocker spaniel, ran on ahead of them. It followed the retriever into the bushes.

Howard, a tall, middle-aged man, was frustrated by his pet's refusal to heed his command. Without giving the women a glance, he waded through the bushes in pursuit of Bella.

He succeeded in grabbing her collar and pulling her away from a pile of dead leaves, nettles and bracken. A running shoe lay among the foliage. A blue trouser leg was also visible.

The two women behind him had left their woodland track and caught up with Howard, who had stopped still.

'Whatever's the matter?' yelled the younger woman, who was swinging a dog chain. She peered into the thicket and screamed. 'There's a body in there,' she gasped. She backed away and started to cry. The other woman rushed to comfort her.

It was clear that, lying here, partly obscured by greenery, was the corpse of a man. He was lying on his back with his legs close together. Beneath his wavy hair, his blue eyes, staring up at the sky, were open and lifeless. A metal object was protruding from his blood-splattered shirt.

'Alisha, get hold of the dog. Come away, Harley!' the older woman cried.

The younger woman put Harley on his chain before turning to Howard, who had a shocked expression.

'Do you think we should take a closer look – just to make sure the fellow's dead?' she said.

'I don't mind doing that,' he replied.

He stepped back among the bushes and brambles. He tapped the corpse twice with the toe of his right foot. There was no movement. He kicked at it more forcibly. The body jerked freely from side to side in rhythm with his shoe. Then he stopped prodding and the body fell back, motionless.

'Yes, he's dead,' he informed them. 'Poor bastard.'

'Oh my God!' said Alisha. 'Are you all right?'

'A bit shaken,' he admitted as he shook his head and looked down at the leafy ground. 'I'll be fine in a minute. It's just that it's bringing back memories of my poor old brother when he passed away. You don't expect to go for a little walk and find some poor fellow like that, do you?'

Then he added, 'We'd better call the police. Have either of you got a phone? I've left mine at home.'

Alisha produced a small, black handset.

'There's no signal here but I think it'll work in the car park. Shall we–?'

'Yes. Let's try in the car park. There's bound to be a signal there,' he said. 'I'm Howard, by the way.'

'I'm Alisha. And this is my mother Fariza.'

As they trudged along the main pathway, one of the women took some tissues from a pocket and they both dabbed their eyes. Bella and Harley sniffed each other out of canine curiosity. The mutual interest quickly waned. The retriever had no wish to befriend the boisterous spaniel and rushed ahead with the smaller dog close on her tail.

'I think I'd better put mine on her lead. Bella! Bella!' Howard called.

This time his pet obediently scurried to his side. He clipped on the lead and walked determinedly back towards the car park, keeping a few paces behind the women.

The sun was at last peeking through the tops of the trees. It promised to be a warmer day than Howard had expected. He took off his lightweight jacket and undid the top two buttons on his shirt.

'Do you often walk your dog here?' he asked the two women as they approached the parking area.

'No,' replied Fariza. 'My husband usually brings him.'

'We run kennels and I sometimes bring two.'

'How lovely.'

'I haven't been here for a while,' he admitted as they emerged with their dogs in the bright daylight.

He gazed slowly around. There were more vehicles now – a black, mud-splattered Volkswagen Golf; a red Vauxhall Corsa; a smart blue Volvo XC90; and a grubby, white Toyota van. There was also a grimy, black and white Honda motorbike, which he studied for a few seconds.

The two women waited patiently for Howard as he carefully opened the tailgate of his Ford Focus Estate and helped Bella inside. He removed his black leather gloves and placed them inside the car before walking back to them.

'Do you want to speak to the police?' asked Alisha while brushing a piece of bracken off her denim jacket. 'I'm not very good with things like this. I'll dial it for you.'

As soon as the emergency number rang out, she passed the handset to Howard. After explaining they'd found a body at Foxwell Heath in North Warwickshire, he told an officer in the control room at police headquarters he was in the Yeoman's Lane car park and that the body was a few hundred metres away.

'And you're sure the person's dead?'

'I prodded the body and there was no life,' said Howard in a calm, cultured voice as the women gazed at him.

'OK, sir. A team's on the way. Is it a man or woman and how did you come across the body?'

'I think it's a man. I was just walking my dog and we noticed it in the bushes just a few metres to the left of the main path.'

'You didn't check the pulse?'

'No. I wouldn't really know how to. He was definitely dead.'

'Must have been a bit of a shock. What time did you find the body?'

Howard called out to the women, 'What time did we find the body? Nine fifteen?'

Fariza and Alisha both nodded.

'A quarter past nine,' Howard informed the officer while staring at the ground.

'So about ten minutes ago? All right. Your mobile number's come up here, but what's your name and address, please?'

Howard frowned. 'Well, this isn't my phone. I'm with two ladies who were also with me when I found the body.'

The officer took down all of their details before giving further direction.

'Sir, would you do me a small favour? Because it's in the woods, would you be kind enough to wait for the paramedics and first responders so you can show them the exact spot? It might save a bit of time.'

'Glad to help. I'll be sitting in my Ford Focus, if you want to tell whoever you send.'

'Right you are, sir. I know this is asking a lot, but could you discourage people from entering the woods until the police arrive? That would help tremendously.'

'I'll do my best.'

'Thank you. So, you're in the main car park in Yeoman's Lane, you say? Is there anyone else around?'

'Well, there's a few people – other dog walkers, mainly.'

'Perhaps I should speak to Miss Hamid now?' the officer suggested.

'Well, all right.' Howard passed the phone to Alisha. 'He wants to speak to you,' he said.

Alisha and her mother moved a few metres away to get a better signal. They quickly became engrossed in a conversation Howard was unable to overhear.

Just then a man in black motorcycle apparel, carrying a helmet, emerged from some bushes, started up his Honda and roared off up the road towards the nearby village.

A few minutes later, the three dog walkers took up position on the edge of the car park, ready to bar anyone from passing through the gap in the wooden fence that led to the woods. They chatted for a while in hushed voices as the spaniel continually strained on the lead to get away.

'What sort of age do you think the man was?' Fariza asked.

'Hard to tell,' replied Howard. 'Not a young man.'

'Could have been a tramp.'

'What did he look like – the dead man?' Alisha asked Howard.

'Oh Alisha!' said her mother. 'Fancy asking that.'

'I just wondered if he'd been beaten up and was covered with blood. That's all, Mum,' Alisha explained.

'There was a bit of blood.'

'The whole thing is a real shock, isn't it?' said Fariza.

'There's so much crime and violence on TV these days,' he said. 'You think something like this isn't going to affect you, but it does.'

They stood together quietly for a few moments. Howard was trying not to think about the dead man and the loved ones who would surely miss him. Then his attention was drawn towards Fariza. She was peering at someone.

He followed her line of sight. Her gaze was fixed on a man sitting in the driver's seat of the white van. He was staring directly towards them.

Fariza looked away. But the man in the van continued to stare at them.

Chapter 3

'Helen! Where are you?'

Chief Inspector Gavin Roscoe's voice echoed round the hallway of his family home before his wife yelled back from the living-room.

'I'm going to be late for work,' he moaned as he entered the room. 'Has Mel left for–' Then he stopped abruptly.

He was confronted by the unexpected sight of his blonde wife receiving a back and shoulder massage from her own mother. The older lady relaxed her hands when she noticed her son-in-law.

Carol Lloyd raised her arms and turned towards him.

'Oh, I wondered when we were going to see you,' she said.

'What brings you here on this rather overcast Monday morning?' he asked.

'Sorry, darling!' said Helen, rising in a towel. 'I didn't have a chance to tell you Mum was coming to help with my back.'

'I just wondered if Mel had left for college,' he continued.

'I think she left a while ago. Hey, you're going to be late yourself, aren't you?'

'I'm leaving now,' he replied, stepping into the hall to find his coat.

Carol called out, 'I've been talking to Helen about her father's retirement party.'

He returned to the doorway. 'So Dennis is finally giving up work? That's brilliant.'

Helen smiled. 'Yes. Sometime in the new year. They might want to hold it at the tearooms.'

Carol shrugged. 'Well, we're not sure. We also thought about the Crown and Sceptre in Queensbridge.'

Roscoe nodded. 'You'd have to look at their menus, but all their food comes from a frying pan.'

Helen interrupted to say, 'I'm sure that's not the case.'

'It is,' Roscoe insisted. 'Just go and see.'

'It's just amazing you've got Dad to give up work,' said Helen as she slipped on a blouse.

'Yes, I know,' said Carol. 'But it's time for him to put his feet up.'

'You both deserve some leisure time together,' said Roscoe.

She eyed him with the kind of disappointed look a mother might give her son after a poor exam result. 'Hard work's in his nature. It's the same with Helen. Unfortunately, others are often too ready to take advantage. I'll see myself out.'

Helen waved her goodbye through the leaded light windows.

'That was a little uncalled for,' said the chief inspector.

'What, darling?'

'Well, saying you and your father both work hard and others take advantage. That was obviously aimed at me.'

'Don't take it to heart, darling. She worries about me. That's all.'

Roscoe kissed Helen goodbye, slipped on his navy-blue coat and set off for the headquarters of Heart of England Police.

* * *

On arrival, the burly detective with ruddy cheeks and short grey hair strode up to the second floor and straightened his tie before knocking on Chief Superintendent Nicola Norris's door.

'Come in, Gavin!' she declared in a shrill voice.

The chief inspector murmured 'Morning, ma'am' as he strode across the beige carpet.

Norris, whose grey hair had been neatly combed back, was sitting in her wheelchair behind a large, oak desk, surrounded by photographs of police award ceremonies. She had been badly injured in a horse-riding accident and had lost use of her legs. She was due to retire at any moment.

She had the air of a harassed head teacher as she peered over the top of her reading glasses.

'Sit yourself down, Gavin. I've been meaning to ask how your lad's faring in Warwick?'

'George? He's loving every minute of the job,' said Roscoe, drawing up an office chair in front of her desk. 'He can't understand why he didn't join the force earlier. Now, you said it was important.'

'Yes. I called you in because one of these campaigning criminal justice lawyers has been stoking up some trouble. Giles somebody. It's come to the Assistant Chief Constable's attention, and he's asked us to prepare a report. There are claims that two men were "fitted up" and wrongly convicted. So we need to look into this ourselves and find out if there's any evidence at all of police wrongdoing,' she said.

'Gavin, this is a confidential assignment we've been entrusted with. Obviously, what I tell you now must be kept strictly private. There's a suggestion of a crooked cop being involved,' she continued.

Roscoe folded his arms. 'Beyond the pale, ma'am.'

'I know this isn't your normal field of expertise,' she went on, 'but the Assistant Chief Constable wants to set up a small unit under your command to investigate. He decided that, on this occasion, this wasn't a case the professional standards department should handle for confidential reasons.'

He smiled. 'I'm happy with that.'

'I'm giving this inquiry the codename Operation Sepulchre,' she continued, 'and I'm placing DI Vickers in charge of it. So, you'll be liaising with him.'

'Extremely good appointment, if I may say so, ma'am. Tom's very hard-working and conscientious.'

'Staffing and resources will be down to you. I hope you won't feel slighted that I've asked him to take day-to-day charge of the work rather than yourself, Gavin.'

He leaned back in his seat. 'Police misconduct's not my speciality. I'd feel like a man going to play tennis with a cricket bat. I'm fascinated by homicide, ma'am. I'm intrigued by the psychology of the murderer and what leads him or her to take another's life. I try to avoid re-examining old legal cases or hanging about in draughty streets outside people's houses and snooping on phone calls. Maybe it's a sign I'm getting old.'

She shook her head. 'No, I believe in choosing the best person for the job and a DCI's role is supervisory, of course. Vickers must start work at once.'

As he left her office and climbed down the stairs to his office on the floor below, the chief inspector realised the creation of Operation Sepulchre had implications for the whole of CID. They were already working within tight budget restraints.

'I'm damned if Tom's going to get any extra staff and money,' he muttered to himself. 'Let's see if he can manage on his own for a while.'

Soon after reaching his desk, his mobile phone rang and an image of his sergeant, DS Sunita Roy, appeared on the screen.

'Sir, sorry to bother you,' she said in her educated voice. 'A man's body has been found in the woods at

Foxwell Heath. I'm on my way over there with DC Khalid to take a look.'

'Thanks for letting me know. Who found the body?'

'A man walking his dog.'

'Body in the woods, eh? Suicide or something else?'

'Not suicide, sir. A metal spike's been driven into his chest.'

Chapter 4

Sunita Roy clung onto the door handle and her seatbelt as her colleague, DC Omar Khalid, sped along the main road towards the village of Foxwell Green.

She knew their mission was urgent, but her heart was in her mouth whenever he swerved to avoid a pothole or overtook on narrow stretches of the road.

For most of their journey from Solihull, along the M42 motorway, they had been travelling at speeds of up to ninety miles an hour with the blue light flashing on his unmarked Ford Focus. But, for the final few miles, they had been travelling south along a trunk road and maintaining a speed of around sixty-five. The pair finally reached Yeoman's Lane at just before half past ten.

The first officers on the scene had closed the lane and cordoned off parts of the woodland. Police were only allowing their own vehicles in the vicinity of the car park. Cars used by uniformed police, scenes of crime staff, the forensics team and pathologists were lined up along the lane.

Other motorists – newspaper photographers and inquisitive residents – had been obliged to park further away, near the top of the lane, close to Foxwell Green village.

Khalid managed to squeeze into a gap between a black Mercedes, partly splattered in mud and grime, and a green Land Rover Discovery that they both recognised as belonging to Home Office pathologist Dr Silas Reynolds.

Dark-haired Sunita, who was slim, five feet seven inches tall and with attractive brown eyes, stretched and yawned.

'That was a hell of a journey,' she muttered to herself. 'Next time, I'm driving.'

They found most of the public car park had already been taped off. The only means of entering the woods was along a narrow access route created by police on the eastern edge of the car park. But as soon as they stepped in that direction a young, lean-faced constable rushed to block their way.

'Sorry, you can't come in here,' said the officer, who spoke with a slight Scottish accent.

'I'm DS Roy and I'm the senior detective here until our SIO turns up,' she explained, reaching into her jacket pocket and removing her warrant card, which she brandished.

'Apologies,' he muttered.

'This is DC Khalid, who's assisting me,' she said, pointing to her colleague who was two inches taller than her with short, dark curly hair. 'Do you know who the first officer on the scene was?'

'Yes,' said the constable. 'It was my colleague PC Nina Kaur. I'll just call her. PC Kaur! PC Kaur!'

A young female officer hurried towards them. Sunita recalled seeing the dark-haired woman several times before in the canteen at the St James Street headquarters.

'Nina, I'm DS Sunita Roy. I gather you were among the first here?'

'Yes, Sarge. Got here just before nine forty-five. There were a few members of the public here. I've got a list of names, addresses, phone numbers and reg numbers. The force photographer came shortly afterwards, and we've got pictures of all the vehicles that were here.'

Sunita noticed only one vehicle remained – a black Volkswagen Golf.

'Oh well done, Nina,' she said as she began scribbling details in a small notebook. 'Where are all the people who were here when you first arrived? Have they all gone?'

'Yes, all gone. We were on our own and some of them slipped away before we could stop them. The only ones to remain for a time were a Mr Cooper, a Mrs Hamid and a Mrs Hussain. These three gave us full statements and we didn't see the need to detain them any longer. Oh yes, and the owner of a blue Volvo, who gave the name Robert Brown. He seemed a bit nosy and said he might come back later.'

'Who first found the body?'

'It was Mr Cooper. Let me have a look at the list. Yes, Howard Cooper. At first, he couldn't locate the body. We found it after a few minutes, and I arranged for an inner cordon to be set up around the location. He was very helpful, and he's only just gone.'

'Sounds like you've done a good job,' said the sergeant as the constable handed her the paper list.

'We've also set up a common approach path so our personnel can enter and leave the woods. It runs roughly parallel with the main path,' PC Kaur added. 'I wanted to be sure no one would contaminate the area where the public were walking earlier on.'

'That's great. We saw Dr Reynolds' Land Rover out in the lane. I take it he's with the body?'

'Yes.'

As they were speaking, Khalid was studying the list of car park visitors. He suddenly turned towards PC Kaur.

'There's one vehicle here that doesn't have a driver listed. The black Volkswagen Golf, which is parked over here.'

She nodded. 'Yes, you're right. No one's been to collect it and it's not on the national computer.' She sounded annoyed that he'd asked about it.

'That's strange,' Khalid remarked.

He walked round the parked car, staring through its windows and taking notes. After a few minutes, he returned to find the two women still talking.

Just then they noticed a man in a shabby black jacket and crumpled green slacks speaking to the young Scottish constable at the entrance. He had unkempt dark-brown hair and black facial stubble. PC Kaur pointed him out to the detectives.

'That's Mr Brown,' she whispered.

Sunita at once stepped towards the stranger, listening carefully to part of the ongoing conversation as she approached.

'Just wondered if you'd picked up on whose body it is, like,' he was saying.

'Can I help?' she asked. 'DS Roy, Heart of England CID.'

The man took a few steps towards her.

'I was here earlier on. I just wondered... was it a tramp, like?'

She was immediately suspicious of the man. She recalled reading in a police training manual that offenders sometimes returned to the scene of their crime to observe the police.

'What's your interest, sir?' she asked.

'Oh, I was here earlier on. That's all. I was chatting to someone who told me a body had been found. I was just curious, like.'

'What's your name, sir?'

'Robert Brown.'

'Have you got any ID on you?'

'No. Not so to speak.'

'Date of birth?'

'It's 5 April 1990. Look, I was here earlier and just wondered who it was who died.'

As she beckoned DC Khalid to join them, Sunita asked, 'Why were you here earlier, sir?'

'I was on my way back from the shops in Queensbridge and my engine began overheating. I've been carrying water round. I let it cool down for twenty minutes and then topped up the rad.'

She stepped away and held a whispered conversation with Khalid.

'I'm suspicious about why this man has returned,' she told him. Then she announced that they would search Mr Brown under Section 60 of the Criminal Justice and Public Order Act.

'No problem,' said the man. 'I've got nothing to hide.'

Khalid tried to ignore the man's slight body odour as he removed his jacket and carefully examined the contents.

'Got any sharps?' he asked Brown.

'No. Never carry knives,' the suspect replied.

After Khalid got the man to empty his trouser pockets, the pair inspected the contents. There was a set of Volvo keys, some house keys, a black comb, a pair of nail scissors, a blue ballpoint pen, a wallet containing ten pounds and three pounds fifty pence in coins. There was also a council demand for a sixty-pound parking fine, giving an address in Field Crescent, Shawley Green.

'Is this your address?' Sunita asked, unfurling the letter.

'Yes, number twenty-three, Field Crescent.'

'All right,' she said. 'Look, Mr Brown, we've no information at the moment on this suspicious death. So we suggest you leave the area and don't return. But before you go, I want to ask you something.'

She took out her notebook and pen. Then, on a fresh page, she sketched out a rough map of the car park.

'Sir, would you like to mark here the approximate position of your Volvo when you parked here before?'

He took the pen and book from her and drew a tiny oblong shape near to the centre of the car park.

'That's fine. Thank you,' she said.

'Will that be all then?' he asked.

She nodded. He put his jacket back on and shuffled away up the lane towards Foxwell Green.

* * *

A few minutes later, Gavin Roscoe arrived. He walked briskly past the car park entrance and joined her. Then, along with Khalid, they marched along the access path into the woods.

'What's the strength of this then, Sergeant?' he asked.

'We haven't been in the woods yet, sir. We thought we'd wait for you. Just been briefed by a PC Kaur, who was first on the scene, and then we interviewed a man showing an unusual interest in police activity. We've got his details. Could be something or nothing.'

'Good. Then let's go and see Silas.'

They traipsed for several hundred metres along the pathway between the lines of tape, Roscoe looking around him as he went. Sunita and Khalid followed close behind. Eventually they reached the location of the body. It was now sheltered by a small white tent, which was surrounded by scenes of crime officers in white suits.

'Silas! Are you about?' Roscoe called out.

Within seconds, the overweight, grey-haired pathologist raised his head above the far side of the tent.

'Good morning, Gavin!' he boomed. 'Just like you to turn up when most of the hard work's done.'

The chief inspector gingerly approached the tent while his two colleagues looked on from the access path.

'What have we got then, Silas?' Roscoe asked as the pathologist stepped out of the tent.

'He's a white male, aged about fifty and he's a hundred and seventy-five centimetres tall. He's wearing a light-blue sweatshirt and light-blue tracksuit bottoms with white stripes. There's a laceration to the skull and red marks round the neck, suggesting an attempt was made to strangle him.'

'So there's no doubt he's been murdered?' said Roscoe.

'No doubt at all.'

'So how did the poor man meet his end?'

'It appears to me the killer made an initial attempt to throttle his victim using some kind of ligature and, when that failed, he resorted to causing a sharp force injury.'

'My sergeant heard there might have been some kind of metal spike involved.'

'Not a metal spike, but there was a barbecue carving fork embedded in the poor fellow's chest.'

Chapter 5

The chief inspector was used to bizarre weapons cropping up in murder inquiries, but he had never encountered a carving fork before.

'So, the killer first attempted strangulation and, when that failed, switched his technique and used the fork. Is that what you're saying?' he asked.

'Yes. More tests are required, old fruit. But the red marks tell us it wasn't a rope or cord that was used round the neck. I'm thinking maybe a scarf or a pair of women's tights – some kind of fabric. Scratches round the neck suggest the victim struggled with his assailant and grappled to remove the ligature. Somehow the killer's chanced upon this sixteen-inch carving fork and plunged it into the man's heart. Death would have been almost instantaneous.'

Roscoe had an image of the man's last moments in his mind and it filled him with disgust.

'Is it possible there was a struggle and that the dead man impaled himself on the fork by rolling onto it or falling onto it?'

'Impossible. It's been driven into his chest with some force.'

'Anything else we need to know?'

'Well, there are no bruises or lacerations on his knuckles,' he said, gazing at Roscoe over his horn-rimmed glasses. 'That suggests that, apart from struggling with the material round his neck, he had no proper chance to fight back and was quickly overpowered. His sweatshirt is snagged in places. It looks as if he's come up against something sharp – possibly barbed wire or a metal fence.'

Roscoe's eyes lit up. 'So he met his death somewhere else and was then brought here?'

'Yes. There are signs his body was dragged into the undergrowth.'

'I'll ask DS Roy and DC Khalid to conduct a search. Might find some barbed wire.'

The doctor nodded. 'We're going to check his clothing thoroughly and will have more to report to you in the next week or so, Gavin.'

'Nothing under his fingernails that might link to the killer?'

'Might be traces of the killer's DNA there. We'll check everything thoroughly.'

'Any idea what time he died, Silas?'

'I'd say between seven thirty and nine thirty this morning. Rigor mortis hasn't set in yet.'

'So this has only just happened? We get so many cases where a body's been decaying for days or weeks.'

'Yes, we should be grateful for that. It's much harder to collect the information when the body's been around a while.'

'Right, thanks very much, Silas. Can I just take a peek at the body – so I've more of an idea what we're dealing with?'

'Yes, of course.'

Roscoe peered through a flap in the tent. There on the ground lay the lifeless body of the fitness enthusiast with the murder weapon still implanted in his chest.

'Not a pretty sight, Silas,' Roscoe declared.

'No, old fruit. I see dead bodies every day. But it still shakes you up, I can tell you.'

'Absolutely,' murmured Roscoe, as he felt just for a moment that he might retch. But he recovered.

'Strange to be here in such a beautiful place, dealing with a hideous murder,' Roscoe remarked.

Reynolds nodded. 'This poor guy could have expected many more happy years.'

Thoughtfully, the chief inspector walked back to where Khalid was waiting.

'Where's our sergeant?' he asked.

'She just wandered off without a word,' Khalid replied.

A few minutes later, Sunita walked breathlessly back to join them.

'Sir, I think you should come and take a look at this,' she said.

The two men followed her until they reached a woodland glade fifty metres away. It was a secluded spot on the far edge of the woods with extensive views across nearby farmland.

'Look at this, sir,' she insisted, pointing to the charred remains of a campfire. 'It looks as if someone's been roasting food on the fire. There's some blackened knives, forks, and a couple of tin mugs. I was just wondering if the barbecue fork might have come from here.'

'Very well spotted indeed, Sergeant,' said Roscoe.

He peered across the autumn fields, the neatly cut hedgerows and clumps of trees. Then his eyes came to rest on a rickety barbed wire fence that marked the boundary between the woods and the farmland.

He walked towards it, looking for any signs of recent human activity. Finally, he came to an abrupt halt. If he was not mistaken, he could see signs of scuff marks in the soft earth. He stopped to examine the ground and what appeared to be the traces of two sets of footprints.

Then, as he rose to his feet again, he noticed a tiny wisp of blue cloth snagged on one of the fence's sharply pointed barbs. Sunita had been walking close behind him and saw the material at the same time.

'Could be from the dead man's sweatshirt,' she remarked.

'That's what I thought,' he replied. Then he turned to Khalid, who was standing a few metres behind. 'Khalid, can you call the SOCO team over? We need to cordon off this area. This looks like the scene of a struggle between the killer and his victim. And can you inform Dr Reynolds as well? Thanks.'

As he began to walk back for another word with Dr Reynolds, Roscoe noticed his sergeant was studying the ground between the abandoned campsite and the wire fence.

'Sir,' she said, 'there's something else. It looks like either the killer or the victim arrived on two wheels. There are fairly fresh cycle tracks in the earth. I'm going to see if I can follow them.'

* * *

An hour later, the chief inspector was on his way back to his St James Street office when his mobile phone rang. He pulled over to the side of the road and cut the engine.

'Roscoe,' he replied as he answered the call.

'Dad,' said a voice he knew well. 'How are you doing?'

'Oh, it's you, George,' he said. 'Not bad. I'm just on my way to the office.'

'I'm getting on well, Dad. The duty sergeant hasn't got anything for me right now, so I thought I'd find out how the family are doing.'

'We're all fine.'

George tutted. 'I just called my sister, and she couldn't speak to me because she was washing her hair. Who washes their hair at half past eleven on a Monday morning, Dad?'

'Mel's meant to be at college. I'll have to have a word with her. How's Warwick? Job still going well?'

'Couldn't be better. I arrested my first shoplifter yesterday. I felt sorry for the woman though. She was a single mother with three children. I got called to a fashion store where she'd been caught trying to walk out with an expensive winter coat.'

Roscoe shrugged his shoulders. 'Some of those shoplifting cases can be upsetting.'

'Dad, I wanted to mention something. I was having a chat with Amanda and Sean.'

'Your friends from the training course?'

'Yes, Dad. We're all fully fledged constables now. Listen, all three of us have heard rumours about a CID department in North Warwickshire which failed to properly investigate the murder of an artist. Apparently, two men have been jailed for it, but my sergeant can't understand it. There are strong suggestions that one of the men was miles away at the time. The sergeant says the evidence was flimsy and the charges against both men should have been dropped. He says it's probably incompetence, but there's been talk of corruption.'

'That's very concerning,' his father said. 'At one time corruption was rife in the police, but I've not heard of it being a problem for years.'

'It's very dispiriting, Dad. Even just the suggestion that there might be police corruption is disheartening for someone like me. You join up full of good intentions, vowing to help the community. You swear an oath promising to act with fairness. You promise to uphold human rights and respect all people. So it's a shattering blow when you learn not everyone's honouring those principles and they're as crooked as a witch's hat. Not only that, it has a devastating effect on our relationship with the public. How can they put their trust in us if we're breaking the law ourselves? The whole system starts to break down.'

Roscoe was moved to hear his son's words. He momentarily recalled his own introduction to the police nearly thirty years before. He too had experienced revulsion on learning the lives of some colleagues had become debased by the canker of corruption.

'As you know, I'm very proud of you, son,' said Roscoe, who didn't reveal the details of his conversation with the chief superintendent earlier that day. 'Don't worry, George. The top brass must be aware of these rumours. I'm sure they'll take action if there's any evidence.'

'I hope you're right, Dad, because it's very worrying. Oh, I'm sorry, Dad. We've just had a shout. Got to go. Bye.'

'Bye,' said Roscoe.

As he placed his phone on the passenger seat, a faint smile crept across his face. George was twenty-two and had been in the force for less than a year. Yet the lad had reminded him of the reasons he himself had joined – the need to uphold the law, prevent crime and serve the public. He still believed in those key tenets.

His son was right. Any crooked officers had to be rooted out. But allegations were often made against the police by dedicated defence lawyers. He'd seen no proof yet of any misdemeanours committed by his fellow officers.

Nonetheless, perhaps he had been hasty in ruling out financial support for DI Vickers' new unit. Perhaps he should do more to help if it was a question of nailing a crooked copper.

Chapter 6

Sunita Roy carefully weaved her way past a series of police vehicles as she approached the thatched cottage where Scott Deeley had been living. His mother had reported him missing the day before and officers had accompanied her to the mortuary at Alexandra Hospital for the heartbreaking task of identifying her son's body.

Bouquets of late summer flowers had been laid next to the white picket fence in tribute to the man found dead in the wood. Sunita stopped to read some of the messages.

One handwritten note on a white card said, 'RIP Scott. In our thoughts always'. Another said simply, 'You didn't deserve this'.

She pushed open the wooden gate with its faded green paint and walked briskly up the garden path, admiring the roses as she passed. Her colleague, Omar Khalid, trailed a few metres behind.

She rapped on the heavy oak door of the cottage. After a few minutes it creaked open. She found herself being greeted by the cheerful face of a police colleague, Pam Listers, a family liaison officer.

'Hi, Sunita. Hi, Omar. You'd better come in and we'll talk in the kitchen. The local doctor's just been, and Mrs Deeley is sleeping, but I can probably help you with some of your questions.'

Listers, a short, stout lady, led the pair through the dark hallway and into a surprisingly spacious, rustic kitchen which had a picture window overlooking a side garden. In the centre of the rather dated room stood a modern oven and hob surrounded by cream-coloured cupboards. Their wooden, spindle-backed chairs scraped on the black-tiled floor as all three sat round an oak table.

'Would you like some tea?' Listers asked.

Sunita shook her head. 'No, thanks. How long have the forensic team been here?'

'They arrived an hour ago – about the same time as me.'

'So, what do we know about our Mr Deeley?' Khalid asked, as both officers drew notebooks and pens from their pockets.

'Well, he's not a "mister". He's a doctor,' she explained, taking a sheet of paper from her handbag and consulting it. 'He was fifty-three. He was born on the 27 March 1965. Neighbours say he grew up round here and helped run a practice in south Birmingham. Then he moved down to Kent for some reason and worked at a GP surgery down there. He recently moved back to care for his mother, Sarah. She's got dementia.'

'She must be devastated at the news.'

'We haven't told her exactly what happened yet. Just relating that he's died was enough for the moment.'

'Has some of this information about the victim come from her?' Sunita wondered. 'Can we rely on it?'

'Most of this has come from one of the neighbours.'

'When exactly did he move back from Kent?' Khalid asked.

'July or August. He wasn't married and, as far as people round here know, he didn't have a girlfriend.'

'Any idea what he was like as a person?' said Sunita.

Listers picked up a colour photograph from the kitchen table which showed a slim man with chiselled good looks, a wide grin and greying hair.

'Here he is,' she said. 'By all accounts, despite good looks, confidence and intelligence, he never got round to tying the knot. He's one of those guys who just focussed on his career. Oh, and he was a fairly placid guy. Not the kind who would get involved in any confrontation.'

Khalid gazed towards her. 'He was possibly gay?'

'I asked about that, and people said emphatically no. He had a woman friend in Kent that he saw regularly, but everyone says he was the sort who could never commit.'

Sunita looked blank. 'I see,' she said, although her facial expression suggested she didn't.

'Anyway, he'd put his whole life on hold to care for his mother, whom he was devoted to,' Listers went on. 'As an only son, he valued the bond with his mother.'

'Where had he been yesterday morning?' Khalid asked. 'I mean, how come he was in the woods?'

'He was a bit of a fitness fanatic. He regularly went for an early morning run round Sinton Bank and Foxwell Green. He's quite well-known round here, by all accounts. I ought to mention that a few years ago he was a part-time script advisor for a medical TV show made in Birmingham. Do you remember it? *Morning Surgery*, it was called.'

Sunita shrugged. 'Vaguely,' she said, while her colleague nodded.

Listers continued, 'Do you remember the lead character, Dr Frank Sutton? It was based on Dr Deeley and his time as a Solihull GP.'

At that moment, a forensic officer, clutching a laptop computer she'd found upstairs, burst into the room with a smile.

'Oh Pam, we've finished and we're all leaving. So, feel free to take our colleagues upstairs,' she said.

Listers rose to her feet with her smile. 'Thanks very much,' she replied.

Sunita also stood up. She began walking round the kitchen, examining some of the fixtures. She came across a wall calendar tucked behind some crockery on the white Welsh dresser. Sunday, 28 October had been ringed with a black pen. Someone – presumably the doctor – had written 'Mum's Birthday' in small letters beneath the date.

'So, Mrs Deeley is turning eighty-four later this month?' she asked.

Their friend nodded. 'That's right.'

'Shame she's got dementia.'

'Yes, it's pretty bad.'

At that very moment, they heard an elderly woman's voice calling from upstairs. The kitchen fell silent.

'That's her. I'd better see what she wants,' said Listers. 'Will you excuse me?'

'Of course,' said Sunita. 'By the way, which is Dr Deeley's bedroom?'

'First on the left upstairs – immediately opposite his mother's room.'

As Listers went off to the old lady's bedroom, the two detectives climbed the oak stairs and pushed open the door of the room opposite. They found themselves in a dark room with a low ceiling and centuries-old brown wooden beams, which was crammed with medical equipment. A small window overlooked the front garden, while an ornate, metal-framed double bed stood by the right-hand wall.

The doctor had found space on a small, antique writing bureau for a defibrillator and stethoscope, which he'd presumably brought back with him after his ten years or more spent in practice in Kent. In the far corner stood a treatment couch, an exercise bike and a rowing machine. The bureau was cluttered with medical books, medical magazines and some old crime novels.

Sunita strolled over to a modern, white dressing table with three mirrors – which appeared out of place in the character cottage – and searched in the drawers, while her colleague gazed through the window into the garden.

As he glanced over the top of the hedge at the front, he noticed all the police cars except theirs had departed. Then he spotted something else. Just across the street, his eyes settled upon a tall, grey-haired man in dark clothing who was holding a bicycle and staring directly towards him.

‘What the–?’ Khalid began.

Sunita turned round. ‘What’s the matter?’

‘There’s a suspicious-looking man on the far side of the road. He’s staring straight up at the house. Have you seen him before? Was he at the car park at Foxwell Heath?’

She joined him at the window. ‘No, never seen him before.’

‘I’m going to run down and have a few words. You never know,’ said Khalid, racing out of the room and down the stairs.

Sunita returned to the dressing table. Her attention had been attracted by a single item of jewellery which she’d found in a small white box in a left-hand drawer. The box contained a gold necklace with a rose-gold flamingo pendant. Alongside the box was a handwritten receipt from a firm of Birmingham jewellers. She gasped when she noticed the price of nine hundred and fifty pounds.

Khalid was breathless when he slowly walked back upstairs.

‘He’s got away on his bike, but I got a good look at him, and I’d definitely recognise him again.’

‘Take a look at this, Omar,’ she said. ‘Have you ever seen anything so beautiful?’

‘What is it? I’m a bloke. I don’t know about these things.’

She sighed. ‘It’s a necklace with a golden flamingo pendant. Nine hundred and fifty quid, it says on the receipt.’

‘A lot of dough. Maybe it’s meant for his mother. Her birthday’s coming up, you mentioned.’

‘I doubt it. Looks more like a gift for a girlfriend. A gift he no longer has a chance to give. That’s sad, isn’t it?’

‘I can guess why a lot of men don’t go in for buying flamingo jewellery,’ said Khalid. ‘As soon as a fella learns the price in the shop, he flaming goes.’

‘You’re such a comedian!’

Khalid's attention was drawn to a piece of paper on the floor.

'Hey, what's this, Sarge?'

He stooped down and picked up a bus ticket, which he handed to her. She took it to the window to study it in the natural light.

'Looks like he made a bus journey to the Alvechurch area on 1 October. That was exactly a week before the murder, wasn't it?'

'That's right, Sarge.'

'Seems strange he didn't take his car.'

Just at that moment, they heard a series of shouts coming from Mrs Deeley's bedroom. They were unable to make out exactly what the old lady was saying. It sounded like, 'Lots of 'em! Lots of 'em!'

After quickly slipping the jewellery box and receipt into a transparent evidence bag, Sunita stepped onto the landing. Khalid followed close behind. An old lady in a white nightgown with long, grey, straggly hair hobbled out of the bedroom with wild, staring eyes. Mrs Listers caught her by the left arm and tried to calm her down.

Sunita was startled. She'd never seen anyone ranting like this before.

The shock of her son's death must have tipped her over the edge, she thought to herself.

'She doesn't believe me!' Mrs Deeley yelled into the young detective's face.

'What doesn't she believe?' Sunita asked her.

'She doesn't believe me when I say lots of men have been coming into the house.'

Mrs Listers stood directly behind the old lady, looking perplexed and shaking her head.

'She's confused,' she insisted.

'I'm not confused,' the old lady screamed defiantly. 'It's true. Men have been breaking in while Scott's been out. It's not safe round here. One of them must have done for him.'

Chapter 7

The chief inspector always tried to leave DI Tom Vickers to his own devices, except when he was seconded to his CID team. So, he wasn't a frequent visitor to the inspector's office on the other side of the headquarters building. But on Thursday afternoon that week, he knew it was time for a face-to-face meeting.

He strolled out of the main CID office, crossed the landing and remembered the inspector's room was on the left. He knocked gently before stepping inside.

It was a bright, medium-sized room containing four desks, a filing cabinet and some video equipment. Both Vickers and his colleague DC Wendy Hopkirk, were engaged in phone calls. Hopkirk sat up straight when she noticed Roscoe and smiled across at him.

As the inspector ended his call and hurried to greet him, the chief inspector reflected on how much his former sergeant from Wolverhampton had changed. Vickers, who was slightly overweight and with short brown hair, had once dressed shabbily. Now he was wearing a smart grey suit with a blue tie. Although he had shaved off his ginger moustache, there were signs it was trying to make a fresh appearance.

Roscoe smiled as he shook his hand. 'Tom, I wanted to hear your thoughts on Sepulchre.'

'It's so good to see you, guv,' he said. 'Won't you take a seat?'

'It's good to see you as well, Tom,' said Roscoe as he drew up a chair next to Vickers.

'I gather you've had a chat with Norris,' said Vickers, resuming his seat.

'Yes,' said Roscoe. 'You've got a heavy responsibility here. It makes us look bad if the wrong men have been convicted. So you'll have to let me know what help you want.'

'Absolutely.'

Roscoe smiled. 'I hear you and Sunita are talking about moving in together,' he said.

'Yes, I've been seeing a lot of her. I think the world of her, guv. She's certainly keeping me on my toes now!'

'I have to say you're looking extremely smart these days, Tom.'

He recalled how, just after Vickers' wife left him, he was often to be found in crumpled clothing after having slept in the CID office.

'Oh, I'm sorry, Tom,' he said. 'I probably spoke out of turn.'

Vickers shook his head. 'No, that's OK. You're right, guv. Sunita's made a lot of difference to my life. She's helped me to get my act together. She's a smart woman. She's talking about taking her inspector's exams. Do you know she keeps careful count of the beers I have on an evening and always remembers whose turn it is to drive?'

'I didn't realise she'd been aiming to become an inspector so quickly.'

'And it won't be long before she's bidding to reach even higher. Right now she's working hard on the Deeley case. But we always try to avoid talking about work when we're together.'

'It looks as if it will be a challenging case – especially since it took place in dense woodland. No end of characters could have been in the wood at the time of the murder and no doubt many of them were long departed before the first responders arrived.'

'Foxwell Heath's a really popular place with walkers, runners and cyclists. I don't envy Sunita. After the body was discovered, at least ten minutes went by before the first 999 calls started coming in. On top of that, there's the problem of securing the site when it's such a vast area.'

Roscoe shrugged. 'Hopefully, somehow or other, there'll be some DNA.'

'That's right. Anyway, I'd better tell you about Sepulchre. It's very early days, guv, but it involves the "body in the bath" murder case in Sedgeworth. Do you recall it?'

Roscoe nodded. 'Didn't that concern an artist called O'Sullivan?'

'That's right. Brendan O'Sullivan. He was found dead in his bath in January last year and the word was that he'd managed to upset some seriously heavy people involved in a drugs gang.'

Roscoe folded his arms. 'I seem to remember his body was riddled with bullets.'

The inspector nodded. 'Yes. Nasty case. Two guys were arrested and charged with his murder, and it went to trial this summer at Warwick Crown Court. They denied having anything at all to do with O'Sullivan and consistently claimed they'd been set up. But they were convicted by a majority verdict and got sent down.'

'So now their lawyer's mounted a campaign for a retrial and is making serious allegations against Heart of England?'

'Yes. I think it's generally accepted that the two men who went down weren't angels. They'd definitely been involved in the drugs trade. But one of the suggestions this lawyer, Giles Farquhar, has made is that two men from a rival gang carried out the killing. And among his more contentious allegations is that corrupt police assisted in framing them.'

'Why would officers from Heart of England do that? What would be the point?'

Vickers shrugged. 'Well. The allegation is that a corrupt detective arranged it because he or she is in league with the rival gang.'

Roscoe shook his head. 'The more I think about it, the more I'm convinced this is a pack of lies created as part of a campaign by the two convicted men to get a retrial.'

'But what if it were true and one of our guys is playing for both teams, guv?'

'That's a different matter, I agree, and we've got to come down on him or her like a ton of bricks.'

The inspector leaned back on his chair. 'I've had a look at the file and I must say the evidence against the two defendants was flimsy, to say the least. Looks like they might've been set up.'

'We've got our work cut out here, Tom,' Roscoe mumbled. 'If you need any help from my underworld contacts, just let me know.'

* * *

As the chief inspector returned to his office, he found Sunita Roy waiting impatiently for him.

'Sir, you know this murder at Foxwell Heath? We've received an interesting tip-off. Do you remember the TV soap *Morning Surgery*, which was based in Birmingham?'

Roscoe unlocked his door, then turned to face her.

'Yes, of course. The main character was a fellow called Dr Sutton. Frank Sutton, if I remember rightly. You got that from Pam Listers, didn't you?'

She looked up at him from her desk. 'That's right. Well, this caller, who wouldn't give his name, was explaining how Deeley became involved in the show.'

'That's interesting.'

'He said Deeley was once a pal of the show's creator. Not only that. We've had a look in the archives because his name rang a bell with one of the older DCs. I found a report from 2007 that appeared in the *Queensbridge Gazette*. Deeley was once accused of failures that led to the death of an eleven-year-old boy.'

She glanced at some notes she'd made.

'Dr Deeley diagnosed gastroenteritis and dehydration. He told the parents there was no need to take him to hospital and instead he was sent away with painkillers. A few hours later the lad, Jerome Harper, was rushed to hospital after becoming critically ill at home. He died later the same day in August 2007 from what an inquest described as "sepsis created by meningococcal septicaemia". Blood poisoning, in other words.'

Roscoe frowned and took a seat beside her.

'I vaguely remember something about this. I was a DI at the time. I think the family lived in Queensbridge.'

'That's right. Pershore Road.'

'Didn't the parents try to take the doctors' practice to court?'

'Yes, but as far as I can tell, they failed. Shortly afterwards, Deeley retired from the practice and moved away. If it's all right with you, sir, I've got a little more research to do. But, tomorrow morning, I'll go over to see the parents with DC Khalid and see what they've got to say about their old adversary being found murdered.'

Roscoe stroked his chin. 'It's coming back to me. The lad was a talented footballer, if I remember rightly. It was a terrible tragedy, and the parents were finding it difficult to recover from their loss.'

'You never know, sir. The death of their son might've provided a motive for murder.'

Chapter 8

The semi-detached Edwardian villa in Pershore Road, Queensbridge, was one of eight houses in a terrace. But the home of David and Amy Harper stood out from the other seven.

Cream paint was peeling from the masonry. The black timber gables had been allowed to decay. The windows were grimy. The front garden was unkempt.

Sunita Roy noticed that the front gate was missing as she waited outside the address for Omar Khalid. Once her colleague arrived, they negotiated their way through the overgrown garden and found the gate lying, rotting, beside the stone path.

They set off towards the front door, looking down continually to avoid tripping on the creeper and brambles. Here and there, red chrysanthemums and yellow dahlias fought to raise their heads from among the unbridled weeds.

'It's lucky I haven't got my best clothes on,' she confessed to Khalid, whose trousers were briefly caught on a bramble.

Within a few minutes, they reached the porch. Paint was peeling from the dark green front door. Shabby curtains hung loosely across the two main downstairs windows. One of the panes was cracked. Passers-by may well have thought the house was empty and the residents long gone.

Sunita rapped five times on the black metal knocker. The house appeared uninhabited, but she persisted. There was a black-framed bicycle at the side of the porch. She knocked three more times. There was no sound from within. Then she heard distant footsteps and bolts being drawn back. After a few seconds, the head of a tall, grey-haired man appeared round the door.

'Yes?' the man demanded.

'So sorry to bother you,' Sunita began, producing her warrant card. 'Heart of England CID. You've obviously heard about the death of Dr Deeley in the woods at Foxwell Heath?'

'Yes. I wondered if you'd be calling. You'd better come in,' said the man.

She was taken aback. She'd expected some reluctance to speak to the police.

The house was as neglected inside as it was on the outside. The dim hallway had a threadbare, red carpet. The house was colder than the chilled aisles at a supermarket.

The man led them into an equally drab front room with a partly stained green carpet, woodchip wallpaper which had been painted in a light peach colour and a grey three-piece suite with fraying fabric.

The room reeked of alcohol. The visitors quickly understood why. As he slumped down on a brown, leather armchair, they could see two opened cans of lager stood next to a half-filled pint glass on a coffee table. On the carpet was a half-empty whisky bottle.

'Can I offer you a drink?' asked their host, slurring his words.

She glanced at her colleague, who shook his head.

'No, thank you, sir,' she replied. It was ten o'clock on a Friday morning. Too early for anyone to be drinking alcohol, she felt.

'Haven't got any tea or coffee – it would have to be alcohol,' the man added.

'Oh, no, thank you, sir. So, you're Mr Harper?'

'Yes, David Harper.'

'Is your date of birth 3 April 1973?'

'Yes, you've missed my birthday.'

'I'm DS Roy and this is DC Khalid. Just wanted to ask a few questions.'

He nodded and pointed to a grey settee near the fireplace.

'You'd better sit down over there.'

Sunita collected up some magazines that littered the settee and the detectives sat down. She slipped a notebook from her jacket pocket while she focussed her attention on their host. He was unshaven, had receding hair and was slovenly dressed in a partly unbuttoned shirt, blue jeans and moccasins.

Khalid was also staring at him. 'I've met you before, sir,' he said. 'A good few years ago.'

Harper raised an eyebrow. 'Have you?'

'Yes, you were campaigning over your son outside the police station. I was a schoolboy and stopped to ask what your campaign was about.'

'You can't expect me to remember that.'

Khalid shook his head. 'No, I don't but I'm pretty certain I also saw you earlier this week at Honeysuckle Cottage in Sinton Bank, the doctor's home.'

'That wasn't me. I've been keeping well clear of the doctor's house. I'm glad you took an interest when I was running my campaign. I was doing my best to get the people on my side but, in the end, I realised it was a bloody waste of time. No one listened. I hired a top brief for the inquest. He tried to pin Deeley down, but the bastard wriggled out of it. And the coroner was on Deeley's side from the start. He was never going to let Deeley be done for murder or manslaughter. I'm convinced of it.'

'Your son Jerome was just eleven?' said Sunita.

'Yes, the doctor turned him away with some pills. He said the boy wasn't ill enough for hospital. A few hours later, he was dead at Queensbridge General.'

'I'm so sorry,' she murmured.

'I'm bloody sorry as well,' said Harper as he sat down on the second settee. 'He was a brilliant young footballer, you know, young Jerome. His sports teacher had high hopes for him. His life was just snatched away, and everything went downhill from then on. I couldn't focus on anything. I lost my job, and my marriage nearly went down the pan. Now we're being evicted.'

'I'm very sorry to hear that,' said Sunita. 'So your wife… Amy, isn't it?'

'Yes, that's right. We're still together… just.'

'Could we ask where she is now?'

'I don't know and, to be totally frank, I don't bloody care. She's out somewhere.'

Harper opened the whisky bottle and poured himself a measure.

'I worshipped the ground that boy walked on,' he continued. 'Do you know Amy had years of IVF and we were told she'd probably never conceive? Then she fell pregnant. It was a difficult pregnancy, but at the end she produced this really beautiful baby. I've never seen such a beautiful little boy.'

He slumped forward, putting his head in his hands. When he looked up moments later, the pair could see tears running down both his cheeks.

'A lot of people had it in for Dr Deeley. It's no surprise to me he met a grisly end.'

Khalid raised an eyebrow. 'Did you ever get any compensation over the death of your son, Mr Harper?'

'No, nothing. The doctor moved away, and everything was dropped. I don't blame the bastard for running away. He wanted to get on with his life. I've tried to get on with my life too, but I can never put the death out of my mind. It's there every day when I wake up. It's there every night when I go to bed.'

Then suddenly his manner changed.

'Do either of you drink whisky,' he began. 'No?'

They shook their heads.

'Don't blame you. It's a fool's game, but it's keeping me happy for the moment. I go to the regular clinics and meetings, but I think they're about to give up on me. Do you know something? I'm bloody glad that doctor's dead. Here's a toast.'

With a quivering hand, he raised his glass.

'Let's toast to our enemies' demise,' he exclaimed. 'Let's take pleasure in the doctor's death. Will you have a drink with me?'

Deeley's death appeared to have brought him a brief moment of comfort in the dark abyss into which his life had plunged.

Khalid brought them back to the present.

'Mr Harper, we need to ask where you were between 9 a.m. and 9.30 a.m. on Monday of this week.'

'Is that when the bastard was killed?' Harper asked. 'I was at my little part-time job at a cafe.'

Footsteps sounded outside before they heard a key turning in the front door lock.

'This must be Amy now,' he muttered as he placed his glass and cans on the floor so they were less visible. An amiable woman in her mid-forties with dark curly hair and clutching two shopping bags appeared in the doorway.

'Oh, you've got company,' she said as Sunita and Khalid rose to their feet out of politeness.

'It's all right, love. It's the police. They're just asking a few questions.'

'Oh, right. I'll just put these in the kitchen.'

Moments later she was back, leaning against the doorpost.

'So, this is about Dr Deeley?'

Sunita nodded.

'They were just asking about Monday,' Harper said. 'What were you doing, love? Were you at work?'

'I went to visit my mother in Norton Prior between half past seven and half past eight to check she was all right. She's been falling out of bed a lot recently. Then I went to the supermarket in Queensbridge, where I work. Anyone at Tesco's will tell you. I was there all day on the checkout.'

'What line of work were you in before, Mr Harper?' Sunita asked.

'I was an architect, wasn't I? But after the boy died, I couldn't focus on my work. I took a lot of time off and, in the end, they gave me the boot.'

She frowned. 'Whereabouts is the cafe where you're working now?'

'It's called Mike's Café. It's in the main street in Sinton Bank.'

'I noticed a bicycle outside here. Is that yours?' she asked.

'Yes. I use it to get to work.'

'I'm afraid we're going to have to impound it.'

'What? I'll have to get a bus and then walk. For God's sake–'

'I'm sorry.'

'Why do you need my bloody bike?'

'Possible evidence. Fresh cycle tracks were discovered in the woods at Foxwell Heath. We just need to eliminate your bicycle from our inquiries.'

Harper was becoming agitated.

'What? You think I cycled into the woods and bumped him off? That's ridiculous. Tell her, Amy.'

'It does sound far-fetched,' his wife insisted. 'David is kept extremely busy at the cafe. They don't allow him breaks to go off gallivanting on his bike. In any case, how would my David know the doctor was going into the woods?'

Khalid interrupted her. 'We're not going to argue, Mrs Harper. We're going to take the bike. Don't worry. We'll give you a receipt and we'll return it as soon as our forensic people have finished with it.'

As he spoke, Sunita removed her phone from her trouser pocket and began an online search for a phone number.

'I'm sure it was you I saw at the cottage,' Khalid went on. 'It was Tuesday morning at about eleven or twelve. I spotted you from the window and ran down to talk to you, but by the time I got outside you'd pedalled away. The man I saw was a tall, grey-haired man. I'm pretty certain it was you.'

'You must be mistaken. I was at the cafe.'

'We can easily check,' Khalid said.

'Check, if you like. I'm an honest man.'

'Look, I'm not bothered whether you were snooping around at the doctor's cottage on the Tuesday or not,' Sunita said. 'But I *am* concerned about your whereabouts at the time of the murder.'

She dialled the number she had obtained for Mike's Café through her smartphone search and moved into the hall as a voice answered.

'Mike Griffin?' she said. 'Hi, it's Sunita Roy here from Heart of England Police.'

A faint buzzing sound could be heard as he responded.

'Yes, that's right. I was with my colleague, Tom. I'm glad you remember me. I think we dropped in during August to sample some of your coffee and cake. Listen, I'm part of the team investigating the death of your neighbour, the doctor. You've got an employee named David Harper? … Good. We're actually with him now … No, he's not in any trouble – not at the moment, anyway–'

'Now just hang on a minute,' said the man in the armchair.

She ignored him.

'Was he working for you on Monday morning? … He's listed on the rota? … Yes, but did you actually see him turn up for work yourself? … You did, but he wasn't there the whole time because he'd got a problem at his home to sort out? … OK.

'What about the following day, Tuesday? Was he at work then at around eleven o'clock? … You can't account for his movements all the time, you say? … We'll call you back later and make an appointment to visit you in person and take a statement. Thank you for your time, Mr Griffin.' She then ended the call.

'So, you see, Mr Harper,' said Sunita, looking into the man's slightly bloodshot eyes. 'It pays to tell the truth.'

'OK. I wasn't there all morning on Monday. We did have a problem at home. A water leak, didn't we, love?

'Er, yes,' said Amy, although she hardly radiated confidence with her note of confirmation.

'I was at the cafe most of the time,' her husband insisted but his demeanour had changed. He had slumped back into his seat. He was fading like a flower in the frost.

'And I definitely didn't visit the Deeleys' house on the Tuesday. Why would I do that?' he insisted.

Sunita stood up. 'Mr Harper, don't leave Queensbridge without letting us know. I'm sure we'll have further questions for you at some point.'

Chapter 9

Tom Vickers sat in a corner of his bright, spacious living room, studying his computer screen. He was learning about the North Warwickshire market town of Sedgeworth, where 'body in the bath' murder victim Brendan O'Sullivan met his fate. He was digesting the fact that Queen Boudica fought her last battle against the Romans in that area in AD 60, when his doorbell rang.

He peered through the blinds. At first, all he could see was a car travelling down the dimly lit hillside of terraced houses. He ventured through the hall to the half-glazed front door of his modern terraced house in Halesowen, and turned on the outside light. He detected the faint shadow of a figure standing on his forecourt. It was like a phantom, slipping in and out of view.

'Who is it?' he asked.

A voice with the softness of cotton wool whispered back, 'It's Chloe.'

He heaved the door open. 'What the hell are *you* doing here?'

'Tom, I'm in trouble. Can I come in?' asked the woman.

She was short with bright red lips and strawberry blonde hair. He noticed her grey Ford Fiesta, loaded with belongings, was parked beside his white Audi A3.

He backed away from the door, allowing her to step into the hall. He frowned.

'What do you want?'

Chloe, who looked pale, tutted. 'Can I come in and sit down? I've got a bit of explaining to do.'

'You've got five minutes,' he said.

She pushed open the door to the living room and strolled inside.

'Oh, you've had it decorated,' she said with a smile. 'It looks very nice.'

'Cut the small talk,' he snapped. 'Why are you here?'

She sat down on his white leather settee, taking care not to crease her short grey skirt. All the while her eyes were darting around.

'Oh, you've moved the sideboard,' she said. 'And where's the rug that was in front of the fireplace?'

'I got tired of the rug. I never liked it.'

'And you've allowed the creeper to spread round the porch.'

'Chloe, why are you here?'

'Pete's thrown me out. I've got nowhere to go.'

He sat down at the dining table where his computer screen displayed a page detailing the life of the ancient warrior queen who defied the might of the Roman Empire.

'I repeat my question. Why are you here? Our divorce is nearly completed.'

She shrugged. 'I know, but I'm in a bit of a tight spot. I've got nowhere to sleep. I'm getting so much hassle and I'm worried about losing my job.'

He smirked. 'Well, you're not going to be staying here. I've moved on with my life since you walked out on me. You're the one who decided to shack up with lover boy.'

She stared down at the beige carpet.

'It would only be for a short time. Please, Tom.'

She swung her head so that her hair tumbled back across her shoulders. The inspector thought he detected a slight fluttering of her eyelids.

'You've got a bloody cheek coming here,' he insisted. 'You walked out on me nearly a year ago, telling me our marriage was over. You started proceedings and I'm left unsure whether to sell the house or not. Now you tell me your fling with Pete's over and you're homeless.'

'I know. I'm sorry.'

'Why can't you stay with your mother or your sister?'

'They haven't got any room.'

'What, not even for a short time while you sort yourself out?'

'No.'

'Well, you're not staying here. I'm in a new relationship now.'

Chloe scowled. 'What with that Asian sergeant you work with?'

'It's none of your bloody business whom I'm in a relationship with. The point is the world's moved on since you and I lived here in our little semi, stuck in our dreary life in the Birmingham suburbs. I'm happy now.'

Chloe stood up and walked towards him.

'I've just left Pete's flat for good. I've loaded up the car and it's packed with nearly all my worldly possessions. Pete's warned me he's changing the locks and I'm worried he'll turn violent if I do turn up there again. He's already hurt me a couple of times.'

Vickers folded his arms. 'I'm sorry to hear that. You know my views on violence. No man should ever strike a woman, but you've got yourself into this predicament and you're going to have to get yourself out of it. Come on. You're leaving.'

He took to his feet and stepped towards the living room door.

'Hold on, Tom. Can't I at least have a cup of tea?'

She adopted a melancholy expression. He'd never seen her like this before. He felt a modicum of pity for her. Her plight was beginning to melt his heart.

'Just a cup of tea then,' he said, marching into the kitchen and filling the kettle.

'Why didn't you phone me and tell me what was going on?' he shouted.

'It only came to a head just now,' she explained. 'We had a row and he threw me out two weeks ago. I went to stay with my friend Jade, but she's got a full house. Pete's been on at me to clear my stuff for over a week now and his demands were getting nastier. This has been building for a while. Tonight I decided I'd had enough. I just loaded up the car and left without saying a word. I just want to be out of his life now.'

A few minutes later, he returned to the living room with two cups of steaming hot tea.

'Still one sugar?' he asked.

She nodded. He passed her cup to her and then sat down at the table with his.

'How's Jade now?'

'She's getting on much better with her husband.'

He nodded. 'They went through a bad patch, didn't they?'

'Yes. But he's got a new job now and everything's going steady for them.'

'Look, Chloe, you can stay for a few days till you sort yourself out. But after that you'll have to go.'

She smiled. 'Really? Oh, thanks, Tom. You're an angel.'

'I'm a fool. Listen, Chloe, I want you gone by next Thursday because I've got builders coming to fit a new bathroom.'

'Have you? I always said that bathroom needed updating.'

'You can sleep in the back bedroom until you find somewhere more permanent.'

'Thank you so much, Tom. You won't regret it.'

Chapter 10

'Sarge, I've got a woman on the line who used to work with Deeley. Do you want to take it?' Omar Khalid asked, cupping his hand across the receiver.

It was the morning of Monday, 15 October. Sunita Roy sat at a neighbouring CID desk.

'No, you're all right. I'm busy going through David Harper's statement. See what's she's got to say.'

The constable helped himself to a coffee from a tray of drinks a colleague had brought in. Then he rested his feet up on a nearby chair and resumed his conversation.

'So, your name's Sandy? Is that right?' he said.

'Yes,' came the response from the confident, mellow voice of a woman in her mid-forties. 'Some negative things have come out about Scott. He's been made out to be some kind of heartless medic who made a monumental blunder over a child's death and then ran away to another part of the country to escape his critics. It wasn't like that at all.'

'Can I ask how you knew him?' he asked.

'I worked with him for a few years when he was on the staff at a Midlands hospital.'

'Oh? Which one?'

'I'd rather not say. But he was a dedicated professional. I know he was devastated when that boy Jerome died. But meningitis is incredibly difficult to diagnose. After the death, he felt immense sympathy for the family and, while he was cleared of any serious professional misconduct by the GMC–'

'That's the General Medical Council?'

'Exactly. While he was cleared, he was so overcome with remorse that I happen to know he donated twenty thousand pounds to the charity founded to help the family and other families in similar situations. Unfortunately, the charity wasn't set up properly. The father got his hands on the money and he spent a lot of it on booze.'

'That's an interesting claim,' said the constable, 'although I'm not sure what we can do with it. By the way, I was wondering what your surname is, Sandy?'

The caller became silent for a moment.

'I don't want to give my full name. Just let's say I was a close friend who worked with him. You know he was a part-time script advisor for the TV show *Morning Surgery*, don't you?'

'Yes. How did that come about?'

'More by chance than anything. The writer who devised it was in a doctor's waiting room in Staffordshire or Leicestershire, listening to patients chatting to the receptionist. He thought a soap about daily life at the surgery would make a successful show – and, of course, he was proved right. While research was being conducted into the proposal, a production assistant who was one of Scott's patients recommended him to the writer.'

'We gather Dr Deeley was a very successful doctor. Is that right?'

'Yes, when he died this week, he was still officially a partner in his Kent practice. He also had an income from the TV show and from a string of properties he rented out. He was pretty well off. That's one of the reasons he was able to take a long break from work so he could look after his mother, who was very frail.'

'Did you know his mother at all?' Khalid asked, recalling the frail but formidable woman he'd met at the cottage.

'No, but he was always talking about her. She was once involved in medical work herself.'

'Oh really? That's interesting. Despite the trappings of success, he doesn't seem to have had a wife or girlfriend though.'

'That's right. I'll be honest. I was very close to him once, but he wasn't the settling down sort.'

'We wondered if he might've had a girlfriend in Kent?'

'Well, I've heard through work colleagues he had a girlfriend in Kent. I heard she might have been a surgery receptionist, but I've also heard it was nothing serious. Men like that are devoted to their work. The practice is your whole world.'

* * *

Gavin Roscoe gazed around at his team. Five of his staff were conscientiously working at their desks – either on the phone or tapping away at their computers.

He found it difficult to admit, but he missed the presence of Tom Vickers – loyal, hard-working Tom who had now been given his own department at the other end of the building. He missed his jokes, his tales from the Black Country and his camaraderie.

He strolled over to Sunita Roy's desk, which was close to his office door. She was engrossed in a phone conversation.

He beamed at her. 'Sergeant, when you've got a moment.'

She nodded back while her phone remained pressed to her ear.

'I'll be right with you, sir!' she assured him.

Moments later, she knocked gingerly on his office door and entered, clutching a newspaper.

'Sorry, sir!' she began.

'How are we getting on with the Deeley case and how's poor old Mrs Deeley?'

'Social services have become involved, sir. Carers are going in every day, but it looks as though she'll be placed in a home eventually.'

'Dear oh dear!'

He glanced through the window at cars driving in and out of the car park at the front of the building.

'Sir, have you had a chance to go through David Harper's statement?'

Roscoe nodded. 'Yes, just finished it. Very sad case. The gist of it appears to be he went off the rails when his son died. He became obsessed with the notion that Dr Deeley's negligence had cost his son his life. He lost his job as an architect and became an alcoholic.'

He leaned back in his padded leather chair.

'As the American architect Frank Lloyd Wright once said, "A doctor can bury his mistakes, but an architect can only advise his clients to plant vines".'

'That's very apt in this case, sir,' she said, taking a seat near the doorway.

'Now Harper claims to have taken time off from his job to attend to a plumbing leak. We need to be certain what time that was and whether there were any witnesses to confirm it.'

'I'm hoping to speak to his boss at the cafe later today. Sir, if you've got a minute, I wanted to tell you about the doctor's will. Scott Deeley was quite a wealthy man. He owned property which he rented out in Kent, and he also sold health products online. It's believed he was worth something in the order of two or three million pounds. Some of his money's been set aside to ensure for his mother's welfare and needs, but the bulk of his assets and property will go his aunt, Valerie Stanbrook, and her husband. They live near Tewkesbury.'

The chief inspector's eyes lit up.

'That's very interesting, Sergeant. That's another aspect of the case we'll have to consider. By the way, have you found out any more about the people parked in Yeoman's Lane car park?'

'We've got someone calling round to see the three people who found the body. They live in Redditch and a nearby hamlet called Loman's Green. So far we can't find who owned a black Volkswagen Golf nor the white Toyota van. We've also had a bit of bad news. You know the man we searched at the car park, Robert Brown? I'm afraid he's given a false address.'

Roscoe looked down at some notes.

'Number twenty-three, Field Crescent, Shawley Green?'

'Yes, sir. Khalid went round there last night. They'd never heard of anyone called Robert Brown. There was a Robert Bowcott at the address five years ago, but he moved away.'

'Don't tell me. They don't have a forwarding address?'

'That's about the size of it, sir.'

Roscoe stood up and placed his hands on his hips.

'Very challenging, this case,' he remarked. 'Very challenging indeed. Oh, by the way, I've asked Kent Police to make inquiries at Deeley's surgery and his former home in Deal. And I want them to look into the situation with the properties he let out. All Kent Police will say at the moment is they believe one of the doctor's tenants had been causing problems for him.'

Just then, he noticed someone standing outside his half-glazed office door.

'Come in!' he barked.

Omar Khalid peered round the door.

'I don't know if you're aware, sir. Mrs Deeley's been found dead at her cottage.'

Chapter 11

As the chief inspector's blue BMW glided to a halt outside Honeysuckle Cottage, he appeared to recognise the Land Rover Discovery parked by the gate.

'Isn't that Silas Reynolds' new vehicle?' he asked his sergeant, who was sitting in the passenger seat beside him.

'Yes, sir. He's passed his Mercedes on to his wife.'

'That Mercedes is only three years old. They must be paying him a fortune,' he muttered as he pushed open the gate and strode up the path, past the red and white rose bushes, closely followed by his colleague.

The front door was ajar. He gave it a gentle nudge and it creaked open, revealing that Dr Reynolds was kneeling just a few metres away, close to the bottom of the stairs.

They quickly realised the pathologist was bending over the lifeless body of Sarah Deeley, who was dressed in a pink nightgown and whose face was covered by long, grey tresses.

'Good to see you, old fruit!' said the doctor as the pair stepped into the drab hallway. He hauled himself to his feet.

'I won't shake your hand,' he told Roscoe. 'I've been playing with some fluids.'

'What do you make of this, Silas?' the chief inspector asked. 'Has she been attacked, do you think?'

'There are no obvious signs of an attack,' the doctor said. 'But I need to show you this.'

He led the pair to the top of the stairs where a scenes of crime officer was examining the banisters along the landing.

The pathologist pointed to the handrail, close to the top step.

'It looks as if some kind of lubricant may have been applied here,' he said. 'There's a small trace of a lubricant on her left hand. I'll know more when we've carried out our tests.'

'What? Some kind of grease or oil?' asked Roscoe as he stared up from his position halfway up the stairs.

'Just not sure at the moment,' said the doctor. 'It may have been applied to the rail by someone intent on causing the poor lady harm. On the other hand, she may have had the grease on her hand before she took to the stairs and placed it there herself. I'm keeping an open mind.'

'The poor woman,' Sunita remarked. 'Where are all the care staff anyway?'

'Apparently she was on her own when the incident happened. She was found by one of the carers, who tried giving her CPR, but it was no good. The good lady seems to have died a short time after her fall. When paramedics arrived, she was declared dead. The carer let the ambulance crew and police into the house and then she went home as her shift had finished.'

'You'll have to speak to this carer, Sergeant,' said Roscoe. 'Find out as much as you can about the circumstances in which Mrs Deeley was found. But, before you do that, examine the bedroom and bathroom. See if there's any moisturiser or ointment around that Mrs Deeley might have been using.'

'Yes, sir,' said Sunita, disappearing into the old lady's bedroom.

Roscoe shook his head. 'So do we know how she died, Silas?'

'Well, I'd say a brain haemorrhage is the most likely cause of death. Probably oedema of the brain on account of the swelling to the head. I'll carry out a full examination in the lab.'

'Fair enough.'

'We also need to carry out toxicology tests – just in case there's something in the body that shouldn't be there, if you get my drift.'

'Of course. Any idea about the time of death?'

'I'd say sometime between 2 a.m. and 8 a.m.'

'I don't know,' said Roscoe. 'I thought the poor lady was meant to have virtually full-time care. It's disgraceful the way some of these care firms operate.'

'I hear what you're saying, but inevitably there can be short periods of time between shifts. Perhaps she was thought to be tucked up in bed and safe to be left for a short while.'

He then wandered out of the cottage in the direction of his vehicle. Sunita appeared at the top of the stairs.

'Sir, I've checked Mrs Deeley's room and the bathroom. There's no sign of any grease around.'

'No signs she was wiping away make-up or moisturising her skin?' Roscoe asked.

'No, sir. But there's a bottle of liquid soap on her dressing table and it looks as if it's been recently opened.'

'OK, get forensics to bag it up. We'll have a word with them later and see if there are traces of the same soap on the handrail.'

As he continued speaking to her from the stairway, Roscoe became aware that someone was ringing the doorbell.

He went down to the hall and drew open the front door. A dark-haired woman in her late twenties wearing a pale-blue uniform was standing outside.

'Please, sir, I'm Colette Hayward from Queensbridge Carers,' the visitor said timidly.

'Oh, so you were the young lady who had the misfortune to find our Mrs Deeley, are you?'

'That's right, sir.'

'I'm DCI Roscoe. I just want you to have a word with my sergeant.'

He took a few steps towards the foot of the stairs, where the body of the dead woman was lying covered with a blanket.

'Sergeant!' he called. 'There's a lady for you to speak to here.'

* * *

Sunita led Colette into the kitchen at the rear of the cottage. The pair sat down either side of the oak table. Sunita saw that Colette was only a few years older than herself and petite. She wondered how she could bear the weight of her elderly patients when helping them in and out of bed.

'I'm Detective Sergeant Roy,' she explained. 'And you are?'

'I was just explaining to the other policeman – I'm Colette Hayward. I work for Queensbridge Carers. It was me who called 999.'

'You found the body?'

'Yes.'

The young woman removed a paper tissue from a box in her handbag. She blew her nose and, when she looked up again, Sunita could see tears in her eyes.

'It's obviously been a bit of a shock to you,' she said.

'Yes. I went home because I was so upset, and I wanted to be with me mum. She urged me to come back and tell the police what I saw.'

'We're glad you did. We'd have had to come to find you ourselves if you hadn't. Tell me, what time did you arrive for your shift?'

'It was seven o'clock. Mrs Deeley doesn't have care through the night, but me supervisor says I should be here from seven in case she needed the toilet first thing.'

'What did you see when you arrived at the cottage? Presumably you've got a key. Did you let yourself in?'

'That's right. The agency have a key. I collected it from my colleague last night and let meself in. Of course, I saw her lying there where she is now. Oh my God – I was so frightened. I ran over to her, but she was as cold as ice. I checked her pulse – nothing. And then I got my mobile out and dialled for an ambulance.'

She paused for a moment as a tear appeared below her right eye and began to roll down her cheek.

'Poor Mrs Deeley,' she cried. 'I know her mind was starting to go, but she was a dear old soul. She'd been very upset by the loss of her son. She didn't deserve to die like this, falling down the stairs.'

'How long had you been her carer?'

'I only started coming on Friday of last week, when the police had finished working here.'

'But, in that short time, you got to know her quite well?'

'Yes. She used to say some funny things sometimes. The other day I brought in her breakfast, and she said, "Don't let the man with the bicycle in." I said, "What on earth do you mean?" She said, "The bicycle man. The bicycle man. Don't let him in." I'd no idea what she was on about. I went out the door and looked up and down the street to see if anyone was there. I never saw no man with no bike.'

Chapter 12

Tom Vickers rose from his office desk and strolled to the sink in the corner. He glanced across at his colleague, DC Wendy Hopkirk.

'Presumably you want another tea?'

'Yes please, Tom.'

He filled the kettle with water and switched it on.

'Could you do me a favour in a minute? Could you go down to the basement and see if they've got any more files on the Brendan O'Sullivan murder?'

'Yes, sir. No problem.'

'I've read most of the material, Wendy. I just want to double check we're not overlooking anything. Oh, I didn't tell you, did I? Midlands TV have compiled a DVD for me of news reports from last year. I'm just going to run through it in case those TV reporters picked up on something we missed.'

As Wendy left the room, he loaded the disc into his DVD player, which was perched on a nearby empty desk. He drew up a chair and, seconds later, the clear, educated voice of TV reporter John Singleton reverberated round the room.

> *'This evening on our programme, Crime Tonight, we're turning our attention to the gruesome murder of a local artist who was found dead at his home on Monday, 23 January. Brendan O'Sullivan, aged fifty-five, was a well-known artist who specialised in painting landscapes. Originally from Ireland, he settled in the market town of Sedgeworth in the mid-1990s. According to friends, he was a keen supporter of the local arts centre, and he was popular with neighbours. He lived alone and enjoyed a quiet life.*
>
> *'All this changed on the afternoon of 23 January when there was a disturbance at his house. Here is Detective Chief Inspector Ainslie Hill from Heart of England CID to explain what happened.'*

The camera homed in on a gruff-voiced, overweight man with a beard and a solemn expression.

> *'Mr O'Sullivan was on his own watching TV at around 2 p.m. when there was a knock on his front door. He opened it to find two men in their late twenties. We believe they were both known to him, and they were invited in. It's possible there was some discussion about a debt payment*

which they believed was owed to them. It's also highly likely that he asked for time before making the payment, whereupon it appears the men grew angry. It's believed, over the next few minutes, his life was threatened and then, eventually, it seems the visitors' patience ran out.

'Neighbours reported hearing the sound of four gunshots. Two of the residents looked out of their houses to see a pair of men running away up the street in the direction of Sedgeworth town centre. Police were called and the body of Mr O'Sullivan was discovered in his bath.

John Singleton interrupted to say, *'This was a truly despicable crime, Chief Inspector.'*

'Yes, John. As I say, Mr O'Sullivan was only fifty-five and lived a quiet life without causing problems for his neighbours. It appears one of the men drew a gun and used it to terrify their victim. In fear, Mr O'Sullivan may have run into the bathroom in an attempt to lock himself in. It's thought they pursued him, attacked him, and subjected him to appalling violence on the first-floor landing. Then they shot him and dumped his body in the bathroom. A post-mortem examination found four bullets had penetrated his torso. This incident ended just after three o'clock in the afternoon. The two men were afterwards seen running along Albion Road and it's unclear where they went. It's possible they got into a vehicle and drove away.'

'Truly shocking, Chief Inspector. Do you have a description of the two men seen running away?'

'Yes. They were both in their late twenties. One was about five feet ten inches tall with curly black hair. He's of a medium build and from an Afro-Caribbean background. He was wearing a blue denim shirt and trousers. He may have had a tattoo on his neck. The second man was much shorter – about five feet five inches in height and from an Asian background. He had short dark hair and dark clothing.'

Singleton went on to describe the murder as 'an horrific attack' carried out in the middle of a very cold January afternoon.

> *'Heart of England Police are appealing for the public's help in tracing these two men. They've got to be found. This was a brazen attack in a quiet residential street. Some witnesses have already come forward to give their account of what happened. But police believe there may be others who witnessed the two men running away. They're particularly interested in any information about a vehicle that the men may have used to escape the scene.'*

Vickers switched off the DVD and returned to his desk. There he read some police files about the two men who were arrested a few weeks after the television appeal. They were Winston Stevens, a twenty-seven-year-old father-of-two from Coventry, and twenty-eight-year-old Raj Kumar from Sedgeworth.

But as he clicked through the pages on his computer, he felt uneasy. He'd read newspaper reports alleging a miscarriage of justice. One report claimed Stevens had been shopping in the Bull Ring, while Kumar had been at a Summerstoke dentist's surgery at the time of the incident. The alibi evidence was only referred to in the files fleetingly.

***

Half an hour later, Wendy Hopkirk returned after her trip to the basement. She placed two folders on his desk.

'That's all I could find, Tom. I think you may have read them already. There's nothing more in the archives.'

'All right, Wendy. I'll have a look in a minute.'

As she resumed her place at her desk, Vickers began reading the words of the prosecution counsel at the time of the men's trial in June. The prosecutor told the jury at Warwick Crown Court, 'This is a tale of simmering conflict and brutality in the cruel world of drug addiction.'

The barrister claimed Brendan O'Sullivan was a part-time drug dealer who owed money to a drugs gang. A series of text messages had passed between him and one of the defendants, Stevens, in the days before the murder, it was claimed.

> *Over the next two weeks, members of the jury, we'll be peering into the dark heart of the West Midlands drugs world. The court will hear a dossier of evidence that will show these two men, Stevens and Kumar, did in fact burst into O'Sullivan's home and subjected him to appalling violence. The beating was so severe that he was left with nine rib fractures, a fractured skull, and twenty-six injuries to the head alone. Injuries were consistent with being repeatedly punched, kicked and stamped on. He was finally shot with a Beretta pistol, since recovered from the home of Mr Stevens.*

Another file showed the two defendants were both convicted of murder by majority verdicts and jailed for life.

He glanced across at his colleague.

'Makes grim reading,' he told her. 'You know, Wendy, we've got a massive task on our hands here. I'm going to have to see if the DCI can pull something out of the hat with his Birmingham contacts. We've got to see if these men were framed over the murder of Brendan O'Sullivan and, if so, by whom? And, if they were innocent of the crime, who were the real killers? It's a hell of a challenge. And, by the end of it all, we might discover our police colleagues over in Summerstoke made some appalling blunders over the evidence.'

Chapter 13

The following morning, Gavin Roscoe drove to central Birmingham, to the streets of Digbeth where he had spent several years on patrol as a young constable. During the Victorian age the district had been an industrial powerhouse with vast factories operating at all hours.

Easily reached by rail or canal, the location was once a hive of activity and a bustling city hub. It had passed through an era of neglect as city planners struggled to dream up new schemes for the disused warehouses, factories and mills.

But now old buildings were gradually being given new lives as community centres and art galleries. New flats were springing up. The age of neglect was slowly being replaced by an era of hope.

After finding a parking space for his car, Roscoe walked to the housing estate he had once patrolled with its mix of tower blocks, low-rise flats and maisonettes.

As far as he recalled, his old friend, Pat Clancy, lived in a flat beneath one of the ten-storey tower blocks which had been built during the 1960s. He was one of five resident caretakers.

He knocked on the door of the ground-floor flat where he believed his friend still lived.

Pat had wide contacts throughout the city. He was so well-known and well-liked that people from various walks of life trusted him with information and gossip. He came from a family of ten and each of his brothers and sisters worked in a different industry. Each of them, like him, had become a walking database of facts and figures.

In particular, Pat had vast knowledge of the residents of the Cumberland Estate, many of whom were on first name terms with him.

The door was opened by a dishevelled young mother with a bawling child in her grasp.

'No, Pat don't live here no more,' she said. 'We ain't got no caretaker since he retired, but they've give him a flat on the first floor. I think it's number fifteen.' With that, she closed the door.

Roscoe entered the lift, which stank of urine, and moments later emerged on the first-floor balcony above. He quickly found number fifteen and rang the doorbell. After a short wait, his burly, silver-haired Irish friend emerged in the doorway.

Pat was a cheerful, middle-aged man with receding hair and a gentle manner.

'Gavin! What a pleasant surprise, to be sure,' he said. 'Won't you come in? What are you doing round these parts again? Have you fallen on hard times now?' He embraced him like a Frenchman greeting a D-Day liberator.

'It's been a long time, Pat,' said Roscoe. 'How are you keeping? How are your family?'

'We're all fine, thank you,' said Pat. 'And how are you? How's it going down in the country with the carrot crunchers?'

'It's fine, Pat. But don't ever think it's quiet down there,' said Roscoe. 'If you're ever down our way, we must go for a drink, Pat. I never forget all the help and friendship you've given me over the years.'

'Not at all, not at all. Won't you come in?'

Pat led the chief inspector down a long, narrow hallway, past a kitchen, bathroom and two bedrooms, to the living room at the end. It was a bright room with pale yellow walls. There were blue floral-patterned curtains on either side of the large window at the end of the room. But the only views from the window were of flats, concrete walkways, and parked cars.

Roscoe made himself comfortable on a grey, three-seater settee while Pat sat opposite in a matching armchair.

'Is it three years now since you were promoted?'

'That's right,' said Roscoe. 'I don't think I want any higher rank than I've got. My father-in-law is retiring now and it's made me wonder about doing the same.'

'Oh, I see,' said Pat, opening a packet of cigarettes. 'Would you like one of these?'

Roscoe declined as Pat struck a match and lit one.

'Pat, just between us, I'm looking into the "body in the bath" case.'

'Oh, poor old Brendan. Such a nice fella. What a terrible thing those guys did. What were those two bastards called? Stevens and Kumar, if my memory serves me well.'

'It serves you very well, Pat. Yes, Winston Stevens and Raj Kumar, but you've heard about the men's campaign for justice, haven't you? They both claim their alibis at the time of the murder have been completely ignored.'

He smiled as he blew out a cloud of tobacco smoke.

'Nothing much escapes old Pat. I've seen some recent press reports. Those guys have got some good PR.'

Roscoe sighed. 'Pat, those convictions don't look safe at all and there are rumours about possible police interference with the evidence.'

'Oh really? I didn't know that.'

Roscoe nodded. 'What we need to know is whether any of your contacts have any inkling as to whether any of this is true and, if so, does anyone have an idea who the real killers might've been.'

Pat scratched his head. 'Well, now you're asking something, old friend. All I can do is ask around. I keep my ear to the ground, as you know, but no little titbits have come my way. Listen, for an old friend, I'll put some feelers out and I'll get back to you. Of course, this case involves the murky world of drug dealing and it might be a tough nut to crack.'

Roscoe said goodbye to his friend and drove out of Birmingham. He'd been pleased to see his long-term informant again and he was certain Pat would not disappoint him. He'd proved extremely reliable in the past.

* * *

Delayed by heavy evening traffic in the city, the chief inspector took more than an hour to reach his home on the outskirts of Queensbridge. But finally, after a twenty-five-mile journey through the Birmingham suburbs and Warwickshire countryside, he arrived in the narrow, tree-lined lane that led to his detached 1930s home, The Willows.

His wife Helen must have been listening out for the hum of his engine. She was standing at the front door as he locked his car away and stepped past the leaded light windows.

'Hi, love,' he said, planting a kiss firmly on her cheek. 'Everything all right?'

She beamed at him. 'Think you'd better come in and sit down. George is here. He's got the day off.'

'Is he OK?'

'He's getting married,' she said with a smile that could have lit up a darkened street.

'You're right. I think I'd better sit down,' he said, striding into the living room and settling himself down on the settee. 'It's a bit sudden, isn't it? I assume Amanda's the lucky lady?'

'Yes,' said Helen, following him into the room. 'He says he's completely smitten with her and wants to spend the rest of his life with her.'

'So, when's the happy event?'

'Not till next year. They need to save up for it and, as you know, neither of them is on brilliant money at the moment. I think Amanda wants a summer wedding.'

'But where are they going to live?' asked Roscoe. 'He's in digs and she's in a flat-share.'

'It'll be difficult for them, I know, but they're hoping to get a small flat together.'

'They might have to settle for a broom cupboard, the way property prices are going. Oh well, good for George. Next summer, he'll be what? Twenty-three?'

'Yes, and she'll be nearly twenty-two.'

'I suppose we were roughly that age when we got engaged. So where's George now?'

'He's upstairs. He'd wanted to tell us both together, but he was so excited he blurted it out to me as soon as he arrived. He's been on a night shift. He's gone up to bed now. He was so shattered, the poor love. He's going to bring Amanda down here soon – so we can all have a chat together about their plans.'

'That's wonderful because we've only met her a couple of times and they were quite brief. I'd no idea what he was planning. He's a lad, isn't he? Any idea about the best man?'

They heard the thud of a footstep on the landing and a creaking sound on the stairs.

'Is this George coming down now?' Roscoe asked.

Helen glanced behind her. 'Yes, here he is. I thought you were sleeping, love?'

George, in a dressing gown and slippers, plodded through the hall, rubbing his eyes, and stood in the living room doorway.

'I've had a nap,' he mumbled. 'Hi, Dad. I heard the car. What do you think?'

Roscoe smiled. 'I'm delighted,' he said, rising from his seat and stepping towards his son. He gave him a quick hug. 'You'll have to bring Amanda over so we can warn her about you.'

A slight hint of alarm flashed across George's face until he realised his father was joking.

'Have you got a best man yet?' Roscoe asked

'I was thinking of asking Sean Munro.'

'Oh, your friend from the course?'

'Yes.

'Oh, that's good. I like Sean. His dad was a high-ranking officer in the Met. Will it be a church wedding?'

'I'm not sure, Dad. There's still a lot to be decided.'

'Yes. It's early days. So, you're officially engaged now?'

'Not yet. We've got to go shopping for a ring.'

'And I've got some other news,' Helen said. 'My mother called in this morning. They visited the Crown and Sceptre and realise it's not suitable. So, they want to book the tearooms for my father's retirement party next year. By the way, I don't want you playing any of your silly jokes – you know, giving him a colouring book and set of crayons, for example.'

Roscoe laughed. 'We could get one of those mugs which says, "You can't make me – I'm retired".'

Chapter 14

Ten days after interviewing Robert Brown in the car park at Foxwell Heath, PC Nina Kaur was strolling along a busy road in the town of Redditch when a motorist drew up.

Despite her and PC Graham McDonald being in uniform, the driver drove up onto the pavement and prepared to lock his car – ignoring the brightly-painted double yellow lines intended to deter parkers.

The twenty-eight-year-old officer knocked sharply on the window of the Peugeot hatchback as shoppers tried to shuffle past. The male driver wound the window down.

'Just what do you think you're doing, sir?' she demanded, bending down towards the errant driver.

'Sorry, miss. I'm in a bit of a rush. Didn't see you there.'

'Drive on and find somewhere sensible to park,' the constable said.

The man wound his window up, checked over his left shoulder for any approaching traffic and pulled away.

As she re-joined her colleague, she caught a sudden glimpse among a crowd of shoppers of a face she appeared to recognise. It was just a partial view, but she recalled the unkempt, dark-brown hair and black facial stubble of the man who'd given his name as Robert Brown.

'Quick, Graham!' she said. 'That dodgy guy we saw at Foxwell Heath, Robert Brown – I've just seen him. He's just walked past us.'

'You mean the guy who gave a false address in Shawley Green?'

'Yes. He's still got the same black jacket on. Let's get after him.'

PC McDonald broke into a run. He could see a man with dark-brown hair and a dark jacket moving steadily along the pavement ahead of them. With any luck, Brown would not notice he was being pursued and they would quickly catch up with him. PC Kaur was sprinting after her colleague, although he was more agile than her. They managed to keep the man in their sights. They were edging closer.

Then, inexplicably, Brown glanced over his right shoulder. He noticed the two officers hurrying towards him and took to his heels.

'Damn!' the policewoman muttered as they were forced to exert themselves even more. Then, mysteriously, their quarry vanished.

'He's run into the shopping centre!' said PC McDonald. 'That's going to make our job a hundred times harder.'

'Never mind,' said his colleague, breathlessly. 'We've got to try and catch him somehow.'

The pair raced through the revolving doors at the centre, nearly knocking over two elderly ladies as they passed.

'There he is!' yelled PC McDonald, as Brown wove his way in and out of a cluster of people directly ahead of them.

'Stop that man – the man in the black jacket!' he screamed at the top of his voice.

It was as if his prayers had been answered. Three men and a woman who were close to the fleeing man quickly realised the loud entreaty came from a policeman. They sprang into action and surrounded Brown in a circle, preventing him from proceeding further. McDonald arrived seconds later and slapped handcuffs on him.

'Robert Brown, I'm arresting you for obstructing a police officer in the course of his duties by giving a false address.'

He then recited the remaining words of the police caution. Brown said nothing in response. PC Kaur struggled for breath as she thanked the shoppers who aided them.

'We're so grateful,' she told them. 'We'd been chasing him for a quarter of mile, so you've all been a great help.'

As the pair led their prisoner out of the shopping centre, she called CID at St James Street to tell them of the arrest.

'Yes, just nabbed him in the centre of Redditch,' she told a member of the murder investigation team. 'We're bringing him in right now.'

* * *

Later that afternoon, Gavin Roscoe walked into the main CID office and was informed of the arrest. He called his sergeant in.

'Remind me who this guy is, Sunita,' he said.

'He's the man with the blue Volvo parked in the Yeoman's Lane car park at the time of the doctor's murder,' she said. 'He gave a false name and address. His real name's Robert Bowcott. He's twenty-eight and lives in

Foxwell Green, just a short distance from the murder scene. I've asked Khalid to see if he's got any form.'

'Why did he give a false name?'

'No idea, sir.'

'All right. So, if we've got him in the cells, we'd better haul him up and have a little chat with him. Are you free to sit in with me?'

'Yes, sir. Of course.'

'All right. Can you see if Interview Room One is available?'

* * *

Half an hour later, two custody officers accompanied Robert Bowcott into the small ground-floor interview room which boasted cream-coloured walls and the smell of fresh paint. Roscoe and Roy arrived shortly afterwards.

As he turned on the recording equipment, the chief inspector announced, 'DCI Roscoe at two thirty. Interview with Robert Boycott.'

'Bowcott, sir,' Sunita reminded him.

'Of course, Robert Bowcott,' said the chief inspector. 'Also present is DS Roy.'

The two detectives then sat down at the mahogany table, opposite their suspect, who appeared downcast.

'Right,' said Roscoe. 'It looks like you've been playing games with us, Mr Bowcott.'

'I don't know what you mean,' said the suspect, looking the chief inspector in the face for the first time.

Roscoe was unimpressed by the man's greasy, unkempt hair and facial stubble.

'You gave us a bogus address in Shawley Green which you've used before to dodge paying parking tickets and other bills,' Roscoe said. 'You also told us your surname was Brown. What've you got to say for yourself?'

'I didn't mean no harm.'

'Well, your behaviour's been highly suspicious. Tell me what time you first arrived in the car park at Yeoman's Lane on 8 October.'

'It was about half past nine.'

'Why did you go there?'

'Well, I've been having trouble with me motor, like. I was on the way home from Queensbridge, and I needed somewhere to stop.'

'Your morning began with a trip to Queensbridge?'

'That's right.'

'What did you go there for?'

'I needed a bit of shopping, like.'

'Like what, for instance?'

'Just groceries. I like the supermarket there.'

Sunita frowned. 'What time did you leave your home, Mr Bowcott?'

'It must have been around eight o'clock. I like shopping early in the day. There are fewer people around.'

'What time did you leave Queensbridge?' the chief inspector asked.

'Must've been about five past nine, like. I should think I reached Yeoman's Lane about nine twenty-five or nine thirty.'

'Why did you drive into the car park?'

'Well, my engine's been overheating. I'd topped up the rad with water before I left home, but the temperature gauge suddenly shot up. I stopped to let everything cool down. Then I topped up the rad with some water.'

Sunita interrupted. 'Have you had your car fixed yet?

'No. Not yet.'

'Good,' she said. 'I think we'll have to take a look at it – just to check you've been telling us the truth.'

The chief inspector grinned. 'That's a good point, Sergeant.'

'Why do you need to check me rad's buggered?'

'Just to ascertain you're telling us the truth,' the chief inspector retorted. 'You've told us so many lies that, from now on, we'll have to check and double-check everything you tell us. Anyway, why did you stop in the car park? Why didn't you carry on until you reached home? You only live a few hundred metres further on.'

'I simply didn't think I'd make it. Steam was starting to pour out of the engine.'

'What time did you finally leave the car park?'

'Oh, I was only there a short while, like.'

Sunita shook her head. 'That's nonsense. You were there at quarter to ten when the first officers arrived on scene.'

'That's right, but I was just leaving then.'

'Why did you return after ten thirty?' Roscoe demanded.

'I was just curious. You don't often get a murder round our way. It's a bit of gab, int-it? A bit of gossip, like?'

'A bit of gossip, eh? Well, we're going to give you a little more to gossip about. We're going to keep you in custody for a few more hours while we examine your car and search your house. If we find there's a definite problem with the cooling system, we'll probably let you go. But if there's nothing wrong with it, we'll have a few more questions for you. Do you understand?'

'Yes, sir.'

'All right,' said the chief inspector. Then, turning towards the recording device, he declared the interview was over.

Shortly after Bowcott had been returned to his cell and the two detectives had returned to CID, DC Khalid took Roscoe aside.

'Sir, I've just been checking, and our friend Robert Bowcott has a number of antecedents,' he told the chief inspector. 'He's served time for theft, dishonesty and affray. But his longest sentence was for attacking a man with a samurai sword.'

Chapter 15

It was a mild, foggy evening as Tom Vickers drove into the car park at the quiet roadside pub. He found a parking space and cut the engine. He was followed seconds later by Sunita Roy in her Peugeot 208. The inspector got out and called to her through the open window.

'Do you remember this place?'

She gazed across at the stone-built inn, surrounded by rolling countryside and smiled.

'Of course. It's one of the first places you brought me when we started seeing each other.'

'I was trying to think where we could go this evening,' he told her. 'Then I remembered this place.'

Sunita had a few fond memories of the Wheatsheaf Inn, near Redditch. She recalled it had flagstone floors, dark oak beams with low ceilings and wood panelling. In the depths of winter, a roaring log fire greeted visitors.

A waitress in a dark-blue apron with short, dark, curly hair showed them to a spot in a quiet corner of the bustling gastropub and brought them menus. Then she lit a candle in the middle of their table before walking away. Vickers looked up from reading his menu.

'I'd been thinking of taking you to the White Swan at Shawley Green, but the guv'nor reckons the food's terrible there.'

'Yes, he's got firm ideas about food and drinks. I suppose that comes from being married to someone who runs a tearoom.'

When the waitress returned, the inspector ordered beef Wellington, while Sunita opted for grilled salmon. They chose a bottle of pinot noir.

She smiled at him across the table. 'By the way, I won't be able to spend any time with you the first weekend of next month.'

'Why's that?'

'My ex-flatmate, Rupa, is coming to stay for the weekend. She's splitting her time between being with me and her sister in Leamington.'

'Not to worry. I'll probably spend that weekend throwing myself into the Sepulchre work.'

'It's taking a lot of your time, isn't it?'

'Too right. It's annoying the guv'nor can't spare any extra staff at present, although he's promised to try very hard to find me someone. Don't mention this to anyone else, but Wendy's not a great help. She's very slow. Don't think her heart's in the job. Anyway, how about the doctor in the woods? You were telling me about this shifty character, Robert Bowcott. Forensics were checking his motor?'

She nodded. 'His car does have a problem overheating, so he was at least telling us the truth about that. But he's got a bit of a violent past and we're going to be interviewing him again tomorrow. The boss thought a night in the cells might do him good.'

'But has he got any connection with the doctor? Is he a former patient or former neighbour or something?'

She shook her head before taking a sip from her wine glass.

'We can't find any link between him and the doctor. It looks like we'll have to let him go.'

'So, the search for the killer goes on.'

'Yes. The boss is getting agitated, but I've found you have to be patient with murder investigations. You have to take things one step at a time.'

'I agree. Ah, this looks like our food now.'

The waitress set their plates down on the table and asked if they required any sauces, which they declined.

'This salmon's delicious,' said Sunita. 'Tom, you promised to show me the delights of Halesowen this weekend. Are you still up for that?'

The inspector tried to remain calm despite an inward sense of alarm.

'I'm not sure that's a good idea, Sunita. This investigation I'm on is taking up so much of my time.'

'But I thought it was all planned. We were going to visit the shopping centre and have a walk in the park.'

He finished a mouthful of food. 'Did I say that?'

'Yes. You've been full of praise for the town. You said that if you forget about the Hagley Road, it's a great little town.'

'I think we'll have to leave it for now. Let me come over to Warwick tomorrow evening and we can go for a few drinks.'

'Tom, I'm disappointed. I don't often come over to your place. You're not hiding anything, are you?'

He glared. 'Why on earth would you say that? Of course, not. It's just that this Sepulchre business requires a lot of background research, which I do best when I'm on my own at home.'

* * *

The inspector was incandescent with rage when he arrived back at his house just after eleven o'clock that evening to find his wife's car was still on the drive.

His wife, Chloe, had faithfully promised she would only be staying a few days. He'd insisted she leave by Thursday of that week at the latest.

It was now Friday evening and she was still in the house. The outside light had been left on – perhaps an attempt by her to curry favour with him. And he recognised the strains of one of his Ed Sheeran tracks being played.

'What's the meaning of this?' his voice boomed as he marched into the living room. 'You said you'd be gone by Thursday.'

Chloe was lounging across his three-seater settee in a white negligee with a pink pillow under her head. She glanced up on hearing his voice.

'Sorry, Tom. Is the music a bit loud? I'll turn it down. I love the album.'

'You agreed to be gone by Thursday and today's Friday.'

'I'm sorry, Tom. I've tried, but I just can't find anywhere to go.'

'We can't go on like this, Chloe. You've got a choice. Either you drive off tonight and stay with one of your relatives or I'll call the police and have you made to leave to avoid a breach of the peace.'

She swung her feet round and sat up straight.

'What? You'd risk the humiliation of calling in your colleagues from the West Midlands force to have your own wife thrown out? You'd be a laughingstock.'

The red-faced inspector glared at her.

'I know. You wouldn't think my life's reached such a low point, would you? But here I am having to threaten my own wife with the police in an effort to get my own privacy and freedom back.'

'You're not serious.'

He slipped his mobile phone from his pocket. 'I *am* serious. I'm very serious. I'm going to dial the emergency number now.'

Chloe stood up and walked towards him. He noticed her blonde hair had been newly styled with ravishing curls, while her body exuded an attractive fragrance.

'Don't be a silly boy,' she said. 'Put your phone away, Tom.'

'Look, you're leaving, God dammit!'

'Tom, darling, I'm sorry. I didn't think you meant it when you said you wanted me out by Thursday. I thought that maybe – who knows? – maybe I could talk you round.'

She reached across and fondled his chest. He immediately backed away.

'Those days are over, I'm afraid, Chloe. Look, I've spelt it out as clearly as I bloody can. I put you up for a few days because you seemed desperate, but I now want you out. And I'm taking no excuses. I want you gone by Monday night at the latest or, seriously, I'm going to have a crazy moment and call my mates from West Midlands. And hang the consequences.'

Chapter 16

Gavin Roscoe drew back his bedroom curtains on the Monday morning and gazed across his rear lawn to the golden, bronze leaves of the ash and beech trees beyond. Summer was now a fading memory. Only white asters and mauve cyclamen, those hardy stars of autumn, were thriving now and the nearby orchards were bearing the final fruit of the year.

He left Helen to sleep and, after slipping on his dressing gown, stepped downstairs to make himself a coffee. He'd only taken a few sips when his phone, which he'd placed on the kitchen table, began to ring.

The soft tones of Pat Clancy's voice echoed down the handset. 'Gavin, I'm not calling too early, now?'

'No. I've been up for a while. How are you doing?'

'I'm fine and dandy. Listen, I've asked around and I've got the names of two fellows who work as enforcers for the 101 Crew. That's the band of folk your bent coppers are meant to be mixed up with. But this was a tough nut to crack, Mr G, and it's going to cost you a good drink.'

Roscoe smiled. 'Don't worry, Pat. You'll be well looked after, as always.'

'It was no easy task to come up with them. No one likes a grass, but, by the same token, folk living on the wrong side of the law don't like to see two innocent guys take the rap for something they didn't do,' he continued. 'Listen, I'm never totally at peace talking on the phone, so I'll text you over the names later. Good to see you the other day, Mr G. We must get together sometime.'

Then the line went dead.

Within minutes, as the chief inspector was drinking the rest of his coffee and reading his morning paper in the living room, a text came through with the two names he sought.

Three hours later, he was at St James Street sitting behind his office desk when Sunita Roy tapped on the door.

'Sir, are you busy?' she asked.

He shook his head. 'No, come in. What's going on?'

'I'm just about to set off for Tewkesbury to see the Stanbrooks.'

The chief inspector leaned back. 'Oh yes – Dr Deeley's aunt and her husband.'

'I was going to ask DC Khalid to come with me.'

'No, I've had a bright idea this morning. I want him to revisit all the witnesses who were in the woods and in the car park at Foxwell Heath. While he's at it, I want him to have another look at the CCTV around Heath Road, on the other side of the woods. I've got a feeling we might be missing something. I want to build up as precise a picture as possible of all the movements made by the people in the area at the time of the murder. I particularly want to eliminate anyone in the car park or parked in Heath Road. Khalid's best placed to do that since he's been involved in the investigation from the start. I think you should take DC Dawson with you to see the Stanbrooks because his last job's fallen through.'

'All right, sir. I'll go and find Dawson now.'

'Good, and can you send Khalid in?'

* * *

'So, how have you been, Brett?' asked Sunita as they set off in her car at midday for their forty-five-mile journey to Gloucestershire.

'Not too bad, Sarge,' said Dawson, as he began ruffling his spiky blond hair. 'Of course, you couldn't say the same for my football team. Villa got thrashed last month by Sheffield United, although we had a good result against Swansea.'

Sunita shrugged. 'As you know, Brett–'

'You're not interested in soccer. I know. What you been up to?'

'Went for a nice meal in Redditch the other night.'

Dawson glanced out of the window as they approached the M42 motorway.

'I've got a girlfriend now,' he murmured. 'She's a paramedic.'

'I'm glad for you, Brett.'

'Yeah, she's a nice girl but it's like taking a brisk walk over hot coals when I go round her house.'

'How come?'

'Her dad's a City supporter. Sarge, no one's explained why we're heading to Tewkesbury.'

'Well, you know the murdered doctor wasn't a poor man, don't you?'

He nodded. 'Yeah. The papers reckon he was worth up to three million quid.'

'Yes, well, most of it goes to his aunt Valerie. That's who we're going to see. Do you remember that Gloucestershire marriage that caused a bit of controversy because the groom was so much younger than the bride?'

'Yes. He was in his forties, and she was in her seventies, if I remember right. Is it the same couple?'

'Yes, it is. Rufus and Valerie Stanbrook. She's the widow of a dairy farmer. They met online. He was a penniless carpet salesman. Now they're running the farm together.'

'I doubt whether they'll be happy to see us,' he muttered.

'Well, you never know.'

After travelling a few miles along the M42, they turned off near Redditch and picked up the A46 near Queensbridge. The dual carriageway took them through farmland on the Warwickshire and Worcestershire border. Just outside Evesham, they passed over the River Avon and the Cotswold Line, which links Oxford and Hereford by train.

Dawson played a game on his tablet that involved killing as many crazed zombie characters as he could. Every now and then he would cry, 'Gotcha!'

After a while, Sunita found it irritating. She thought to herself, 'Grow up, Brett. You're twenty-three.' Then, out loud, she asked, 'Do you ever grow tired of playing those games?'

'Come on, Sarge. You take life too seriously. It's just a way of easing the tension. You should try it. I tell you what. I'll try and make you laugh. What did Fred Flintstone say when he heard he'd won a holiday to Abu Dhabi?'

'I don't know. What did he say?' she replied.

'Abu Dhabi-doo! Here's another. What do plumbers tell their customers? Every time you flush a toilet, you put food in my family's mouths!'

'I think that'll do for the moment,' she said dryly.

She drove them past Evesham football ground, a garden nursery and a lake before taking a left turn down a country lane which led to the quaint Gloucestershire village of Bishop's Stoke.

Just before half past one, after travelling down a narrow lane for a few miles, she spotted a sign saying 'Lower Clavington Farm'.

She frowned as she glanced at the ramshackle buildings.

'This must be the place, but it looks a bit run-down.'

The wooden five-bar gate was rotten. A barn on the right had part of its roof missing. Another building was largely covered by ivy.

Sunita drove through the entrance and parked next to the barn. Then they got out and walked slowly towards a white, detached dormer bungalow, which they assumed to be the farmhouse.

'Lunchtime's probably as good a time as any to find a farmer at home,' Dawson remarked with a grin.

The air was cold. Sunita wished she hadn't left her coat behind in the car.

Suddenly a dog began barking inside the bungalow. A man with short black hair and a short-sleeved shirt undone at the neck opened a window to the left of the oak front door. He peered out while the dog continued barking.

'What do you want?' he demanded.

'Sorry to bother you. Mr Stanbrook?'

'I might be. Who wants to know?'

'Heart of England Police. Sorry to call at a sad time, but we want to ask you and Mrs Stanbrook a few questions.'

'It's not very convenient.'

'We'll try not to take up too much of your time.'

'Hang on a minute.'

He closed the window and withdrew. Seconds later, he opened the front door as the dog began barking again.

'Stop it, Major!' the man shouted. 'Now, young lady, what did you want to talk to us about?'

'We're investigating the death of Dr Deeley and thought you could help us with some information.'

The sergeant observed that the man was stocky, about five feet ten inches tall and had a plump face with a goatee beard. She waved her warrant card towards him as he stepped out of the front door.

'I'm DS Roy and this is DC Dawson,' she said.

He frowned. 'I suppose you'd better come in.' Then, as the young German shepherd dog came towards them, he explained, 'This is Major. He won't hurt you. As soon as you've said hello and patted him, he's your friend for life.'

The pair followed his advice and stroked Major. Dawson wasn't convinced the animal would be his friend for life. It seemed to regard him with suspicion. After Major had spent more than a minute growling at the constable, the householder took the dog away and locked him in the kitchen.

He then led them into the large living room at the back of the house which overlooked some fields. Sunita noticed a baby asleep in a pushchair in front of the patio doors.

Observing her glance, the man said, 'I'm babysitting. Now what can I do for you?'

'I take it you're Mr Stanbrook?' she asked.

'The very same,' he replied, sitting on a brown leather settee close to his baby grandson. 'My wife's in bed. As you can imagine, she's been very upset. The doctor thinks that, on top of the bereavement, she may have eaten something that doesn't agree with her.'

As he invited the two detectives to sit on two dining chairs next to a table, he continued.

'We're both devastated. The doctor worked hard and, until now, he'd been a lucky man. He didn't deserve to die – not in that horrific way with a carving fork in the chest.'

Sunita, whose eyes had been fixed on the baby, turned her gaze to him.

'You've been reading the press reports?'

'That's right. Whoever did it is meant to have picked up the murder weapon after finding it lying beside an abandoned campfire. Is that right? Doesn't sound as though the perpetrator was well prepared for the task, does it?'

She nodded in agreement as she made a note of his remarks in her notebook.

'No,' she agreed.

'I won't pretend I liked Deeley,' he went on. 'He'd let the cottage in Sinton Bank fall into disrepair. The place was badly neglected, and Valerie was upset about that. It had been her childhood home, you see.'

The visitors glanced at each other, recognising the irony of the situation. They were listening to a man in a neglected property complaining about his relative's neglected property. But they said nothing.

Stanbrook showed no signs of stopping now.

'You wouldn't think a man with so many houses would let a place get so run-down, would you? Valerie's sister, Sarah, was always complaining about the cold and damp at the cottage.'

Dawson's face was blank. 'He owned several places, did he?'

'More than fifteen houses and flats. But, like the man or not, he didn't deserve to die like that, stabbed to death. What's adding to my wife's upset is we can't even organise a funeral. The coroner won't release the body until you people have finished making inquiries and that could go on for months.'

Dawson leaned forward in his seat. 'We've heard all the money and property goes to you and your wife. Is that right?' he asked.

Mr Stanbrook's demeanour suddenly changed.

'Who told you that?' he demanded.

'It's just a rumour.'

'Well, you shouldn't listen to bloody rumours. If that's why you've come round here, prying into our affairs, I suggest you leave,' he bellowed. His shouting prompted the baby to cry.

'I'm sorry if we've upset you,' said the sergeant. 'I realise you've had a terrible time.'

Stanbrook rocked the baby's pram until the infant fell silent again.

'Well, you people should be a bit more sensitive when you come bursting into people's homes without being invited.'

Sunita tried to overlook his growing annoyance.

'Mr Stanbrook, I want to ask you about Monday, 8 October. I need a detailed account of your movements.'

Stanbrook stroked his straggly beard. 'I was at the farm all day.'

'What sort of jobs were you doing?'

'I remember it because we did a lot of clipping. Clipping the ewes around the tail end. Tiring work, but it's got to be done. We've got a hundred and sixty ewes.'

'Anyone with you?'

'Only my flock manager.'

'What time did you start?'

'Six thirty. Had a bit of a lie-in, you might say. It's a pity Valerie wasn't well enough to see you. She'd have a lot more to say. I have to be careful because the doctor and his mother were *her* relatives – not mine.'

She nodded. 'We understand.'

He rose to his feet. 'Now, if you don't mind, I've got lot of things to do.'

'All right. Thank you for your time, sir,' said Sunita. 'I hope Mrs Stanbrook gets better quickly.'

'So do I,' he replied.

Dawson remained silent as they stepped out into the chill late October air.

He had found it hard to warm to the man who had become an overnight millionaire. He glanced at the sergeant. 'He flew off the handle a bit just then, didn't he?'

'Suppose it's been a traumatic time for him and his wife.'

'Yeah, but you'd think three million quid would help ease the pain.'

Chapter 17

Tom Vickers' desk phone rang out on Monday evening as he was about to leave his office for the day.

'Vickers,' he announced as he grasped the handset.

Roscoe's genial voice boomed out. 'Tom, I've been trying to reach you all day.'

'Sorry, sir. I was meaning to get back to you. It's just been so busy.'

'Look, I've got the details of two men who are believed to have been Brendan O'Sullivan's regular dealers. Have you got a pen?'

The inspector raced round his desk, sat down, and, with the phone cradled between his shoulder and ear, searched for his pen and notebook.

'I'm all set,' he informed him.

'Right. The first name I've got for you is Tyrone Blake. I've had Dawson making some quick inquiries for me. Dawson says there's a man on the database with that name who's more than six feet tall with close-cropped dark hair and he's got a tattoo of a dagger on his right arm. He's from a Jamaican family.'

'What sort of age would he be?'

'We understand he's around thirty and he's got form for drug offences and violent crime. The second guy is Tahir Khan, who's about the same age. Dawson says he's five feet eight inches tall, of average build and from an Asian background. He's also got form for drugs and violence, and both men have done stretches in Ashwood Vale. They're believed to have regularly sold drugs to O'Sullivan, mainly cocaine.'

Vickers smiled. 'Very useful information. I won't ask where it came from.'

'I wouldn't tell you if you did,' said the chief inspector. 'But rest assured it's from a highly reliable source.'

'Thank you, sir. I'm busy interviewing all the officers who were involved in the case at the moment and all the witnesses. DC Hopkirk's been helpful up to a point, but–'

'I'm sorry, Tom. We're very stretched – particularly with this Deeley case. I can't spare you any officers at present.'

* * *

As Vickers set off for his home thirty miles away, his mind was troubled. He'd given his wife an ultimatum: leave by Monday night or he'd be forced to take drastic action.

As he travelled nearer and nearer to Halesowen, he dreaded the prospect of finding she had defied him again.

Sure enough, as he drew up outside his home, Chloe's car was still standing on the forecourt – just as it had for the past ten days.

He found her hobbling about in the living room.

'Oh, Tom,' she cried as he emerged from the hall. 'I'm in agony. I think I've either sprained or broken my ankle. I can't walk on it.'

She screwed up her eyes as though in pain. He threw his grey coat and mobile onto an armchair.

'Oh, very bloody convenient!' he exclaimed. 'You know this is the night you're meant to be leaving.'

'Oh, Tom. I haven't been able to find anywhere. None of my relatives can help. But, right now, I'm in agony. Can you drive me to the doctor's? I certainly can't drive.'

The inspector sighed. 'Won't they be closed?'

'They said that if I can get to the practice in Redditch by six o'clock, they can see me.'

He shook his head. His patience with his wife was wearing thin. He harboured doubts about whether she had genuinely injured her ankle. Was it just another ploy to delay her departure from the house? He suspected it was. On the other hand, what if she had a genuine injury? He wasn't a cruel man and didn't want to see anyone suffering – and that included the woman who had brought so much suffering into his life in recent times.

'All right,' he relented. 'I'll drive you there now. I suppose this means you'll have to stay living here a little longer.'

'Thank you, Tom. I didn't think you'd let me down. Could you fetch my coat?'

* * *

Five minutes later, at a quarter to six, the pair set off for Redditch in the inspector's car. After twenty minutes, he drew up outside the large, red-brick Victorian house in the Worcestershire town where Chloe was registered with a GP.

There were double yellow lines on the main road outside. Vickers knew he couldn't park there for long so he took the precaution of turning the car's hazard lights on as he left the vehicle parked partly on the pavement and began to help her out of the passenger door.

Fully focussed on the task in hand, he failed to notice the driver of a passing blue Ford Focus slowing down as he put his arm round Chloe. The driver watched as Vickers allowed Chloe to lean on him while helping her across the block-paved forecourt and through the doors of the building.

Once they reached the reception area, a practice nurse took over and Chloe was eased into a waiting room chair.

'Are you the lady who phoned up with an ankle problem?' asked the middle-aged receptionist as she peered at Chloe over the top of her glasses.

'Yes. I think I've just sprained it as I came downstairs earlier on.'

'All right. Stay where you are. Dr Robbins won't be long.'

'Phone me when they've finished with you,' Vickers muttered as he returned to his car and drove off to find somewhere to park.

An intriguing thought crossed his mind. He could drive off home and leave her there. But it wouldn't look good to the doctor and reception staff if a serving police officer were to act in that way. In any case, her car and all her belongings were still at his home. He would just have to be patient and let events take their course.

Chapter 18

The sun was dipping behind the clouds as Omar Khalid arrived at the nineteenth-century cottage in Loman's Green where Howard Cooper lived with his wife Jessica.

A green board outside proclaimed: 'J.H. Cooper. Golden Retrievers and Labradors. Breeding, boarding, quarantine.'

Right on cue, as he was reading the sign, several dogs heard his car door slam and began to bark. He gazed across at the grey, stone cottage, which stood close to woodland. He wasn't sure where the noise was coming from but noticed some high wooden fencing to the left of the cottage and decided the kennels must be behind it.

Clutching a folder of documents, the constable opened the latch on the wooden gate and walked slowly up the stone path to the blue cottage door. As he did so, he was almost dazzled by a bright security light triggered by his arrival.

Within seconds of him pressing the doorbell, Howard Cooper drew back the door and peered out.

'Can I help?' he asked. The householder's face, illuminated by the security light, appeared smiling and friendly. 'Goldies or Labradors?'

The visitor grinned. 'No, I'm from Heart of England Police. DC Khalid. We're re-interviewing witnesses. Do you remember I phoned you? You said any time after 4.30.'

Cooper nodded. 'Yes, of course. I'm sorry. I can't invite you in. Some of the puppies are loose in the kitchen.'

'No Mrs Cooper?' the constable asked while searching for Mr Cooper's police statement in his folder.

'She's gone to her mother's.'

'Oh, I see.'

The constable went through the statement, question by question. Mr Cooper confirmed all the information as correct.

'Where were you before your trip to the woods, sir?'

'Well, here, of course.'

'And how come you only took your dog Bella for a walk – not any of the other dogs?'

'Bella had some veterinary treatment a few weeks ago and in September we were advised to take her for more frequent walks.'

'Is there anything you'd like to add to your statement, sir?'

'Well, it's probably not important but there was one thing that's been on my mind,' said Mr Cooper. 'You know the Honda motorbike in the car park? For some reason, I've remembered part of the number plate.'

'Really, sir? That's interesting.'

'Yes. The registration began with MD66.'

Khalid wrote the number down in his notebook. 'You didn't think to mention that before?'

'Never really had the opportunity.'

'Did you see a man on a bicycle at any time?'

'No. I'm sorry. I didn't.' He paused. 'How's the investigation going anyway?'

'I think we're making progress, sir. These things often take time.'

'I've had some counselling sessions – it upset me so much.'

Khalid nodded. 'Extremely good idea, sir. A problem shared. My colleagues need a chat with a counsellor sometimes after some of the things they have to deal with.'

'It definitely seemed to help me.'

Khalid glanced towards the gate as he prepared to leave. 'Don't you worry, sir. We're fairly confident of catching the offender before he strikes again. Now I'd better go. I've got other people to see.'

'Good evening, officer. Thank you very much for coming.'

* * *

Fifteen minutes later, the constable reached the nearby town of Redditch, where he planned to speak to Fariza Hussain and her daughter, Alisha. Fariza's Victorian semi-detached house, 31 Cornmeadow Road, stood halfway up a hill. So, to be safe, he parked further down the road in a level side street and walked back to their home.

Fariza Hussain welcomed the young detective in and offered to make him some tea, but he declined.

'That's very kind of you indeed, but I'm anxious to get home for my evening meal,' he explained as she led him into a small sitting-room, which had a bay window overlooking the street. 'Is your daughter around by any chance?'

'Alisha's still at work. She and her husband have their own place nearby but she's dropping round here at seven thirty.'

He shook his head. 'I don't want to wait. I've got her phone number and, if I need to, I can easily call her.'

He sat down on a settee while Fariza remained standing.

'Can I ask how you came to notice the body on Foxwell Heath?' he asked.

She shrugged her shoulders. 'Well, it was Mr Cooper who first saw the body. His dog was sniffing around, and he found it in the bushes.'

'Was there anyone else around at the time – a man on a bicycle, for instance?'

'No. We didn't see anyone else until arriving back at the car park.'

Khalid withdrew a copy of her statement from his folder and checked through the details with her.

While they spoke, he noticed a camping stove, a torch, a sleeping bag and some insect repellent in a corner of the room.

'Mrs Hussain, are you planning a camping trip?'

'They're Alisha's,' she explained. 'She's going on holiday abroad with her husband.'

He smiled. 'I was going to say – a bit cold for an outdoor holiday in the UK at this time of year. Well, I think I've finished for now. If there's anything else, I can always catch you on the phone, can't I?'

She nodded. Just then a burly, sullen-faced man burst into the room, whom he assumed to be Fariza's husband.

'Who are you?' the man demanded.

Khalid stood up as Fariza quickly explained their visitor was from the police.

'Well, you should have asked my permission before you came in here, bothering my wife,' insisted the man, who was tall with dark curly hair.

'This is my husband, Abdul,' she explained to the detective.

'It doesn't matter who I am,' the man went on. 'You have to ask me before you come waltzing into my house.'

Khalid shrugged. 'Very sorry, sir, but I'm on police business. Your wife is a witness in a murder case.'

The man placed his hands on his hips.

'I know all that. She's made her statement. Why are you bothering her again? You should be out there, trying to find the killer. He could kill someone else, couldn't he? We're having to use the local park until this maniac's caught.'

'Look, your wife's been very helpful, sir. I was only checking the details of her statement. My boss believes that we often solve cases by being thorough.' Khalid made his way towards the front door. 'I've got everything I need now, thank you, Mrs Hussain.'

'I'm sorry, officer,' she said.

'There's nothing to be sorry about. I'll find my own way out and please tell Alisha I'll be in touch.'

Khalid was annoyed as he walked back to his car. 'There was no need for that guy to act like that,' he told himself. 'None of his bloody business anyway. He wants the bloke caught, doesn't he?'

He had other calls to make, but he was tired after a long day. His girlfriend had promised to cook a chicken supper. He was eager to get home.

But as he left Cornmeadow Road and joined the main road out of Redditch, he saw a familiar figure stepping out of a white Audi. His suspicions were confirmed as he drew nearer. His colleague, Tom Vickers, was escorting a woman into the entrance of a doctor's surgery. If his eyes weren't deceiving him, the inspector had his arm round his estranged wife, Chloe.

Chapter 19

The chief inspector peered out of his office door just after ten o'clock in the morning on Monday, 29 October. Sunita

Roy and Omar Khalid were busily pinning a huge map of the Yeoman's Lane car park to the whiteboard.

'Sergeant!' he yelled. 'Did you tell everyone about the meeting in five minutes?'

'Yes, sir.'

'Are they all able to make it?'

'Yes, sir. Dr Ling apologised. She said she might be a little late because she had to collect something from the lab. Nina Kaur and Graham McDonald, who arrested Bowcott, are also attending – just in case they can contribute something.'

'Yes, that's very helpful, particularly with their knowledge of the Foxwell Green area,' he said, returning to his office. 'Nice work, Sergeant.'

A few minutes later, he peered through his internal window. The buzz of conversation was becoming louder as his team began settling in front of the whiteboard. He noticed two scenes of crime officers had joined them. DS Roy was fastening photographs of suspects and witnesses to the board.

'Good morning, everybody,' he announced while clasping a sheet of paper in his hand. 'Sorry to keep you waiting.'

He smiled and glanced at the board, where his sergeant was in the process of writing names, ages and occupations beneath seven photographs.

'Right. Listen carefully, please,' he told the nine people present. 'I wanted to bring everyone up to date with what's been happening on the Deeley case. Dr Reynolds believes the killer confronted his victim in an area close to the disused campsite at the edge of Foxwell Heath woods. There was a struggle in which the victim fell backwards, striking his head on a tree branch, causing concussion and a subdural haematoma, a bleed on the brain. The killer then attempted to strangle the doctor with a ligature – probably a scarf, tie, towel, or sash.'

He glanced around at his team, who were listening intently.

'Microscopic cotton fibres were found embedded in the victim's skin. Finally, the two-pronged barbecue fork was thrust into the doctor's heart with force. We've tried to trace where the murder weapon came from, but it's a common brand and, in any case, it looks as if the fork wasn't brought into the wood by the killer, so it's unlikely this would lead us anywhere.'

He held up his sheet of paper.

'This is the pathologist's report. I'll read part of it. "The cause of death was a stab wound to the heart which induced severe blood loss in the victim. Death would have occurred fairly quickly."'

He placed the report on a desk in front of him

'Dr Reynolds says no fingerprints were found on the murder weapon. He believes it was wiped clean by the killer. Then he confirms that the body was dragged from the scene of the burnt-out campfire to the location where it was found among the bushes. So much for that. Now here's the most important point I want to make this morning. No ligature's come to light so far in our inquiries and it's imperative we find it.'

He turned towards Sunita Roy, who was standing behind him. 'Sergeant, would you like to repeat what you told me earlier about Robert Bowcott?'

'Yes, sir. Our vehicle team have examined his car and they've confirmed there's an overheating problem caused by a leaking hose. So it appears that when he told us he stopped at the car park in Yeoman's Lane because of a problem with steam under the bonnet, he was probably telling the truth. We also found out the incident with the samurai sword was ten years ago when he was fairly young.'

The chief inspector interrupted. 'I think most of you know we decided two days ago to release him on condition he reports to police daily. He's still a person of interest, though, because he gave a false name and address and because of his strange behaviour near the murder scene.'

A few polite chuckles rippled round the room.

His eyes lit up as Alice Ling, the senior forensic scientist, arrived, taking a chair near the front.

'Ah, Dr Ling. Welcome to our briefing,' he said. 'I'm glad you're here. I gather there's no fresh news about Sarah Deeley?'

She shook her head. 'No, sir. As you know, Dr Reynolds has requested toxicology tests and the results always take a few weeks. This is because so many different specimens of fluids have to be taken from the body and some have to be tested at specialist labs. So, we could easily be looking at the end of November.'

'OK. Thank you for that,' said Roscoe. 'Now I understand someone in your department's been examining David Harper's bicycle. How've they got on with that?'

'Well, we've compared the tread of Mr Harper's bicycle with the tracks found in the wood and initial results suggest a match, but we've got to make comparisons with other styles and makes of tyre before we can be certain.'

This elicited murmurs of approval from some of the team members. Roscoe folded his arms.

'We need to check his alibi thoroughly and ask him some serious questions.'

Sunita Roy interrupted. 'I should mention a woman from Sinton Bank has come forward to say she saw a man fitting Harper's description cycling towards the woods just after 8 a.m. on the day of the murder. DC Khalid is going to see her and take a statement.'

'Thank you, Sergeant,' said Roscoe.

PC Kaur, who was sitting at the back, raised her hand.

'Sir, I was wondering if you'd considered holding a reconstruction of the scene? I know it would involve a lot of organising, but I'd be happy to help.'

'That's great,' said Roscoe. 'We've been looking into that already and we've pencilled in Monday, 19 November

– exactly six weeks after the murder. Could you liaise with DS Roy on that?'

PC Dawson had remained quiet at the side of the room until now. He ruffled his hair before interrupting the chief inspector.

'Sir, I don't know if you're aware of this, but there's an interesting report in the latest issue of the *Queensbridge Gazette*.'

'I haven't seen it. What's the gist of it, Dawson?'

'Two of their journalists went down to Tewkesbury to interview Rufus Stanbrook, whose wife's due to inherit the doctor's estate. He's thrown the woman reporter out and attacked their photographer.'

The chief inspector waggled his finger.

'Interesting, Dawson. I'd like to have a look at that. Right, I've got some information I need to share with you. I've had a fascinating call from Kent Police. They've been doing some digging around for us. Apparently, our Dr Deeley wasn't such a cold fish after all. He had a girlfriend down there, a lady by the name of Michelle Goodrich. She's a doctors' receptionist.

'DS Roy, as you've been the lead investigator so far, I want you to visit Deal in the next few days and interview this lady. Take DC Dawson with you. We may get a lot of personal detail about the doctor's life that can lead us off in a new direction. Now we've been trawling through the CCTV in the Foxwell Heath area and checking number plate data. Can you tell us what you found, please, Sergeant?'

Sunita Roy stepped towards the centre of the whiteboard.

'Yes, sir. You should all be able to see this sketched map of the car park on the morning of 8 October. Let me know if you can't. It shows the position of all the vehicles at a quarter to ten, when the first officers arrived.'

Once assured everyone was watching, she continued.

'The vehicle here, marked Number One, is a black and silver Honda motorbike registered in Manchester. It was stolen from Stockport in June. We've a grainy image of a man in black leathers driving to the heath from the Birmingham direction and inquiries are on-going.

'The vehicle marked Number Two is a grubby white Toyota diesel van registered to a man named Denzel Hughes. He's been traced and gave a full statement. Number Three is the blue Volvo driven by Robert Bowcott, whom we've discussed.

'Number Four is a mud-splattered Volkswagen Golf which is unregistered and doesn't appear to have been picked up on CCTV. The last two vehicles, the red Corsa and the green Focus Estate, belong to the dog walkers who found the body and called us. They've also given statements.'

Roscoe interrupted to ask, 'Any other vehicles of interest caught on CCTV?'

She nodded. 'Well, two I should mention. Cameras at the filling station on the main road close to the heath picked up a white Ford Transit van. The male driver was in his twenties, of average height and of slim build. He was wearing an open-necked white shirt, black trousers and a white baseball cap. He stopped opposite the garage to buy a sandwich and a takeaway coffee. Then he walked into the woods at ten minutes to nine. He's seen returning to his van forty minutes later. We're trying to trace him.

'One of the filling station cameras also shows a grey Mini Hatch which stopped near the same place. It was there just before 9 a.m. and left an hour later. No one can be seen leaving the vehicle, but the footage is hazy. Someone might've got out. The car's owner lives in Gloucestershire and the team are making efforts to trace him as well.'

Sunita paused for a moment to catch her breath and then turned to the chief inspector.

'Sorry, sir. There was one other thing I wanted to mention. Scott Deeley was a member of a running club. He'd only just joined, so it was hard to find anyone who knew him. Eventually, I found someone who'd had a few conversations with him. Apparently, the doctor was in the habit of running through the wood until reaching the village of Foxwell Green. Then he'd run back, so we're not entirely sure how long he was in the wood before his death. But we think it fair to assume he'd been on his run for anything up to an hour.'

As the meeting broke up and staff returned to their duties, the chief inspector watched as Khalid took the sergeant aside.

He heard him tell her, 'Sarge, I'm sorry about this but there's something I think you ought to know.'

Chapter 20

It was an icy cold morning on Wednesday, 31 October when Tom Vickers set off from St James Street for the market town of Sedgeworth. His mind was full of questions about the criminal trial four months earlier at Warwick Crown Court involving Winston Stevens and Raj Kumar.

Gavin Roscoe's son, George, had phoned him the night before, filling him on details about the men's families and their campaign to have the case reopened. The young constable had been unsettled by what he'd heard while attending a public protest outside the court.

Relatives and friends of the pair were claiming alibi evidence given by the defence had been brushed aside by the court.

Both had previous convictions for possession and intent to supply drugs. But the prosecution case had appeared weak. It was likely the jury may have been swayed by the passionate final speech given by prosecution counsel.

George Roscoe's words kept swirling through his mind: 'It's pretty clear these men were framed.'

The inspector shared the young constable's concerns about the way police colleagues and the Crown Prosecution Service had handled the murder investigation.

As his white Audi approached the outskirts of the town, close to the Leicestershire border, he vowed to do his utmost to find out what really happened on the afternoon of 23 January of last year, when Brendan O'Sullivan was brutally slaughtered in his own home.

Eventually, his sat nav brought him to Albion Road, where the murder had been committed. It was a quiet suburban street on the western side of town consisting mainly of Victorian terraced and semi-detached houses.

He parked directly opposite the murder victim's house – number one hundred and sixty-seven, an end-terrace property with a concrete parking area to its right. He turned off the ignition and spent a few minutes gazing across at the red-brick house that had once been O'Sullivan's home. It was a drab-looking, undistinguished property, the likes of which can be found in any town. Faded white net curtains fluttered from the bay window and the first-floor sash window. The garden looked barren and untended.

On the side of the street where he had parked stood a row of Victorian houses – similar in style to Mr O'Sullivan's home – and then a block of fifteen flats, which bore the name Hatton Court.

Vickers locked his car and knocked on the main door of the dead man's home, which lay down an alley at the side of the house. There was no reply and, after he'd peered through the letterbox, the pile of unopened post on the hallway carpet told him the property was unoccupied.

The inspector then spent an hour knocking on the doors of the flats. Most residents were pleasant at first but proved reluctant to speak to him once he'd explained he was from the police, and inquiring about the murder.

'We've had the world and his wife here before you,' one grey-haired elderly lady in a ground-floor flat explained. 'The press, the police. Then more press. I'll tell you the same as I told them: I didn't know the man and, after what I saw on TV, I'm glad I didn't. I never heard no shots and never saw no one run away.'

He then ventured into the front garden of the house adjoining O'Sullivan's place and knocked loudly on the door. At first there was no reply but, after a couple of minutes, a middle-aged woman with short, grey hair and silver-framed glasses came to the door.

'I'm so sorry to bother you–' he began.

She leaned across the door. 'What are you selling?'

He displayed his warrant card. 'Nothing. I'm from Heart of England Police. We're taking a fresh look at the terrible murder in January last year.'

'You're out of luck, darling. We've only just moved in. But you can try over the road – Mrs Shah. We've been told she was around when it happened, but don't tell her I told you.'

With that, she stepped back inside and closed the door.

The house in question, almost directly opposite Mr O'Sullivan's property, had been built in an identical style to the murder victim's home. But, in contrast, it was kept in pristine condition. The homeowners' privacy was protected from prying eyes by made-to-measure wooden shutters around the bay window. The side alley, leading to the composite navy-blue front door, contained a row of various plants in colourful ceramic pots and troughs.

Mrs Shah, who was smartly dressed and in her early thirties, was hesitant in opening the door when he pressed her doorbell. She insisted on Vickers showing his identification.

Once he had explained he was re-investigating the murder, she was delighted to hear it and quickly invited him in. She explained her first name was Nisa and that she lived there with her husband, Asad. She brought the inspector into a bright front room with white walls and two black leather settees.

After she had handed back his warrant card, the inspector sat down beside the front windows and smiled.

'I recall from reading the files that you gave a statement to police at the time of the murder.'

Mrs Shah nodded. 'That's right. I heard the shots. I saw two men running away. I was one of several people who dialled 999. I was here when the ambulance crew and police arrived. It was absolutely terrifying.'

Vickers looked puzzled. 'But you didn't appear as a witness in court?'

She shook her head. 'No. I wasn't called.'

'But that's astonishing. You should have been one of the key witnesses. What reason did they give for not calling you?'

'They just said, "You've made your statement. You may be called as a witness. You'll probably receive a letter requesting you to attend." But the letter never came.'

The inspector shook his head while gazing down at the carpet.

'I find that absolutely amazing. Anyway, I want you to tell me, in your own words, what happened that afternoon, Mrs Shah. But first, if you don't mind, I'd like to get my video camera so I can film your account.'

Within a few minutes, the inspector had fetched a camera from his car. He placed it on the edge of the dining table, pointed it towards Mrs Shah, who was now sitting on the second of the two settees, and pressed 'Record'.

'Just ignore the camera and focus on my questions,' he said as he took a seat at the table next to the camera.

'Now, tell me the first strange thing you noticed that afternoon.'

'Well, it was around three o'clock. My husband was at work. I was about to leave to collect our two children from school. Suddenly there was a bang. It sounded like a gunshot. Half a minute or so passed. Then it was followed by four more shots.'

Vickers brought out a notebook and began jotting down details. 'Are you sure about that?'

'Yes, I was sitting in this very room, and I counted each one.'

'According to the trial notes, there were only four shots and when the police found a Beretta pistol at the home of one of the defendants, only four shots had been fired from it.'

She shrugged. 'There were definitely five shots altogether,' she said. 'Shortly afterwards – I'd say less than a minute after the final gunshot – two men came running out of the house and tore up the street in the direction of the town centre.'

'Can you give me a description of them?'

'Yes. One was a black man – possibly Jamaican or from the Caribbean at any rate. He was about thirty and very tall. He had close-cropped, dark hair and some kind of tattoo on his right arm. I couldn't see what it was. It all happened so fast.'

'What about the other man?'

'He was an Asian man – possibly Pakistani. He was about the same age, but nowhere near as tall.'

'How tall would you say?'

'Average height.'

'His hair?'

'I don't remember. I only caught a glimpse.'

'This doesn't fit at all with the descriptions of the two jailed men. Mrs Shah, can you tell me what they were wearing?'

'I can't remember much, except the tall man was in faded blue denims.'

'Anything else? Don't hurry. Take your time.'

She nodded. 'What did you say your name was? Is it Vickers?'

'Yes.'

'Mr Vickers, the only other thing I can remember is they were shouting at each other, but I couldn't hear what was being said. It looked like the taller man was angry with the other man. I don't know if that helps.'

'That'll do very well, Mrs Shah. You've been incredibly helpful. Do you have a job at the moment?'

'No, Mr Vickers. I've taken a few years off to raise the children.'

'Quite right too. But how were you employed before you married and had children?'

'I was an airline stewardess. Flew all over the world.'

'So I imagine you were educated to a good standard.'

'I've actually got a degree in Geography from Birmingham University.'

'So, if the prosecution or defence had called you to appear as a witness, I imagine you'd have given a clear and precise statement of what you saw?'

'I've never been to a court, Mr Vickers, so I couldn't say. I kept expecting a letter or email any day, but it never came. I'm wondering now if I wasn't called because what I saw conflicted with other evidence the police were given.'

The inspector frowned. He was already becoming convinced Mrs Shah had not been called for exactly that reason. He had the impression her evidence had been extremely inconvenient for someone. Leading officers from North Warwickshire CID had come to a decision about the pattern of events that afternoon and about who was responsible. Her testimony had been at odds with that. She had been omitted from the court proceedings on purpose.

'By the way, we've been talking about this terrible crime, but I haven't asked you about the victim himself,' said Vickers. 'What was he like?'

'We didn't see much of him. He kept himself to himself, but he was a pleasant enough man on the rare occasions I spoke to him. He always asked politely about my husband, Asad, and our two children. He had black, rather greasy hair. He was overweight – probably over sixteen stone. He had tattoos on his neck and arms, and he used to receive visitors at all times of the day and night.'

'Did you ever suspect he was involved in drugs?'

'We suspected, of course, but I tried to put it to the back of my mind that we might be living opposite a drug dealer or drug user.'

'I don't think it's been suggested he was actually a dealer himself,' said Vickers. 'But there's certainly evidence from the court documents he was buying cocaine and amphetamines.'

'We heard that, and we were shocked, naturally.'

'I'm told he was an artist. Do you know if that's how he made his living?'

'I think his parents left him money. I can't imagine he made much money from art. He specialised in landscapes. I've seen a few of his paintings on show at the library. They don't appeal to me.'

Vickers hauled himself to his feet. He smiled across the room at her.

'Well, you've been most helpful, Mrs Shah, but it's probably time for me to go.'

He turned the camera off and carried it to the door.

'It's been a pleasure to help the police,' she said. 'I've got to go to the shops now and get one of the kids a new coat.'

The inspector smiled. 'How old are your children?'

'Eight and ten, and they're a real handful. Certainly, don't want any more.'

Vickers seemed distracted as he stepped into her hallway.

'Mrs Shah, I think, in view of what you've said, I feel an even greater need to visit the murder scene itself. But the place seems to be empty. Would you know what's happening about the house?'

'There's no one there at the moment. I think it's being sold. Mr O'Sullivan's nephew was there for a while, but I haven't seen his car for several weeks.'

'What kind of car's he got?'

'A grey Hyundai.'

The inspector opened the front door and cast his eyes along the alley towards Mr O'Sullivan's house.

'There's certainly no car there at the moment.'

He warmly shook hands with her and thanked her for her assistance.

'Goodbye, Mr Vickers, and good luck,' she said.

He stepped across the street and stared through the grimy front windows of Mr O'Sullivan's house. He could see landscape paintings on the living room walls and that it was sparsely furnished.

As he returned to his car, he failed to notice a twitching net curtain inside a first-floor flat at Hatton Court and a woman's face gazing out.

Chapter 21

The man spoke with a confident, educated voice as he answered the phone in his darkened hallway.

'Hello, Coopers Kennels.'

'Is that Howard?' asked a shy female voice.

'Yes.'

'Howard, it's Alisha Hamid. Do you remember? We met you on Foxwell Heath.'

He nodded. 'Oh yes. How did you get my number?'

'You told us you ran kennels and had retriever puppies. We remembered hearing you telling the police you lived in Loman's Green. So it wasn't difficult. We went online and found you in a matter of minutes.'

'The wonders of the internet.'

'Look, the reason I'm calling is I'm thinking of buying a golden retriever puppy. My husband and I've been talking about little else.'

'Have you any past experience with goldies?'

'No, but we've always had dogs in the family and your Bella's gorgeous. I fell in love with her.'

'Haven't you got a dog already? I saw you with a spaniel.'

'That's mother's dog.'

'Well, Alisha, your call is very timely. Our bitch Beauty's recently had twelve puppies. We've sold eight, but there are still four left – two boys, two girls.'

'It sounds as though we'll have to be quick.'

There was a pause. 'They're not cheap, mind. They've got a proper pedigree. I'm afraid the price is currently more than two thousand pounds.'

'That doesn't put me off. I tell you what, Howard. I'll have a word with my mother and get back to you. How old are they anyway?'

Howard thought for a moment. 'They're eight weeks and have had their first jabs. They're having one more next week and they've been wormed.'

'Is this Beauty's first litter?'

'Second.'

'Can we come over and have a look at them?'

Howard paused for a moment.

'Depends when you want to come. Things are a bit difficult at the moment because my wife's away but it's important you should see the puppies with their mother.'

'Would Sunday, 18 November be OK? We should have the money by then.'

'That's fine. Jessica will be away with her mother again, but that's all right. Have you got our address?'

Alisha nodded. 'Your website says it's number seventeen, Church Lane, Loman's Green, near Redditch.'

'That's right. Listen, I'll give you a call in a few days to see if you're still interested and if you should, by chance, speak to my wife Jessica, don't mention the death in the woods, will you? I'm banned from talking about it. She finds the whole thing extremely upsetting.'

'No, of course not.'

'Thank you. She's a very sensitive soul. I sometimes wonder how she finds the strength to take an animal to the vet's to be put to sleep. She can't bear to think of an animal or human being suffering.'

'We quite understand, Howard. We'll be the soul of discretion. Have you had the police round in the past week?'

'Yes, a young detective called in to see me for a few minutes. Have you?'

Alisha nodded. 'Yes. They were asking about a man on a bicycle. But we didn't see anyone like that, did we?'

'Do you know? I've been racking my brains ever since that day in the woods. I couldn't recall anyone with a bicycle, but I've remembered part of the number plate of the Honda motorbike.'

Alisha's voice became excited. 'I remember the motorbike. When we were on the phone in the car park, a man in black leathers came out of the woods, started it up and drove off like a bat out of hell.'

'Yes, that's right.'

'So, you managed to remember its registration?'

'Not all of it – just part of it. MD66. I don't know why but it stuck in my mind. I suppose I must have been thinking of Managing Director or something.'

'Or Doctor of Medicine?'

'Yes, possibly. Well, I told the copper that came round – Khalid, I think his name was. But he didn't really seem too interested and there's been nothing in the press about it, as far as I can tell.'

Alisha sighed. 'I'm afraid the police have been pretty hopeless. I don't think they're ever going to catch the doctor's murderer, do you? They seem to be fumbling in the dark.'

'I entirely agree,' said Howard. 'They seem to be getting nowhere. The doctor's mother died as well, didn't she? Maybe the same person did for her. Anyway, it doesn't do any good to dwell on it, does it? Listen, I've got your number. I'll have a chat with Jess and get back to you about when's the best time for you to visit.'

'That's fine, Howard. Look forward to hearing from you.'

Howard had only just ended the conversation when his mobile rang again. This time, the face of his wife appeared on the screen. Jessica Cooper was a good-looking, shapely woman in her early fifties with long, blonde hair. She had a slender nose, blue eyes, and a constant smile.

'How's your mother?' he asked.

'I'm very worried about her, Howard. She fell out of bed again this morning. I think we may have to ask around about a suitable home for her.'

'She won't want that. She's very independent,' said Howard. 'I've just been speaking to a woman in Redditch who's interested in buying one of the puppies. She's late twenties, married, no children. They're a nice family.'

Jessica shrugged. 'They sound fine.'

There was a pause. Then Howard said, 'Jess, I've been meaning to ask you. Is there anything the matter? You're not worrying about money again, are you?'

She shrugged. 'No more than we normally do. No, there's nothing wrong.'

He was concerned about the woman he had married twelve years earlier. The air of confidence she'd always carried about her had vanished in recent weeks like a snuffed-out flame.

'It's just that when you were here on Tuesday night, I don't believe you slept very well. You seem tired all the time and, if you don't mind me saying, a little irritable.'

Jessica shook her head. 'I'm fine, Howard. Stop worrying. There's been a lot of work with the dogs and particularly with the puppies. That's all. I'm sure I'll be OK soon. I expect I just need to catch up on some of my lost sleep.'

Chapter 22

Sunita carefully carried the tea-tray into her living room and smiled weakly at her guest.

'It's been lovely seeing you again,' she announced. 'I'm just sorry I haven't been very good company this weekend.'

He former flatmate, Rupa Chakrabarty, smiled as she relaxed on Sunita's new leather settee.

'I wasn't going to mention it but you've been rather quiet. Not your usual self at all.'

Sunita glanced out of the window at the rain-drenched street outside. She handed her friend her cup of lemon tea and then sat down at the dining room table on the other side of the room.

'I know. I'm sorry. I'll be honest with you. I'm splitting up with Tom.'

Rupa, a short, slightly plump young woman who at twenty-eight was a year older than Sunita, sipped her hot drink and glanced at her friend.

'That explains a lot, but it's been a great weekend all the same.'

As her friend recalled the weekend's highlights, Sunita thought back to the happy four years she'd spent living with Rupa in a tree-lined suburban street in Birmingham's Hall Green.

Of course, there had been the upsetting episode in which an ex-boyfriend, Arun Halder, had stalked her and attempted to abduct her at gunpoint. But the friendship with Rupa had remained strong and they had become close to each other's families.

So, she had been excited by the prospect of showing Rupa her new flat in Warwick's Crompton Gardens and the sights of the market town.

'I'm so sorry you've broken up with Tom,' whispered Rupa.

Sunita glanced down at the carpet. She had been so looking forward to Rupa's visit. But just days before her friend was due to arrive, she'd been devastated to learn that Tom Vickers, her boyfriend, had been seen with his arm round his ex-wife. It was as if an invisible hand had reached inside her and torn her heart out.

Rupa glared at her friend. 'Sunita, did you hear what I just said?'

'Sorry, I was miles away.'

'I was saying that I'm sorry to hear you've spilt up with Tom. He's such a nice guy, but I'm not totally surprised. Your parents were dead against the pair of you ever getting married, weren't they?'

Sunita frowned. 'My parents would have nothing to do with it if I'd ever felt like getting married. I'm my own woman, Rupa, as you know. But I can't go on seeing Tom when he's still so tied up with his ex-wife. I'm just sorry I've been feeling so miserable this weekend – when you've taken the trouble to travel down from Stoke to see me and your sister.'

Rupa shrugged. 'Don't worry. I completely understand. I've been in the same position. It's never a bundle of laughs when a couple break up.'

'I haven't actually told him it's over yet, but he must know me by now. He knows I can't continue seeing him if he's still involved with his wife.'

Rupa raised an eyebrow. 'You haven't actually spoken to him about it?'

Sunita shook her head. 'No, not yet. I haven't had a chance. He's been doing some undercover work connected with his case, so we've not been in regular touch. I'm going down to Kent tomorrow on a job, but I'll probably catch up with him in the office in a couple of days.'

'Kent? That's a long journey.'

'About a hundred and ninety miles. I'm taking one of the DCs with me and it's an over-nighter.'

'Your boss is putting you both up in a bed and breakfast? He must have found some extra money from somewhere.'

'Yes, I suppose so.'

Rupa sipped some more of her tea.

'Why don't you call Tom?'

'Phone him? When he's with his wife? Anyway, affairs of the heart are better dealt with face to face. He must realise he can't go on like this – having two women in his life at the same time.'

'Of course. The man must be a fool if he thinks otherwise. How long have you been with Tom?'

'Since May of last year. Funnily enough, our relationship began the day I put an offer down on this flat. Since then, I've spent so much of my social life with him over the past year and a half, I'm going to be lost without him to begin with. I'm meant to be interviewing this important witness in Kent tomorrow and I don't really feel up to it.'

She felt her confidence had been ebbing away over the past few days like sand in an egg timer.

'Oh, you'll be fine. I remember you having doubts on that other case – where that woman was murdered in her garden last year. You got over your distress and unmasked the killer in the end. You told me your boss had been full of praise for you afterwards.'

'Pretty much, but this business with Tom's really left me reeling. I'm going to be talking to this woman – if we find her – about the dead doctor and all the time I'm going to be remembering my time with Tom. It's making me upset, thinking about it now. I don't think I told you, but I nearly ended things a year ago over suspicions he was being overfriendly with his ex. Now the same issue has come up again.'

'Office relationships are often difficult. So, you're definitely calling time on it?'

She nodded. 'Yes, I won't be having anything further to do with Tom, except in a work capacity.'

'You need to speak to him as soon as possible. You need to clear the air.'

'Whatever he says won't make any difference. My mind's made up.'

Rupa tried to lift the mood. 'Maybe you need a holiday.'

'I'm having a break at the end of this coming week. I'm going up to Leicester for a couple of days so I can spend Diwali with my parents.'

'No, I mean a proper holiday. The new friend I was telling you about, Latika, wants us to go to Iceland or Norway and see the Northern Lights. Maybe all three of us could do that in the next month or two.'

'Maybe.'

'Come on, Sunita. It's a really cool idea. Seeing the lights is a breathtaking experience.'

'I promise you, I'll think about it.'

'Anyway, this is a lovely flat, Sunita. Wish I could afford to buy one. And it's been a lovely weekend. I really enjoyed climbing the ancient towers and gazing over the ramparts at the castle. Can I have another look at the pictures you took on your phone of the peacocks before I have to go and catch my train?'

Chapter 23

'So, who do you think killed Scott Deeley?' Brett Dawson asked Sunita Roy as they drove out of the car park at St James Street and headed towards the M42 motorway.

His smartly dressed sergeant, who was sitting in the front passenger seat of the Ford Focus, looked surprised at the question.

'It's just too early to say, Brett,' she said with a solemn expression. 'There are several suspects already and I dare say we may find a few more over the next few days.'

'David Harper looks as guilty as hell to me,' said Dawson. 'From what I've seen in the reports, he's got a strong motive because of his son's death. He's got the mentality to do it as well – the obsessive personality bordering on insanity. Since he was cycling through the wood at the same time as the doctor was on his run, I think the case is virtually cut and dried.'

'No, Brett. We don't know that he was in the wood at the same time. We only know that he was seen heading into the woods on his bike. We mustn't be too swift in coming to conclusions. How about Rufus Stanbrook? Don't you think he could be in the frame?'

Dawson nodded. 'Well, I must admit I've had my suspicions about him as well. His praise for his dead brother-in-law in his police statement came across as totally false. He was in a buoyant mood. He was smug. He seemed like a man who's already started counting the money. My mother always said, "Never trust a man who places wealth before kinship."'

'Remind me, Brett. Where did Stanbrook say he was on the morning of 8 October?'

'At the farm all day.'

'Yes. Well, we need to get that corroborated. It's baffling that there's been no word from his wife, Valerie, and no sign of her.'

'That's right. In bed with suspected food poisoning, according to him.'

'We don't have any evidence she was even at the farm when we called. I'm annoyed with myself. We should have demanded to see her at the time. I only thought about it afterwards. What if he's drugged her?'

'You're speaking with the benefit of hindsight. We wanted to avoid upsetting him so we could get the maximum amount of information from him.'

'That's true.' After a pause, she glanced at her colleague. 'As soon as we get back from Kent, we must have words with Mrs Stanbrook's GP. But, getting back to your question, I'm really trying to keep an open mind about the culprit. It seems it might have been a spur-of-the-moment killing. If it had been planned well in advance, you'd have thought they'd have come prepared. He wouldn't have grabbed a barbecue fork from an abandoned campfire.'

Dawson nodded. 'I see what you mean. He'd have come with a chosen weapon.'

'Yes. Normally, these days, a killer would probably use a gun or knife. But his choice was to use a barbecue fork. The only similar case I could find in police files was a murder in a London churchyard fifteen years ago when a man was stabbed in the heart with what was described as a two-pronged carving fork. Two men were later jailed.'

'Yes. Strange weapon.'

'At least we know now we're not looking for a double killer.'

'How do you mean?'

'Didn't I tell you, Brett? The toxicology reports have finally come back on Sarah Deeley. She wasn't poisoned and there were no surprise substances in her body – only the usual drugs she was taking. Dr Reynolds doesn't believe she was murdered. He thinks she simply overbalanced and fell down the stairs, so the family are planning her funeral. The grease on the handrail turned out to be petroleum jelly she'd been using, possibly for chapped lips. That may have played a part in her accident.'

They travelled down the M40 motorway, passing through Oxfordshire and Buckinghamshire, before Dawson turned onto the M25 near London's Heathrow Airport and proceeded into Surrey.

Eventually, they followed the M2 motorway and A2 trunk road to Dover before finally reaching the seaside town of Deal. They spent a few minutes driving along the promenade, looking out for the street where their bed and breakfast accommodation was.

The sea looked cold and uninviting to Sunita. Dawson stopped the car for a moment by the pier so they could step out and inhale the sea air. A yacht was slipping gently through the waves a short distance from shore. An oil tanker was gliding across the horizon. There was a biting wind coming in from the direction of the murky, green water.

'Let's get back in the car. We must have taken a wrong turning and reached Siberia,' she moaned.

* * *

After a quick meal in a cafe near the seafront, they drove round the corner to the guesthouse and took their luggage up to their rooms. The pair spent a while freshening themselves up before they set off to see Michelle Goodrich. They arrived outside her flat in the town's busy London Road just before five o'clock.

The medical receptionist's home was in a white Edwardian house, which had a small lawn at the front. Michelle lived in the basement flat.

While Dawson waited outside in the car on double yellow lines, Sunita strode up the narrow gravel path. She negotiated her way down the grey stone steps to the front door and peered through the letterbox. All she could see were black and white floor tiles, a circular mirror with an ivy-leaf surround on the left-hand wall and, below it, an antique silver-leaf hall table.

The lady's got good taste, she thought as she stood up again and pressed the doorbell. There was no response. She waited for a couple of minutes before pressing it a second time. Again, nobody came, and she returned to the car.

'She's not there,' she told Dawson. 'Looks like we might have a long wait.'

'Hope she's not gone away.'

'A winter holiday somewhere hot? It's possible. I think it's more likely she's gone out for a meal or something. Could be her day off. What was that?'

A firework streaked into the air and a flash of light illuminated the night sky above the town.

'Oh, I'd forgotten it was 5 November,' she said. 'Just think. Instead of being stuck here in the frozen wastes of Kent, we could be shivering in the cold at someone's Guy Fawkes Party.'

By eleven o'clock that night, both officers were feeling tired and annoyed. It had been a long day. How much longer would this damned woman keep them waiting? Sunita wondered.

But eventually, at half past eleven, a black E-Class Mercedes glided slowly towards them and drew up close to the house. It was driven by a dark-skinned man with short, dark hair and glasses. The blonde female passenger appeared to be wearing a black, off-the-shoulder dress with a pink cardigan. As the vehicle came to a halt, the man moved towards her and they kissed passionately.

Perhaps they don't realise we can see them, Sunita thought. Or maybe they just don't care.

After several minutes, the woman, who was grasping a black and gold clutch-bag, got out and strolled to the wooden gate, waving to the man as she went. Sunita took out a small notebook and jotted down the registration number. The woman then proceeded along the gravel path while the Mercedes drew away.

As soon as the car had gone, the two officers got out and pursued the woman, who was about to clamber down the steps to the flat.

Sunita called after her. 'Hello, sorry to bother you! Miss Goodrich?'

The woman turned in surprise.

'Who is it? What do you want?' she asked.

Sunita showed the receptionist her warrant card.

'Heart of England Police. I'm sorry it's late, but we'd just like to ask you a few questions.'

Chapter 24

Michelle Goodrich turned on an electric fire in her front room before inviting her two visitors to take a seat at her dining table.

The pair noticed several of the woman's possessions were pink. A pink clock stood on the mantelpiece. She had a pink bookcase, pink curtains, and the lightshade in the middle of the room had a pink border.

'Would you like tea or coffee?' she asked.

Sunita shook her head. 'No, thank you. It's a bit late, isn't it? We don't want to hold you up any more than necessary, Miss Goodrich. You can probably guess why we're here.'

'Dr Deeley?'

'Yes. We understand you knew him very well. Is that right?'

Miss Goodrich slumped down onto her pink sofa.

'Yes. I first got to know him while I was a receptionist at the surgery. We remained friends when I left and got myself a similar job at another practice in the town.'

'There was a problem where you were working?' Dawson asked.

'I just needed a change.'

Sunita gazed across the room at her while removing her notebook from her jacket pocket. Miss Goodrich was a slender, attractive woman. Sunita knew she was forty-eight but felt she could easily pass for a woman of thirty-eight or even younger. She had an intelligent expression and there was a dignity about her.

'You say you remained friends. Is "friends" the correct word?' Sunita asked. 'Or were you more boyfriend and girlfriend?'

'Well, we had what I suppose you'd call an "on-off" relationship over several years,' she admitted as she began to look tearful.

Dawson interrupted to ask, 'Over how many years?'

She opened her clutch-bag, retrieved a handkerchief and wiped away a tear.

'I'd say over about ten years. He was a terrific man – the kindest, most sensitive, most considerate man I've ever known. His death is such a tragedy.'

'I'm sorry if this upsets you,' said Sunita, who was taking notes.

Miss Goodrich shrugged. 'It's all right. I want to help you in any way I can. Whoever killed him should be caught and locked up. Perhaps I should tell you about my time with him?'

Sunita nodded. 'If you don't mind.'

'He was very hard-working and I felt so privileged to be able to spend a lot of my spare time with him. The problem for me was that he just wasn't the marrying kind. If he'd asked me to marry him, I'd have jumped at the chance. I wanted to spend the rest of my life with him. But he'd never commit to me fully. Whenever I tried to talk about us moving in together or getting engaged, he'd make a joke or change the subject.

'So, as you can imagine, we had a few rows. I really wanted some kind of long-term pledge from him. That's why we had a few breaks in our relationship – a few intervals, you could say – before getting back together again. I ought to explain as well that there was an aura of mystery about him. I worked out that he'd got some kind of secret. I tried to elicit what it was, but he'd always clam up.'

Sunita raised an eyebrow. 'Do you have any idea at all what this secret might've been? I mean, this is important. It might have a bearing on how and why he met his death.'

'No idea at all. It was more of a feeling I had that something had happened in his past which stopped him becoming close to me.'

'Do you think it was something that happened in his childhood or later in life?'

'I've no idea, but I'll be honest with you, I lived in the hope that things between us would change. Then, of course, in the end, his mother became ill and he returned to the West Midlands to care for her.'

'When was that?'

'Four months ago. He told me in April he was going to take unpaid leave. He also informed the other doctors at his practice.'

Sunita smiled sympathetically. 'That must have been very difficult for you.'

'Yes. We both cried. He told me he'd keep in touch, and we'd remain friends. He said he'd probably return if his mother passed away, but I knew it was very likely I might never see him again.'

'Did he keep in touch?'

'He wrote to me twice, but they were fairly formal letters – just saying how his mother was going downhill and how he'd have to spend a lot of money on her cottage.'

Sunita paused for a moment. She looked intently at Miss Goodrich.

'Could I ask you a rather delicate question?' she said. 'When you arrived just now, we noticed you were dropped off by a man. Does this mean you're in a new relationship now?'

She nodded. 'Well, as a matter of fact, I am. But I can't see how that could be of interest to your investigation.'

Sunita was writing furiously. 'I'm afraid everything about Dr Deeley and his circle of friends and colleagues is of interest at the moment.'

'All right. The man who dropped me off a few minutes ago is Dr Ali Hashemi.'

Sunita stopped writing and glanced up. 'Wasn't he Dr Deeley's partner at the surgery?'

'That's right.'

'Could you remind me how you spell the name?'

'H-A-S-H-E-M-I. He's Iranian.'

'You used to work for him, didn't you?'

'Yes, that's right. You've done some research.'

'A little. He's on our list of people to visit while we're down here. By the way, do you know anything about a gold necklace with a flamingo pendant?'

'No.'

'We found a box containing this item of jewellery in a drawer in his room and we're trying to find out why he had it.'

'I'm sorry. I don't know anything about it.'

'You're not a lover of flamingos?'

'Well, they're pink and that's my favourite colour,' she said with a faint laugh. 'But I know nothing about a necklace.'

Sunita shrugged. 'OK. Now, when you heard Dr Deeley had died, I wonder what your first thoughts were? It must have come as a tremendous shock.'

'Of course. I couldn't believe it when I saw it on the television. The news presenters made such a fuss about Dr Frank Sutton from the TV soap being based on him.'

Sunita gazed intently at Miss Goodrich's tear-stained face.

'Is there anything that happened in Kent that might've led to his death?'

'Well, all I can tell you is that a lot of people in this town think they know who killed him.'

'Go on.'

'He had to go to court to evict one of his tenants, a man named Mark Smith. He caused a lot of trouble because he was selling drugs. Scott became very worried about the situation. The man refused to leave the property, and, in the end, he lost thousands of pounds in rent. He even had to call in the bailiffs.'

'Where's this man now?'

'No one knows where he is. After he got thrown out, he moved in with a succession of girlfriends in Dover. His phone was cut off, he came off Facebook and Instagram, and debt collectors were having a devil of a job tracking him down.'

Dawson leaned forward across the dining table.

'So, you think we should track him down and have a chat with him about what happened to Scott?'

'Well, he vowed to cause trouble for Scott after he'd been evicted. If you ask me, he was a bit unhinged. I probably shouldn't say this but I wouldn't be at all surprised if he drove up to Warwickshire and killed him.'

Chapter 25

After spending most of Tuesday in Sedgeworth collecting evidence about the 'body in the bath' case and talking to witnesses, Tom Vickers was ready to head home.

Once he'd called in at his office, he tried again to reach Sunita Roy on her mobile but, as had happened countless times already, her phone simply went to voicemail. In desperation, he left one final message: 'Sunita, for heaven's sake call me and let me know you're all right. We haven't spoken in days.'

As he locked his office and made his way towards the stairs, he found the chief inspector heading towards him, his navy-blue coat draped over his arm.

'I'm looking forward to a pint in the Golden Fleece, Tom,' he called out. 'Are you coming?'

'I might do, sir. Have you seen anything of DS Roy? I've been trying to reach her but her phone's off.'

Roscoe smiled. 'She's due back from Kent any time. Is there any message I can pass on if I bump into her?'

'No, it's OK, sir. It's just she's been a bit elusive.'

'Well, she's been out of town.'

The pair walked down the stairs together and then emerged from the headquarters building into the chill of the November air. At that moment, Dawson's car arrived in the car park. He and Sunita stepped out.

'Just got back?' Roscoe asked his sergeant with a smile.

She nodded. 'Yes, sir. There's a lot to tell you.'

'Good. Well, we're just going up the road for a pint. Do you and Dawson fancy joining us?'

Her companion nodded in anticipation, but Sunita stroked her chin.

'I don't know. I've got my report to do.'

'That can wait. Let's have a chat over a drink.'

'All right, sir. Since you put it like that.' Then she noticed Vickers standing behind her boss. 'I'll catch you up, sir,' she bellowed as the chief inspector and Dawson marched off up the road together.

Vickers walked towards Sunita, who was standing by the entrance steps. He wasn't sure why but felt a cold atmosphere between them.

'Sunita, I've been trying to speak to you.'

She folded her arms. 'I know.'

'I've left you a whole series of messages. Have I done something to upset you?'

She took a deep breath. 'Tom, I'm afraid I can't see you anymore.'

'Why on earth's that?'

'Because you've not been honest with me.'

'What?'

'Last June, I got upset because it was rumoured you were still living at home with your wife.'

'That's right, and I explained she left me in April of last year. Our divorce is nearly finalised.'

Sunita placed her hands on her hips and scowled.

'So how come you've been seen with your bloody arm around your wife? Don't try and deny it. Omar saw you in Redditch.'

Vickers put his hands to his face and took a step back.

'Oh, for God's sake. The bloody woman hurt her ankle and couldn't walk. What was I expected to do? I took her to her GP surgery and, because she couldn't put any weight on her foot, I had to help her inside. That's all.'

'Are you sure that's all? Is she staying with you as well?'

Vickers was unsure what to say. Had she discovered Chloe had moved back into his house temporarily? Or was she bluffing?

'Sunita, the fact of the matter is that the divorce is going through and Chloe will be out of my life soon. All I want to do is settle down with you. You're the only one I love. You know that.'

She glared. 'Don't make this more difficult than it is already, Tom. You were seen fussing over your wife, taking her into the doctor's. Sounds like her boyfriend's kicked her out and she's shacked up with you.'

The inspector looked aghast. 'For God's sake, Sunita.'

She poked him in the stomach. 'She's moved back into your house, hasn't she?'

'She promised it was only for a few days.'

Sunita laughed. 'Just as I thought. You're back playing happy families again, aren't you? You think you can have the cake and the bun, but listen, pal. I'm not going to be part of your little game anymore. It's over between us. It's finished. Now I'm going home. And if you see the boss, you can apologise and tell him I'll see him in the morning.'

Then she hurried over to her Peugeot at the far side of the car park.

'Sunita, wait!' he called, but his words went unheeded.

She started the engine. All he could do was watch in despair as she drove away. He decided not to call in at the Golden Fleece for a drink. He was in no mood to socialise. His colleagues would be bristling with questions: Why isn't the sergeant with you? Where's she gone? You haven't had a row, have you? They would only have to observe his downcast expression to know the truth.

Why had he been such a fool, taking pity on Chloe when she became homeless and helping her when she – allegedly – injured her ankle? Perhaps he shouldn't have been so foolish and allowed Chloe to stay for so long, he told himself.

But, at the same time, why was Sunita being so unreasonable? Couldn't she see that he only had feelings for her and that his marriage was over?

He sat in his Audi for a few minutes, wondering what to do. His mind was filled with anguish. How had he allowed this to happen? To lose the woman who meant so much to him? He felt as if he'd suddenly been struck by a giant hammer and all his hopes and dreams of settling down into a new life with Sunita had come crashing down.

Should he try to phone Sunita again and try to reason with her? No, her phone would more than likely simply go to voicemail. Maybe he should let matters lie for the moment and attempt a reconciliation in a few days. Maybe presenting her with flowers and chocolates might help.

A succession of police colleagues waved to him in his car as they left the building. They were probably wondering why he was sitting there, seemingly staring at the vehicle parked in front. Perhaps it was time to head home.

He switched on the ignition and lights and drove to the car park exit, where he waited for a gap in the traffic. As he glanced to the left, he saw a black BMW was parked a short distance away by the side of the road with two men in the front.

He thought nothing of it but, after turning right into St James Street and heading past the Golden Fleece, he noticed they had set off and were travelling in the same direction. The car continued behind him for a quarter of a mile, with the driver maintaining a respectful twelve metre distance.

When he reached the busy Stratford Road and turned left towards the M42 motorway, the BMW continued to follow him. He could see the men's dark faces clearly in his rear-view mirror. He was sure he'd never seen them before. He was becoming uneasy as he kept within the forty-mile-an-hour speed limit. He reached for his car radio and called his force control-room.

'This is DI Vickers. Being pursued by a suspect vehicle along A34 Stratford Road, Solihull, heading towards Junction 4. Request assistance.'

The control-room inspector asked him to describe the car, which he was able to do, but he was only able to read the last three letters of the registration number, which were PXA.

He continued travelling along the southbound lane of the dual carriageway towards the motorway and then cut his speed to thirty-five miles an hour. The BMW driver followed suit and slowed down while remaining close behind.

The guy's got every opportunity to overtake, but he's choosing to stick with me, Vickers thought to himself. *What's he playing at?* Perhaps they were simply innocent travellers heading, like him, towards the motorway. Perhaps he was becoming unsettled for no reason.

Suddenly, as his car approached the village of Cheswick Green, the suspect car spurted forward and drew up beside him. The driver and his passenger, now wearing black balaclavas, were shouting and waving their hands at him as the two vehicles sped along in parallel.

Then the BMW lurched towards his car and struck his offside front wing. Vickers battled with the controls of his Audi but he was unable to retain control of the vehicle which veered sharply off the road and went careering onto the grass verge.

Somehow he succeeded in slowing the car and narrowly avoided crashing into the line of trees further to the left. Within seconds the vehicle came to a halt and he sat for a moment in shocked silence, hunched over the steering wheel and thanking God for his salvation.

By the time he'd managed to step out, the BMW's lights were disappearing in the distance. He examined the damage. The front bumper had become detached, and he had a crumpled front wing.

Could have been worse, he concluded as his heart pounded. Could have been a lot worse.

Chapter 26

The chief inspector stepped out of his office the next morning and peered out across the CID workspace. Both his sergeant and DC Khalid were engrossed in phone calls.

He raised his voice above the hubbub of conversation and the clatter of computer keyboards.

'Sergeant, I need to speak to you when you're free.'

A few minutes later, she knocked and hurried into his room.

'Yes, sir?'

Roscoe glanced up from his desk. 'We need to have another little chat with our friend David Harper. Forensics are as sure as they can be that the tracks in the woods were left by his bicycle. So we need to see what he's got to say for himself and I think we need to bring him in for questioning – either here or at Queensbridge nick.'

She nodded. 'That's a giant leap forward, sir.'

'Yes, I know. I hear Tom's bill for the damage to his car last night could run to nearly two thousand pounds.'

She shrugged as she took a chair. 'I didn't know that, sir. I may as well explain that we're no longer together.'

Roscoe sat up. 'Really? Oh, I didn't realise. I'm sorry.'

'Nothing to be sorry about, sir. These things happen.'

He nodded. 'Yes, I suppose they do. You'd heard he was run off the road by a couple of thugs?'

'Yes. Of course, I was sorry to hear about that. Must have been very frightening for him.'

'It was. If you're no longer seeing him, I hope that–'

'Nothing will prevent me doing my job, sir, and I expect DI Vickers and I will still be able to discuss police matters without personal feeling getting in the way.'

He looked solemn. 'You've got the right attitude, Sergeant. But if you've any future problems of any kind – you know, if you feel you need time off, for example – I hope you'll feel free to approach me.'

'Of course. Now I'd better go and find Khalid and we should head off to see Harper.'

* * *

Less than an hour later, as rain clouds gathered in the sky above, Sunita Roy and DC Khalid drew up in the sergeant's car outside the Harpers' house. The front path had been cleared, allowing visitors easier access to the entrance.

They strode to the door. 'Someone's been busy,' Sunita remarked.

'Maybe someone's lent them a strimmer or some shears.'

'Or a scythe,' she suggested, knocking five times on the door.

After a minute or two, a woman's voice asked, 'Who is it?'

'Police!' said the sergeant.

Slowly, the door creaked open. Amy Harper stood before them, wiping tears from her eyes.

'If you're looking for David, he's not here,' she said, almost spitting out the words.

'Any idea where he might be?' asked Khalid. 'Has he gone to work?'

She shook her head. 'No idea where he is. He's been sacked from the cafe for bad timekeeping.' She glanced up and down the street, perhaps wary that her neighbours might spot her visitors. 'You'd better come in.'

She led the pair into the hallway and then stopped. When she turned round to face them, they could see she was still upset.

'I'll tell you straight out,' she said. 'David's been suffering a lot with depression. I'm worried he may try to harm himself.'

'When did you last see your husband?' asked Sunita.

'A few days ago.'

'A few days ago? And he hasn't been in contact with you since?'

She wiped her eyes with her hands. 'No.'

'You must be concerned for him.'

'He's done this before – last year. He went off and tried to kill himself. Of course, he was unsuccessful on that occasion.'

Khalid interrupted. 'When exactly was this previous incident, Mrs Harper?'

'August last year.'

'What happened on that occasion? Where did he go?' he asked.

'He was found at a park in Erdington with a bottle of pills. Luckily, he was found quite quickly and hadn't had time to take many.'

Sunita was becoming alarmed. 'Have you reported this new disappearance to the police?'

Mrs Harper nodded. 'I went to Queensbridge police station, and they logged the details, but nothing's happened since.'

It annoyed Sunita to hear the local police had been informed the man was missing but hadn't thought to mention the fact to CID.

'Do you think he might've gone back to Erdington?' Khalid asked.

'It's possible,' she said. 'I don't know what to think. Our lives have been so awful since Jerome died.'

Sunita removed a white card from her pocket and handed it to Mrs Harper.

'Here's my direct number. Please call me if your husband returns. Meanwhile I'll speak to our boss. He may want to make a public appeal for your husband's return because you need him back, obviously, and we need to have a chat with him.'

Mrs Harper closed the door as the detectives walked back down the path and made a call to the office.

* * *

The following morning, Gavin Roscoe arrived at work to find someone had stuck a note to his office door with the message, 'Please see Chief Supt Norris. Urgent.'

He climbed the two flights of stairs to the second floor with some trepidation. He had known his superior officer for many years. She was a perfectionist who could be prickly and difficult to contend with. He always feared he was going to commit a gaffe and appear incompetent in front of her.

He knocked and then waited. His spirits rose slightly. Perhaps the lady had been called away. But then her shrill voice yelled out 'Come in!' and Roscoe knew he had to face her.

The chief superintendent was sitting behind her desk, which was twice the size of Roscoe's. There was a phone on the right of the tabletop and a pile of documents more than twenty-five centimetres high on the other side.

'Ah, Gavin!' she began. 'Sit down. I wanted to find out how the Foxwell Heath murder case is going.'

He took a chair, drew it forward and made himself comfortable.

'Well, ma'am, we've made a bit of progress. We've collected a hundred and thirty witness statements so far. We've got up to sixty officers working on the case in one way or another, and we've got several possible suspects.'

'Have you interviewed this man?' she wondered, thrusting a week-old edition of the *Queensbridge Gazette* towards him.

The front-page story concerned David Harper. It began with the words, 'The death of a family doctor has revived memories of a family tragedy'.

He nodded. 'Yes, ma'am.'

'How far did you get with him, Gavin?'

'Well, we interviewed him the other day at his home. We had our suspicions about him from the start. Not only does he have a motive, but he works not far from the murder scene, and he's got a bicycle. Cycle tracks were found in the wood not far from the body and it's possible he followed the doctor into the wood.'

'Right. So your next move is to arrest him, right?'

'Well, we were waiting for forensic tests to tell us whether it was his bike that left the tracks in the mud. This was confirmed and we went round to arrest him yesterday – but he's gone missing from home.'

'What do you mean he's gone missing?'

'Well, ma'am, Mr Harper's an alcoholic who's been suffering from depression. He's been officially reported to the police as missing.'

'Oh dear, oh dear. What about Rufus Stanbrook? I hear his wife is the main beneficiary of the doctor's estate and he's got a bit of a criminal record.'

Roscoe nodded. 'Yes, ma'am. He's got convictions for assault and wounding with intent. We've been looking at him as well.'

'This guy's been interviewed, has he?'

'Yes, ma'am. But, as you can appreciate, this is a complex case. There are several people we need to speak to and, of course, we've lost Inspector Vickers to Operation Sepulchre.'

'If you need more people, Gavin, that's not a problem.'

'Thank you, ma'am. I'll bear that in mind, but DS Roy and DC Khalid have made a lot of progress.'

'What's the latest news on Sepulchre?'

'Well, as you know, Tom Vickers was run off the road on Tuesday in an extremely frightening incident.'

Norris leaned back in her wheelchair and stretched her arms.

‘I’ve requested regular patrols be set up around the building to add to our security. The DI wasn’t hurt, was he?’

‘No, ma’am, but his vehicle was badly damaged and he’s having to use a hire car.’

She shook her head. ‘Does he have any idea who the two men were who rammed his vehicle?’

‘No. The car they were in was caught on CCTV outside here, but the men’s faces were too indistinct and, as you might well have guessed, it was a stolen car.’

‘And DI Vickers doesn’t have a clue who they might be?’

‘No, ma’am, although he obviously suspects he may’ve been targeted because of his work on the O’Sullivan case. Did I tell you? He is convinced Winston Stevens and Raj Kumar were set up. He’s discovered a very promising witness, a Mrs Shah, who gave him valuable information that could help overturn their convictions.’

She wheeled her chair round the desk until she was just a couple of metres from the chief inspector.

‘When he’s got all his Sepulchre evidence together, we’ll take it to the lawyers and see what they think, Gavin. But I must be honest. The evidence would have to be strong. Our team in Summerstoke allocated a lot of time and resources to the case last year.’

‘I know. But if there were flaws in the original investigation, I’m sure Tom Vickers is the one to find them.’

* * *

While the chief inspector was meeting his boss, Sunita Roy was sitting at her CID desk with her face in her hands. Omar Khalid glanced across from his nearby desk.

‘Come on, Sarge. This isn’t like you,’ he said. ‘You look like someone who’s gone desperately hungry to the canteen and missed out on the last cheese sandwich.’

She looked up and smiled. 'It's this Scott Deeley case. It's been so time-consuming. The DCI's been on my back since that idiot David Harper went AWOL. I spent yesterday and this morning on the phone to various departments inquiring about missing persons. He's been absent for days. He's got no money, no change of clothes, no phone…'

Khalid grinned. 'No bottle of whisky?'

'I don't know about that. He may've taken a whole crate of whisky with him, for all I know. The whole thing makes him look very guilty. And yet–'

'And yet what?'

'And yet he doesn't seem to me to have the makings of a killer.'

'What are the traits that make a man or woman a killer, do you think?'

'I don't know. He seems a bit weak. If someone is capable of stabbing a man to death, you'd expect him to have an energy or a dynamism about him. Maybe also you'd expect them to have some cunning, some inventiveness and some persistence and drive. Those are all qualities that Harper lacks, in my view.'

He sat down at the desk beside hers. 'Interesting theory on the makings of a murderer. But, in my limited experience, all murder cases are different. To me, the men and women who get convicted all have different personality traits. Take the Oxford Lane killer in Norton Prior, for example. Those murders were carried out by someone with a huge grudge. They'd been mistreated as a child and felt the world was no longer their friend. A habitual criminal, who became self-obsessed and would no doubt have killed anyone that didn't fit in with their personal plans.

'Then there was the crossbow killer, who suffered from a traumatic incident. Although there were no antecedents, this single incident caused them such shock that they set out on a course of retribution. Unlike the first killer, the crossbow killer didn't act on impulse. Every step of their murderous career was planned.'

Sunita nodded. 'You've explained that very well, Omar. You're right. There are often differences between the personalities of men and women who commit murder. And clearly different motives that lead individuals to adopt particular patterns of criminal behaviour, but there are also certain similar characteristics that you'd expect to find as well.

'In the case of our killer in the woods, we can be fairly certain he didn't set out that October morning with murder on his mind. If he had, he'd have come prepared. He'd have brought a gun or a knife, probably. Instead it looks as though he – or she – grabbed the carving fork which had been used for a barbecue and then dumped. As far as we know, the doctor had no plans to meet anyone that morning. He was following a fitness regime – going on his daily run to promote his health. So there's a good chance the killer was a stranger that the doctor somehow annoyed or otherwise maybe someone from his past with a grievance.'

'Makes sense,' Khalid said.

'I suppose understanding how a murderer's mind works must come with experience. On the rare occasions I go to the Golden Fleece, I sometimes overhear the guv'nor and Tom Vickers discussing some of their past cases'.

'The DCI must have investigated far more cases than Tom.'

'Absolutely,' she said. 'But from what I can tell after speaking to the DCI, the Deeley case is extremely complex. We have an abundance of possible suspects and yet there could be many more as yet unidentified. Because we'll probably never know the identity of all the people present in the wood at the time of the murder. I'm beginning to become extremely disillusioned with the whole case. We don't seem any closer to catching the killer.'

Khalid shrugged. 'I'm sure we'll catch them in the end, Sarge.'

Chapter 27

Tom Vickers had plunged into the depths of depression. His girlfriend, Sunita, wanted nothing more to do with him. She believed he wasn't wholly committed to her.

He realised this state of affairs was largely his fault. If only he'd stood up to his ex-wife and prevented her from moving back into his home. He should have known that once she had passed across the threshold, she would prove as challenging to remove as a barnacle from a boat.

If only he hadn't taken pity on her and escorted her to the doctor's with his arm around her shoulder. Could he ever undo the damage this had done to his relationship with the sergeant and win her back?

He raised himself from his bed and glanced at the clock. It was nine o'clock on Saturday morning. The calendar gave the date as 10 November. Peering through the curtains into the quiet street outside, he could see it was a cloudy day with a hint of sunshine. This did little to enhance his mood.

Then his phone rang. It was Chloe's older sister, Louise.

'How are you doing, Tom? Hope I didn't wake you,' she said.

'No, I've been up a while. Been unable to sleep much, to be honest. How are you? We haven't spoken in months.'

'That's right. Tom, how are you and Chloe getting on? She's told the family she's moved back with you and you're trying to make a go of it.'

He tutted in exasperation. 'That's not true at all. I said she could stay for a few days. Now she's taking liberties and I can't get her to move out.'

'Really? Is she there right now? Her phone's off and I've been trying to reach her.'

'She was asleep on the settee downstairs when I came in from the pub last night.'

'Can you ask her to call me?'

'Sure thing. Listen, Louise, I think it's extremely unfair that none of your family will put her up – now her boyfriend's kicked her out.'

There was a long pause before she replied.

'Honestly, I don't know what you mean. I'd be more than happy for her to move in here. We've got plenty of space, but she's never asked. She just said she was happy where she was in Halesowen and the two of you were trying to work things out.'

Vickers took a deep breath. 'Really? Well, that's very interesting.'

This was the last straw out of a whole agglomeration of final straws. He'd done enough for his free-loading ex-wife. Now it was time for her to take responsibility for her future life, he decided.

'Are you all right, Tom? You've gone a bit quiet.'

'Louise, get yourself ready for a house guest.' He then ended the call and threw his handset onto the bed.

In fury, he pulled on his dressing gown and marched downstairs, where his wife remained asleep on the settee. He grabbed the bed clothes and shook her awake.

'Your time's up,' he shouted. 'You're leaving this morning.'

She lifted her arm onto her forehead and squinted at him in the half-light.

'What's the matter? What's happened? What's the time?'

'You're moving out. Get your clothes on and pack your bags.'

'Why? What's happened, Tom?'

'I've had your sister, Louise, on the phone.'

'Why'd she call you?'

'Because your phone's off, probably. She says you'd be welcome to stay over there any time, so get moving. You're not staying here a moment longer. You can move in with Louise and her family.'

She swept her legs round and sat up.

'Something's happened, hasn't it? You've not been in a good mood for days. Has someone said something? Is this to do with your road accident?'

'This is my decision. It's the end of the road, Chloe. You're moving out. The divorce is going through. And I want you out of my life forever.'

'I've still got problems walking.'

'I'll help you pack the car, provided you leave in the next hour.'

Chapter 28

As the sun emerged from behind the clouds on Sunday, 11 November, a middle-aged couple set out for a morning walk. They followed the main street through Norton Prior, a country village three miles west of Queensbridge, laughing and joking as they went.

Within a few minutes, Pam Listers and her husband Raymond reached Oxford Park, one of the largest green spaces in West Warwickshire. Their shoes crunched on the frost-laden leaves as they followed the tarmac path along the park's edge. The barren trees formed sinister silhouettes against the dove-grey sky.

She smiled at her husband. 'I'm so glad I wore my thick coat today. It's a lot colder than I was expecting.'

'Yes and it's due to get even colder, according to the weather report this morning.'

Suddenly, out of nowhere, a young woman came sprinting towards them. They recognized her as one of their neighbours, Laura.

'Pam, come quick! Over there! Look!' the woman cried.

The pair followed her gaze. They could see a small group of people several hundred metres away, next to a clump of trees. Someone was lying on the ground beside a park bench.

'Whatever is it, Laura?' asked Listers.

'There's a man over there who's seriously ill. You did a first aid course, didn't you?'

'We'll see what we can do,' she said.

The couple hurried along the path and, accompanied by Laura, quickly reached the spot where the man was lying motionless. Listers knelt down beside him. He was a grey-haired man, aged about forty-five, who was wearing a mauve shirt and slightly torn beige jeans. He seemed to be unconscious.

As her husband dialled 999 on his mobile phone to request an ambulance, she quickly took off her fawn coat, folded it and placed it beneath the man's head. Then she checked he was breathing properly and made sure his airways were clear. She got Raymond to take off his blue anorak and used it to cover the patient's body while they waited.

Within ten minutes, an ambulance arrived. Two paramedics rushed across the field to the small group of bystanders.

'Right, let's have a look,' said the older of the two men, who had a dark moustache and beard. He checked for a pulse. Then he turned towards Listers, who was still squatting beside the man.

'You've been in charge of the patient, have you? You've done well. Right, let's see if there are any signs of an ID.'

He pulled out a wallet after rummaging in one of the man's pockets.

The paramedic frowned. 'Doesn't seem to have any ID at all.'

At that moment, the man stirred, making a guttural noise.

'Ah, he seems to be coming round. Sir, can you hear me?' the ambulanceman asked.

The bewildered man, who had days of dark stubble on his face and smelt strongly of alcohol and body odour, made a half-hearted attempt to sit up.

'No, don't worry. It's all right,' said the paramedic as the patient, his face pale and his eyes bloodshot, stared up at all the gawping faces. 'It's all right, sir. I'm a paramedic. You've been unwell. We're just going to take you to hospital to give you a check-up.'

'I'm all right,' the patient insisted.

'It's for your own good,' said the bearded man.

Their patient was weak and looked to have spent days without food and proper sleep. He was unable to resist as the two paramedics stepped forward, bundled him onto a stretcher and headed back towards the ambulance with him. The onlookers broke into a spontaneous round of applause.

'I've given him a quick examination. I'm sure he'll be all right,' the bearded paramedic told Listers. 'You've done very well.'

Raymond looked on proudly. 'She went on a first aid course in connection with her work.'

'Well, that's proved its worth,' he replied. 'Anyway, must go or I'll have to walk back to town.'

Listers stood up and smiled. 'Where are you taking him?'

'Queensbridge General,' he yelled back as he hurried off in the direction of the ambulance.

'You did a good job there, love,' Raymond said.

Listers was immersed in thought. 'You know who that man might've been, don't you?' she said as they continued their walk through the park.

'Who? The paramedic?' asked Raymond.

'No, you idiot – the rough sleeper.'

'No idea at all. As you say, a rough sleeper. We used to call them vagrants.'

'It might be the missing man. You know, the man the police have been questioning about Dr Deeley. It's been all over the *Gazette* and on TV. The cops have been appealing for information. David Harper, his name is.'

* * *

The following morning, the chief inspector summoned his sergeant as soon as she arrived at work. He peered up at her as she appeared promptly by the door.

'Are you all right, Sergeant?'

'Fine, sir.'

'You look different from normal – not as chirpy.'

She shrugged. 'Probably been working too hard, sir.'

'In your case, that's probably true. You couldn't say that about everyone who works here.'

'My friend says I need a holiday.'

'Well, you've still got some leave to take.'

'We might be going to see the Northern Lights.'

'I always wanted to do that. But the closest I ever got to northern lights was the Blackpool Illuminations. Right, well, I've got some news. David Harper's turned up. He's been sleeping rough over in Norton Prior. Got picked up yesterday and was kept in at Queensbridge General overnight. This morning his wife picked him up and brought him home, so I want you to go over to his house with DC Khalid and arrest him on suspicion of the murder of Dr Deeley. Khalid's just gone to pick up a search warrant. He'll be back in a moment.'

* * *

Soon after midday, Sunita Roy drove to the Harpers' house in Queensbridge with DC Khalid and parked outside.

She strode up the stone path as a police car in Heart of England livery and a white van containing two SOCOs drew up behind her. Amy Harper at once came to the door.

'Can't you leave us alone?' she implored.

Sunita tried an apologetic approach. 'I'm really sorry, Mrs Harper. I know your husband's been unwell, but we need to speak to him again.'

'He's only just been released from hospital,' she moaned as she stood in the doorway. 'He's been away from home for more than a week. Can't you give us a few days together, please? Come back and see us at the end of the week.'

'I'm sorry. We need to see him now,' Sunita said.

As two uniformed constables passed through the gateway and approached the house, Mrs Harper mumbled a question about why so many officers were present on this occasion.

Sunita wasn't listening. She stepped through the hall and found their suspect lounging on the settee in the front room. He looked a different man from the one she'd seen a month before. Now dressed in a simple green T-shirt and blue jeans, he seemed more pale and gaunt than she remembered him. But he was clean-shaven and there was no smell of alcohol in the room.

'Mr Harper, I'm arresting you on suspicion of the murder of Dr Scott Deeley,' she said before reciting the rest of the police caution.

He scowled and shouted at her as the two constables entered the room and handcuffed him.

'I don't bloody believe it. I've been through a horrendous experience. I've been to hell and back. Now, after the doctors have announced I'm on the road to recovery, you're round here, quick as a flash, slapping cuffs on me like I'm a hardened criminal.'

Sunita frowned. 'Take him to the station, please,' she said before turning her attention to the suspect's wife, who was watching events from the hallway.

'Mrs Harper, we've got a warrant here to search this house. We're going to leave some staff here and my colleague, DC Khalid, will be in charge of them.'

She then accompanied Harper and the two constables out of the house. As she stood on the garden path, she turned to Khalid, who was standing in the doorway.

'I'm going to leave you in charge, Omar,' she told him. 'I expect the team will bundle up some of his clothes and take them to St James Street. Obviously, the main object of the exercise is to dig up any possible ligature that could have been used. If you need me, I'll be with the DCI.'

* * *

As David Harper was bundled onto the pavement, a photographer from the *Queensbridge Gazette*, who had been passing, stopped his car and dashed across the road. He snapped a series of pictures of the arrested man being led towards the police car.

'Mr Harper!' the photographer yelled as the camera continually flashed. 'Have you just been arrested? How do you feel?'

'They've got the wrong man,' he called back as he was pushed into the rear of the vehicle.

Chapter 29

By the middle of the bitterly cold Monday afternoon, the chief inspector was becoming convinced that former architect David Harper was responsible for the doctor's death.

His bicycle tyres had left clear tracks in the mud close to the location of the body – and now a new witness had come forward. Her evidence seemed to implicate Harper.

Just before three o'clock that afternoon, two officers brought the suspect up from his basement cell to the ground-floor interview room, where the two detectives were waiting.

He stumbled as he entered the room. He looked haggard and downcast. He took a seat opposite Gavin Roscoe and Sunita Roy. Moments later, the duty solicitor, Roger Sims, neatly dressed in a brown suit, knocked on the door, walked in and took a seat next to his client.

'Right, let's get started,' said Roscoe. Turning to the lawyer, he asked, 'You've had a chance to speak to Mr Harper, I believe?'

'Yes, I have.'

'Good. Mr Harper, I need to remind you that you're still under caution.'

He rose and switched on some video equipment. Then, for the purposes of the tape, he listed the names of everyone present. As he resumed his seat, Roscoe set his eyes on the suspect.

'Now, Mr Harper. I think it would be best if you told us once again how you spent the morning of Monday, 8 October. What time did you leave your house?'

Harper spoke haltingly. 'I left home at about a quarter past seven. I cycled to Mike's Café in Sinton Bank, arriving there just before eight.'

'What did you do as soon as you arrived at work?'

'I– I took off my jacket and started cleaning some of the tables.'

'And you stayed there, working, until what time?'

'The boss, Mike Griffin, let me have an hour off because we had a water leak at home, and I'd got the plumber coming.'

'What time did you go home to see about the leak?'

'Um. I'm not sure. I think it was around nine o'clock.'

'You left before that, didn't you, Mr Harper?'

'No.'

'We've got a witness in Sinton Bank who saw you cycling along Highfield Road towards the woods at around a quarter past eight.'

'Then they must be mistaken. It wasn't me.'

'The lady remembers seeing you because you briefly came off your bike. She was putting out her bins and asked if you were all right. She believes she'd seen you cycling towards the woods on a previous morning as well. She's given us a sworn statement and is ready to come to court. You were travelling towards the woods, weren't you?'

Harper hesitated, glancing at his solicitor again. Roscoe was becoming irritated at the man's lack of frankness.

'Highfield Road leads directly onto Foxwell Heath, doesn't it?' the detective insisted.

Harper made no comment. Sunita went to the back of the room. She retrieved two transparent evidence bags, which she handed to the chief inspector. Roscoe placed one in the middle of the table.

'I'm showing Mr Harper exhibit A,' said Roscoe. 'It's a photograph of a tyre track discovered in the mud at Foxwell Heath which was found on 8 October.'

Harper and his solicitor studied the picture, which Roscoe kept hold of. The detective held up the second bag.

'I'm now showing Mr Harper exhibit B, which shows an impression of a track that your front tyre made when a member of our lab staff placed it in a wooden box filled with mud.'

Harper was beginning to realise the police knew more than he had at first believed. He and his lawyer gazed at the second image and held a brief whispered discussion. Mr Sims glanced across at the chief inspector.

'Could we have a break for a moment?' he asked.

Roscoe nodded. The two detectives moved away from the table so Harper and his lawyer could speak about the exhibits in greater detail. A few minutes later, Mr Sims indicated they were ready to return to the table.

'My client now accepts the tracks in the woods may have been made by his bicycle,' Mr Sims admitted.

Harper leaned forward on the table.

'Yes, you're right. I went into the woods. I left the cafe at just after a quarter past eight. I told Mike I needed a break. I was cycling along Highfield Road when the front wheel must have hit a brick or a stone. I fell off and hurt my leg. It was nothing. I got back on the bike and carried on.'

'What was your purpose?' asked Sunita.

'All right. I'll be honest. I'd noticed, on a few occasions before, that Dr Deeley was in the habit of going on an early morning run. He was a fitness fanatic. On that Monday, I decided to follow him.'

'You decided to follow him and murder him in the wood because you believed he was to blame for the death of your son?'

'No. Definitely not. I just wanted to have it out with him. Look, I don't have a violent bone in my body. I just wanted to confront him – to see what he had to say for himself. I wanted to scare him. There's no way I'd have killed him.'

Sunita glared. 'No way you would have killed him? After everything you've said about him in the past? You told the local newspaper you were glad the doctor was dead.'

'Well, his incompetence led, in my opinion, to the death of my dearly-beloved son – that's true. I did at times express the view that it would be better if he weren't with us. But that's different from actually doing the deed myself. My parents went to church and raised me with Christian morals.'

'Look,' said Roscoe. 'You had an obsessive hatred for the man. That morning you were stalking him. You've admitted heading towards the woods so you could confront him. Your tyre tracks were found at the murder scene. Yet you have the gall to sit there and deny murdering him.'

'Yes,' said Harper. 'Because he was already dead by the time I caught up with him.'

Sunita drew a quick breath. 'You saw Dr Deeley's body then?'

'No.'

'So how do you know he was dead when you arrived at Foxwell Heath?' she asked.

'This is what happened. I followed Dr Deeley into the woods for a few hundred metres, then somehow I lost sight of him. I don't know how. One minute, he was there; the next, he was gone. I'd been delayed by coming off the bike and he got well ahead of me. I walked around the area in a kind of circle pushing the bike, looking out for him. A lot of time must have passed – probably over half an hour.

'Then I noticed, through the gaps in the trees and bushes, a group of people a short distance away from me. At the time, I thought it was three women, but after reading about it in the press, I realise it was a man and two women. They'd got a dog with them. One of them shouted something and another one threw up their hands in horror. It was obvious they'd found something and, whatever it was, wasn't very pleasant.

'I began to panic. I guessed maybe something had happened to the doctor and knew I might be a suspect because of my history with him. So I carried on with my journey in the direction of Foxwell Green and returned to the cafe by following the main road back to Sinton Bank.'

Roscoe scowled. 'You expect us to believe that?'

'I don't really care if you believe it or not. But it's the truth,' Harper said.

'So you didn't have a plumbing leak?'

'No, I'm sorry. I lied about that. I know it doesn't look good now.'

'No. It doesn't,' snapped Roscoe. He shook his head. He'd met countless murderers before and knew how they tried to twist facts to suit themselves.

'No, I'll tell you what happened, Mr Harper. You cycled up behind him and attacked him. You tried to strangle him and, when that failed, you viciously plunged the metal carving fork into his heart.'

'No, that's a lie.'

'Then you realised there were some dog walkers nearby and panicked, fearing you'd be seen, so you quickly rode away. We've found some neckties at your house, and they're being examined. I'm fairly confident we're going to find the tie you used in your pathetic attempt to strangle the doctor before you stabbed him.'

Sunita glared at Harper. 'I think it's possible, sir, that he read about the dog walkers in the press and decided to add them to his story to try to make it sound plausible.'

Harper shook his head. 'No, that's all rubbish.'

'No, Mr Harper. It's your entire testimony that's rubbish,' said Roscoe. 'It's a tissue of lies from start to finish, made in a desperate attempt to defend yourself after your despicable and cowardly attack on Dr Deeley. I'm going to have you put back in the cells. And there's every chance that, sometime tomorrow, you'll face a charge of murder.'

Chapter 30

Tom Vickers glanced up as a flustered DC Hopkirk arrived at work on Tuesday morning, clutching her handbag, a scarf, an umbrella, a newspaper and her lunchbox.

'Sorry I'm late, Tom,' she mumbled as she set the items down on her desk. 'Hold-up at Sparkhill.'

'That's all right, Wendy. Have you finished reading through my report on the court evidence?'

'I'm about halfway through. I'm building up a good knowledge of the case, but I haven't found anything irregular so far.'

'All right. Just keep ploughing away.'

She placed her umbrella on the empty desk beside her, alongside her lunchbox.

'Tom, I know it's probably none of my business, but I've noticed DS Roy hasn't called into our office much recently. I just wondered if everything's all right between the two of you.'

'You're right, Wendy. It isn't any of your business, but, for the record, we're not seeing each other anymore. All right?'

'I'm very sorry, Tom. I shouldn't have asked.'

'No, it's all right. Perhaps I shouldn't have snapped at you. It's just that it's a bit raw.'

'Of course.'

He filled the kettle with water from the sink in the corner. 'I expect you'd like a tea?'

'Yes, please.'

'Wendy, provided you don't find any glaring errors or omissions in my report, I want you to send it out on my behalf. Make sure the chief super, the DCI, the ACC and the legal office all get copies. Don't send it to anyone else for the moment. Is that understood?'

'Yes, sir. No problem.'

A few minutes later, a call came through on his desk phone.

'It's the switchboard here. Is that DI Vickers?'

'Yes.'

'We've got a woman asking to speak to someone called Tom. It's to do with a murder case in Sedgeworth.'

'Yes, I'll deal with it. Oh, before you do that, has her number come up?'

'No. It's number withheld.'

'All right. If you'd like to put the call through.'

The operator's soft voice was replaced by that of a young woman with a strong Birmingham accent.

'You Tom?'

'Yes, Tom Vickers speaking. How can I help?'

'Got some information you might like, darling. It's about that geezer who got done in last year, name of O'Sullivan.'

Vickers frowned as he switched on the phone's loudspeaker.

'How did you get my name?'

'A little bird gave me your name. Said you was raking over what happened.'

He slipped his mobile phone from his pocket and switched on its voice recorder.

'New information comes in from time to time and cases have to be updated. We're always re-examining old cases.'

There was a brief pause before the woman said, 'I got some information you might like.'

'What kind of information?'

'Inside information.'

'Does it relate to the conviction of Winston Stevens and Raj Kumar?'

'Is them the boys that got sent down?'

'Yeah.'

'Yes, it does. It relates to them. Are you interested or not?'

'I might be. How do I know your information's kosher?'

'Well, all I can do is pass it on to you and then it's down to you to check it out.'

'All right. What do you know?'

'I can't do this over the phone. We'll have to meet up.'

'Where do you suggest?'

'Do you know Sidney Road in Sedgeworth?'

'No, but I can find it.'

'All right. Can you make it for two o'clock this afternoon?'

'I should think so.'

'It's number forty-six.'

'Can I take your name?'

'What do you want that for?'

'Well, it's nice to know who to ask for?'

'Vera. Come at two o'clock and don't be late.'

Then she hung up.

DC Hopkirk had been listening throughout the conversation. She stood up and stepped across the room.

'Sounds a bit dodgy to me. You're not going to go, are you, sir?'

'Well, I said I'd go, and it could have a bearing on Sepulchre. So I've got no choice really. I was going to ask for a phone number, but she rang off before I could get the words out.'

Hopkirk took a chair from a nearby empty desk and sat down, facing him.

'Sir, it was only a week ago when those two blokes forced you off the road and damaged your car.'

'I know. But you've got to take chances sometimes.'

'Certainly, I don't think you should go on your own. You need some kind of back-up.'

'That's true, but you can't come because I need someone in the office and our budget's been cut so badly, there really isn't anyone else. I'll have a word with the DCI, but he's stretched as well.'

* * *

The inspector drove his hire car, a blue Citroen Picasso, into Sedgeworth at just before two o'clock. It was nearly two weeks since his previous visit when he had interviewed Mrs Shah.

His sat nav quickly found Sidney Road, a narrow, one-way street on the southern side of town comprising rows of terraced houses with small front gardens. Number forty-six was an end-terrace house with two sash windows overlooking the street – one on the ground floor and one above.

He drove along the street twice, familiarising himself with the house and neighbouring properties. He discovered an alley separated the rear gardens of the properties from similar plots behind houses in the adjoining street. Several vehicles were parked outside the house, so he had to park nearly a hundred metres away, halfway along the street.

He had spoken to the chief inspector before he left St James Street, asking if any officer was free to accompany him, but Roscoe had, with regret, informed him there was no one available at such short notice. Vickers had been so intrigued by Vera's promise of 'inside information' that he decided to take a calculated risk and attend on his own.

As he advanced towards the white UPVC front door, he felt as uneasy as an expectant father approaching a maternity ward. The door was ajar and the front room curtains downstairs were drawn. He rang the bell and a male voice called out in a foreign accent, 'Come in, Mr Vickers.'

Gingerly, he pushed the door and was faced by a pile of unopened mail on the floor of the gloomy hallway. There was a musty, damp smell.

'I'm looking for Vera,' he called out.

'You've come to the right place,' said a voice. 'I'm in the front room.'

That's certainly not Vera, Vickers told himself. That sounds like a man.

He left the front door partly open, as he'd found it, and turned the handle on the living room door. It creaked open and he found himself in a darkened room. A brown leather settee lay beneath the window. At the far side, in a corner amid the gloom, sat a man in a dining chair with a table in front of him set for tea.

He took a few steps forward before he realised the man was pointing a gun at him.

Chapter 31

'I think I might be in the wrong house,' the inspector murmured as he glanced at the middle-aged man pointing the pistol at him. He reckoned it was a Beretta or a Glock.

'My dear inspector! It's OK. You're not in the wrong house at all,' said the man. 'Please forgive the slight use of subterfuge to lure you here. But this a meeting I've been looking forward to for some time. And it could prove beneficial for us both.'

Vickers scowled. 'Who are you? What do you want?'

His host, who was attempting to conceal his appearance by wearing dark glasses, smiled. 'All in good time, Inspector.'

The man was slim with close-cropped dark hair and dressed in a dark-grey suit. Although sitting down, Vickers guessed he was tall. He felt the man might be Polish.

The inspector became aware of a second man's presence behind him. Over his left shoulder he observed a younger man. He appeared to be aged around thirty. He was also tall, casually dressed with short, black curly hair and was of West Indian appearance. Worryingly, he was also clasping a gun.

'Come and join the party,' the Polish man told the newcomer. 'But, before you do, just make a few checks outside. We want to make sure our friend Mr Vickers is all on his lonesome.'

As the younger man placed his weapon in an inside pocket of his jacket and stepped outside, Vickers gazed around the room. The only furniture was the table, two chairs and the settee. A photograph of three children took pride of place above the red-brick fireplace.

'Where's Vera?' asked Vickers.

'No Vera, I'm afraid,' said the man. 'Is all part of a ruse to get you here.' He pointed to a dining chair in front of the fireplace. 'Wouldn't you like to sit down?'

'I'm all right standing up. I don't feel like getting cosy with someone who's pointing a gun at me.'

'Come now, Mr Vickers. No offence intended. Look, I'll put the gun down.'

He placed it on the edge of the table in front of him. 'See? You've nothing to fear.'

At that moment, the younger man strode back and glanced towards the table.

'There's no one else around. He doesn't seem to have any buddies with him.'

'Good. If you'd like to search our guest and relieve him of his mobile phone, perhaps we can begin our little chat.'

Vickers took exception to having to hand over his phone and have his pockets searched. But since both men were armed, he felt obliged to cooperate and let the younger man rummage in his pockets.

'He's good,' said the younger man, handing Vickers' handset across the table.

'Cool,' said the host, who smiled at the inspector as he placed the phone beside the handgun.

'Now, you'd like a drink? Some rum or vodka, maybe?'

Vickers shook his head. 'No, I'm on duty.'

'Oh, the faithful British bobby. How about a nice cup of tea then?'

'No. Just tell me why the hell you've tricked me into coming here.'

'My dear inspector, I invited you here to discuss a mutual problem.'

He turned his attention to the younger man who was now loitering by the doorway, as though awaiting further instructions.

'Go and make some nice English tea, would you?' said the older man. 'And three cups. I'm sure our inspector friend would benefit from a little refreshment.'

As he headed out of the room, the host again suggested Vickers should sit down. He gestured towards the second of the two chairs. This time, the inspector accepted the offer.

'Good. We can now have a little civilised chat, can't we?'

Vickers folded his arms as he tried to make himself as comfortable as possible on the hard, wooden chair.

'Can I begin by asking you who you are?'

'Sorry. No names,' said the host. 'It is enough to say that I have information that may prove useful to you and, likewise, you have information that may be useful to me.'

'This is information about Brendan O'Sullivan?'

The man nodded. 'That's what we're talking about here. Poor Brendan. If only he stuck to the rules.'

'What – paying for his drugs on time?'

The man nodded again. 'I'm glad to see we're on the same page. Yes. His mistake was failing to pay for the service provided. So, Mr Vickers, you're trying to dredge up the whole sorry business of what happened to poor Brendan and treading on people's toes in the process.'

'We've been asked to reinvestigate the case because of fears there may've been a miscarriage of justice.'

The man leaned forward. His glasses slid down his nose a fraction. Vickers guessed that his host was associated with the 101 Crew he was researching.

The man sneered. 'Miscarriage of justice? There was no miscarrying of justice. Is that the reason you bothered Mrs Shah in Albion Road?'

Vickers was perturbed to hear his eccentric host spouting the name of his key witness. But he was careful to avoid giving the man any confirmation of the woman's identity or of the interview he'd conducted a fortnight earlier.

'Who? Sorry, don't think I know that name.'

'Come on. You can be frank with me.'

Just then, the younger man pushed open the door with his foot and entered the room, holding a brown wooden tray laden with cups and saucers, a sugar bowl, a milk jug, a stainless-steel teapot and some teaspoons. He placed it in the middle of the table before leaving the room again.

'Milk and sugar?' asked the man at the table.

'Don't bother making me any tea. I won't be drinking it.'

'Oh, such a shame. In the part of the world I come from, it's drunk all day long and I've been told the Brits drink thirty-six billion cups a year. Very disappointing. I wanted to give you a brief moment of pleasure, Mr Vickers, before I kill you.'

'We'll see about that, chum,' the inspector shouted. He jumped up, grabbed the teapot and hurled the steaming hot tea over the man's head and chest.

The scalded man leapt up, knocking the table over.

'Bastard!' he screamed.

Vickers stooped and picked up the revolver and his phone, both of which had landed close to his feet. He recognised the gun as a Beretta 9000S. His main objective now was to make good his escape from the house in one piece – although, if an arrest was in the offing, that would be a bonus.

He knew he had to act quickly. The second man, whom he'd fathomed by now to be gang enforcer Tyrone Blake, would be back within seconds.

While the injured man sat writhing in agony on his chair screaming abuse at him, Vickers rushed to the door and peered along the passage. He could see a doorway leading to a kitchen at the back of the house.

Then Blake emerged from the gloom, his eyes as crazed as a rabid dog's. The inspector fired the pistol along the passageway as a warning shot. The bullet struck the door frame, causing Blake to duck back into the kitchen.

Blake fired a shot in Vickers' direction, causing him to dive back into the front room. A second bullet followed. Then all was silent, except for the shouts and curses of the scalded man.

Cautiously, taking one step at a time, the inspector ventured along the hallway into the kitchen. The room was empty with the back door wide open.

Believing Blake had fled, Vickers dashed outside after him and found himself in a neglected rear garden with an uncut lawn and overgrown bushes. There was no sign of his quarry.

While standing beside the open door, the inspector called his control room, requesting armed back-up and an ambulance for the burns victim. Then he spied the gunman by a wooden gate at the end of the garden, pointing his gun directly at him.

Vickers tried to evade the first bullet when it came. But he wasn't swift enough and it struck his shoulder, followed instantly by a second one that pierced the side of his chest.

He tumbled onto the grass, clutching his wounds in agony. Blood was seeping through his shirt and jacket.

'Wish I'd listened to Wendy and not come alone,' he mumbled to himself. Then the pain intensified and he slipped into a semi-conscious state.

Blake raced past the inspector, who was now lying motionless on the ground. He hurried into the kitchen and examined the reddening skin on his boss's hands and face.

'Come on, my friend. We must get these burns under some running water and then we'll have to get going. With all that shooting, the street will soon be crawling with cops and we won't look too clever once they've found our guest lying dead by the back door.'

Chapter 32

IT consultant Samir Banerjee was advising a client on the phone about a computer problem when gunfire disturbed the peace of the afternoon. He believed there were at least five shots. They were so loud that they sounded as though a firearm had been discharged in his own house, but he recognised the barrage had probably come from the house next door, number forty-six.

'Something terrible is happening,' he told his caller. 'It sounds like someone is shooting. I must go and see what the matter is. I'll call you back.'

Then he opened his front door and peered out into Sidney Road to see two men – one middle-aged and one in his early thirties – climbing into a black Volkswagen Touareg. The older of the two had a dripping white towel wrapped round his head and shoulders, but neither seemed to be carrying a gun.

He shrugged his shoulders and passed through his house into the kitchen. Then, as he began making a drink, he thought he could detect a cry for help.

He dashed into his back garden and, over the top of his fence, he could see a blood-soaked figure lying on the ground. A male voice was calling, 'Help me, please! Is there anyone who can help me?'

Samir, an intelligent-looking man with black-framed glasses and an enthusiastic nature, didn't hesitate. He undid the padlock on his garden gate. Then he entered his neighbour's garden and rushed to the stricken inspector's side.

He looked aghast. 'Oh, my goodness, you're hurt badly. I must call an ambulance.'

'One on the way,' mumbled Vickers.

Samir was murmuring to himself. 'I must find something. I must find something.'

He raced back inside his kitchen and returned, moments later, with a clean towel. He used it to press down hard on the wound.

'I'm Samir,' he told the inspector.

'I'm Tom,' the inspector murmured. 'Have the men with guns gone?'

'Men with guns? I only saw two men drive away in a Touareg.'

'Car number?'

'No, didn't get it. It's best you don't talk.'

But a few minutes after he began applying pressure to the arm, there was a series of loud knocks on the door of the house.

Warily, because it wasn't his house, Samir ventured inside and found his way to the front door.

'Who is it?' he asked.

'Ambulance service. Someone been scalded with a hot liquid?'

He flung open the door to find two paramedics in the blue uniforms of West Midlands Ambulance Service and an ambulance with flashing lights blocking the street.

Samir gave a sigh. 'Thank God you're here. There's a man badly injured in the back garden. But he's not been burnt. It looks like he's been shot.'

The pair proceeded through the house and found Vickers, still drifting in and out of consciousness and his arm and chest bleeding. The older paramedic, a tall, blonde woman, picked up the towel and pressed on the wound as Samir had done.

'Quick, Lauren,' she yelled. 'Get some gauze and bandages.'

A few minutes later, as police cars began to arrive outside, Samir watched anxiously while Vickers was carried out on a stretcher and hoisted into the back of the ambulance. Samir ran into the street.

'Where are you taking him?'

Lauren whispered, 'University Hospital.'

'Oh, Coventry,' he mumbled as Lauren leapt into the driving seat and the ambulance drew away.

He glanced over his shoulder and noticed a red bag standing in the hall by the sitting-room door. On closer inspection, he found it was the crew's bleed control kit containing gauze, bandages and dressings left behind by the paramedics.

Two police officers in flat caps stepped inside and converged upon him as he bent down to pick up the kit. He'd noticed them a few minutes earlier speaking to Lauren.

'This your house, sir?' asked one, a young, red-haired officer.

Samir shook his head. 'No. I live next door, but I heard shooting and found the guy in the garden in a bad way.'

'Did you see any shooting?'

'No, but I heard it. I've never heard such loud bangs before.'

'Did you see anyone in the street?'

'Yes. I was next door at number forty-four and looked out to see two men getting into a car and driving off.'

'Right. We'll need to take a statement from you, sir. If it's all right, sir, my colleague and I better come inside your house and let our colleagues inspect the crime scene.'

* * *

Half an hour later, after Samir's statement had been written down, his doorbell rang. He drew back the door to find a stocky man with short brown hair standing outside in a navy-blue suit.

He brandished a warrant card.

'Mr Banerjee? I'm DS Bains from Heart of England Police. May I come in?'

He accompanied his host into the small front room.

'Looks as though your prompt actions may have saved a man's life.'

A smile flickered across Samir's face. 'Really?'

'Well, it's early days. He's lost a lot of blood. But it's looking encouraging. May I sit down?'

Samir nodded and drew forward a small armchair.

The detective sat down while his host remained standing.

'He told me his name's Tom.'

Bains nodded. 'That's right. Tom Vickers. He's a detective inspector at headquarters. God knows what he was doing round here. Anyway, I've drawn the short straw and I'm the one tasked with trying to make some sense out of all this. So how long have you lived here, Mr Banerjee?'

Samir made an open-handed gesture. 'I've lived here eight years.'

Bains spent the next few minutes asking about the shooting, the two men who fled, and how he came upon Vickers in the garden.

When Samir had finished answering his questions, Bains's phone rang and he whispered that his boss was calling.

'Yes, sir? … I'm just interviewing a witness … Yes, I'd already considered that … No, I don't think there's any problem … No, the witness, Mr Banerjee, whom I'm with right now, says he didn't think to take a note of the number plate … How's our friend Mr Vickers? … Oh really? … Has he got a wife? … Separated, yeah? … The injury was obviously worse than was first thought. I'll see you later in the pub.'

Bains ended the call.

'My inspector,' he explained. 'Now, can you tell me about the occupants of number forty-six?

'Oh, he's a very sick man. A very sick man indeed,' said Samir. 'He's a Mr Gregory. He's not working, and has visitors at all hours of the day and night. There's been trouble there – lots of trouble. People sometimes bang on my door in the middle of the night.'

Bains, who was writing down some of Samir's remarks in a notebook, glanced across. 'What sort of people?'

'Young people, mainly, and there's always the smell of cannabis in the air late at night. I've spoken to the police about it because I'm worried I live next to a drugs den. But nothing's been happening about it.'

The detective nodded. 'When did you last see Mr Gregory?'

'I last saw him a few days ago. He was just moaning about some noisy children who woke him up, playing in the street. Most of the time we don't speak much. When you were speaking to your inspector, did he say whether he's going to be all right then, that chap Tom?'

'Apparently, he's taken a turn for the worse after losing so much blood. They don't think he's going to make it.'

Chapter 33

Carrying a sheaf of documents DC Omar Khalid approached the chief inspector's door guardedly, and began peering through the glass.

'Yes. What is it, Khalid?' his boss asked. 'I'm very busy.'

'Sir, I wondered if we could discuss the reconstruction?'

Roscoe sighed. 'I suppose I can spare a few minutes for that. You'd better come in. I'm thinking of charging David Harper over the doctor's murder, but there are a few inconsistencies we need to work through and we've had to apply to the court for further time.'

The constable shrugged his shoulders. He placed a folded sheet of paper on the chief inspector's desk before drawing up a chair.

'I've notified the media team and they're putting out a press release tomorrow, sir.'

'Good. So we're all set for next Monday?'

'Yes, sir. All known witnesses have been notified. There are twenty-five altogether, who were either on the heath or close by on the morning Dr Deeley died. On top of that, there are twenty-five officers who'll help them mark their positions and twenty-eight support staff, who'll log findings and direct the public.'

He stared at the sheet Khalid had placed in front of him.

'This is a map of the whole area, is it?'

'Yes, sir. If you open it out, you'll see the positions of witnesses are clearly marked.'

Roscoe leaned back on his chair and placed his hands behind his head.

'This effort to restage the murder scene must be one of the biggest events of its kind we've ever organised.'

Khalid nodded. 'Yes, sir.'

'It'll be interesting to see if any witnesses, so far unidentified, are remembered by the ones who turn up and, hopefully, we'll get a clearer picture of what happened.'

Khalid glanced down at one of his documents.

'We've put up posters about what's happening at bus stops in a two-mile radius. They've also been put up at the car park and round Sinton Bank and Foxwell Green.'

'What about Heath Road Service Station?'

'Not yet.'

'I think we should.'

They were interrupted when Roscoe's desk phone rang. Khalid rose to his feet.

'I'll go and arrange that now, sir,' he said, stepping out of the room and shutting the door.

Roscoe raised his handset. 'DCI,' he replied brusquely and found it was his wife calling.

'It's me, darling,' Helen said. 'What sort of day are you having?'

'An extremely busy one.'

'All right. I'll keep it brief. You hadn't forgotten George and Amanda are holding their engagement party at the tearooms on Saturday, had you?'

He had to confess to himself that the event had slipped his mind.

'Is it *this* Saturday?'

'I thought you'd probably forgotten.'

Roscoe shook his head. 'No, no, it's just that, while I'm at work, some of the social events get thrust to the back of my mind. Of course, it's this Saturday.'

'How many of your colleagues at work have said they're coming?'

'Only DI Vickers and DS Roy. The others don't really know George well enough. Listen, can't this wait till this evening?'

'No, dear. I've got to make final arrangements.'

They were interrupted by a loud knocking on the door. Khalid's anxious face appeared in the doorway.

'It's DI Vickers, sir. He's been shot and he's in a serious way.'

'Got to go, dear. Tom's been shot,' he said. 'Where is he now? Do we know the full SP?' Roscoe asked Khalid as he leapt out of his seat and put on his jacket.

'He's at University Hospital in Coventry, sir. DC Hopkirk says he raced off to Sedgeworth this afternoon after a woman called in, claiming to have information. He called at a house in Sidney Road and he's been shot twice.

'So he was ambushed?'

Khalid nodded as he edged his way towards the doorway.

'Yes, sir. Summerstoke are handling it.'

'Could be the same people who tried to run him off the road. All right, Khalid. You carry on and I'll see you tomorrow. I'm going straight over to the hospital now. Let DS Roy know what's happened.'

* * *

As soon as the chief inspector reached the main entrance building with its distinctive curved façade, he was reminded of a previous visit there last year when his son was stabbed during a robbery. In the event, his son quickly recovered. But Vickers' condition sounded far more serious.

He headed first to the emergency department and was then redirected to the critical care ward on the first floor. His anxiety was growing. He declined to wait for the lift and mounted the stairs, two at a time, until, short of breath, he reached the landing.

'I'm looking for Tom Vickers,' he told a nurse at the reception desk outside the ward as perspiration dripped from his brow.

'You've just missed him. They've just taken him to theatre. Are you family?'

'I'm his boss.'

'He's in quite a bad way. They're operating on him now.'

'Any chance of speaking to someone involved, a doctor?'

'There won't be any news for a while, sir. Your best bet is to go and have a cup of tea and come back in a couple of hours.'

Roscoe was annoyed but followed her advice. He wound his way through a maze of corridors until he found the cafe.

By the time he returned to the waiting area by the ward entrance just after seven o'clock, Sunita Roy had arrived. She was talking to a stout, grey-haired, middle-aged lady who was sitting beside her. Ten or twelve other people were seated in two rows behind them.

He smiled weakly. 'Any news, Sergeant?'

She glanced up with a solemn expression. 'No, sir. But a doctor might be coming out to speak to us in a minute. Sir, can I introduce Mrs Vickers, Tom's mum?'

There was a glint of recognition in the chief inspector's eyes.

'DCI Roscoe. I think I met you once before, Mrs Vickers. How are you? I'm so sorry to meet you in these circumstances.'

'My Tom's been getting into scrapes all his life. He usually comes out of it smelling of roses, but who knows? Maybe he's tempted the gods too far this time.'

Roscoe sat down beside Mrs Vickers. 'This is an awful business.'

'The staff are all too busy,' she replied. 'We'll be lucky to get a word with any of them.'

Sunita leaned forward and glanced at him.

'Sir, apparently, before he was wheeled into the operating theatre, he mumbled something to a nurse. He said he called the ambulance for one of the two men at the house in Sedgeworth, who was scalded with hot tea. But, in the end, the pair fled and it was Tom himself who needed the ambulance.'

'Oh, I see,' said Roscoe. 'So he called his own ambulance before he was injured. That's a bit different, I suppose.'

Mrs Vickers smiled weakly. 'That may have done him a big favour. The paramedics would have seen to him that much more quickly.'

The chief inspector nodded. 'I'm just thinking. They've got a major burns unit here. I wonder if that scalded man came here for treatment.'

Sunita raised an eyebrow. 'Do you want me to check, sir?'

He lowered his voice. 'Maybe you should.'

* * *

While Roscoe accompanied Mrs Vickers to the cafe, Sunita walked to the burns unit, which was in a separate building nearby. There she discovered no burns patient had been admitted from Sedgeworth that afternoon and she returned to the waiting area. She spent some time reading through her emails on her phone. Then, just before half past seven, a slim, dark-haired man in his early thirties stepped out of the lift and walked sheepishly along the corridor towards her.

Seeing there was no one at the ward's reception desk, he strolled across to Sunita. He smiled.

'This is the critical care ward, isn't it?'

She nodded. 'The receptionist will be back in a minute. You waiting to see a patient?'

'Just after some news really about a patient called Tom.'

'Tom Vickers? I'm waiting to hear about him as well. You're a friend, are you?'

He shook his head. 'I'm the person who found him in the back garden in Sedgeworth. My name's Samir, but in England everyone calls me Sam.'

Sunita smiled as she shook his hand. 'Hi, Sam. I'm Sunita, a work colleague of Tom's. My boss and I know so little about what happened. Can you fill us in?'

Samir Banerjee explained about the gunshots at the house next door; how he found the injured detective in the back garden; the arrival and departure of the ambulance crew; and his interview with DS Philip Bains from Summerstoke CID.

'It's very kind of you to travel here to inquire about Tom. But you could have phoned, couldn't you?'

'To be honest, I had a second reason for coming here. The ambulance crew left a red bag behind by mistake.'

'A red bag? With a piece of equipment?'

'It's a bleed control kit – you know, gauze, bandages and dressings. I just dropped it off with the ambulance crew and thought, while I was here, I'd see how Tom's getting on.'

As he sat on a nearby chair, a doctor in a white coat and wire-framed glasses approached.

'Are you Mr Vickers' family?' he asked.

Sunita glanced up. 'We're not family but we're waiting for any information. Tom's mother's gone to the cafe.'

'Could you please pass on some news to her? I'm in a rush to see another patient.'

Sunita nodded.

'We've operated to stop the bleeding in his upper arm and chest,' the doctor said. 'We've found the bullets and managed to remove them. But he's on a ventilator and I'm afraid from now on it's a game of wait and see.'

Chapter 34

Sunita Roy was being plagued by nagging doubts. Throughout her fourteen-mile journey to work on Thursday, 15 November, she remained concerned about the inspector's plight. She was also absorbed by various inconsistencies in the Scott Deeley case.

She was becoming increasingly concerned her boss might be about to charge David Harper over the doctor's murder. The more she thought about the case being made against him, the more weaknesses she found. She sincerely believed the former architect could be innocent and that his version of events might have a basis in truth.

When she arrived at her desk, she turned her computer on and started studying all the evidence again. She knew the chief inspector had taken a dislike to Harper and that he was convinced he had a strong case. She wanted to find as many flaws in the case as she could to satisfy her peace of mind and prevent her boss from making a possible mistake.

At ten o'clock, the chief inspector arrived at the office. After greeting all the staff, he unlocked his door. She gave him a moment to settle in before approaching his office.

Knocking gently on his door, she asked, 'Could I have a quick word, sir?'

'Yes, come in, Sergeant,' he replied. 'Come in and close the door. Tom's still on a ventilator, but I heard this morning there are signs of improvement in his condition.'

'That's good news, sir.'

'Yes, well, I have to mention that the chief super and I view the shooting very seriously. Very seriously indeed. It's quite clear Tom has been targeted by an OCG. We've got to find out who they are and bring them to book. We can't have these thugs following our officers out of police stations and forcing them off the road or luring them to an address on some pretext and putting them under threat.

'So the chief super is quite rightly demanding action. She's paying a visit to Summerstoke CID and she's making it clear she wants quick results. She's insisted that she be kept up to date with their investigation and she's asked me to liaise with them. So, as from now, I'm placing you in charge of the day-to-day running of the Scott Deeley case. I'll be remaining as SIO, of course.'

'That's fine, sir,' she said as she took a seat. 'Thank you for putting your trust in me.'

'No, you've proved yourself very capable. Sergeant, I sense you've got something on your mind.'

'Yes, sir,' she said. 'I've been studying the Deeley case. I think we could be making an error over David Harper.'

'Good. I'm not one of those bosses who try to stifle opinion from among their team. I'd like to hear your view.'

She made herself comfortable on a chair by Roscoe's desk.

'Well, sir, he's an alcoholic in very poor health. I'm not sure he'd have had the strength to attempt to strangle the doctor and I certainly don't think he'd have had the energy required to thrust the fork into his chest.'

'Good to see you're using your brain, Sergeant. Anything else?'

'Well, I've been thinking about the forensics. Striking the doctor in the chest with the fork would no doubt have splashed blood onto the killer, but they've now finished examining Harper's clothes and found no blood. They looked at two pairs of black trousers, a black shirt and a black jacket, because the lady in Highfield Road believed he was dressed in dark clothing. No blood was found on any of them.'

Roscoe nodded. 'Of course, he may've discarded any bloodstained clothing.'

'Yes sir, that's true. But none of his DNA's been picked up at the scene at all. His fingerprints aren't on the murder weapon either and his footprints weren't found at the scene.'

'You're making some powerful points, Sergeant,' said Roscoe. 'So tell me. You've been more involved in the fine details of the case than anyone else. Where do you suggest we go from here? You think we should let Harper go?'

'Yes, sir, I think so. For the moment at least. I think we should turn our attention to three other suspects: Mark Smith, the aggrieved tenant; Valerie Stanbrook, the beneficiary of the will; and Valerie's husband Rufus. We were considering whether Dr Ali Hashemi, the doctor's medical partner, could have been involved. If you recall, he has been dating Michelle Goodrich, Dr Deeley's ex-girlfriend. But he has a strong alibi for 8 October. Several people can vouch for him being at his surgery throughout the morning.'

Roscoe nodded again. He swivelled round on his office chair so that he could gaze through the window at the park across the street.

'We can rule out Valerie Stanbrook as she's an old lady of seventy-eight. Has DC Khalid had any luck in tracing Smith?' he asked.

'No, sir. You'd be amazed how many Mark Smiths there are in the United Kingdom.'

'Go on then. How many are there? Or were you just saying that?'

She smiled and leaned back in her chair.

'There are nearly three thousand men named Mark Smith in the UK, sir,' she went on. 'But Omar is quietly confident. We believe the man is still in Kent somewhere, which narrows it down a lot. He's been checking the PNC and been in touch with letting agents. We think it's just a matter of time.'

'Well, for the moment, that leaves us with Rufus Stanbrook.'

'Yes, sir. As you know, Brett Dawson and I went to see the Stanbrooks three weeks ago and I wasn't entirely happy with the answers Mr Stanbrook gave. I realise also I should have been firmer and should have insisted on seeing Mrs Stanbrook, despite his claim she was ill. I think we need a warrant so we can search the whole farm.'

'I'm one step ahead of you, Sergeant. I applied to the magistrates a few days ago and got one of the DCs to pick it up. Here you are.'

He rummaged in his desk and pulled out a sheet of paper with a flourish. He handed it to her.

'That's brilliant, sir. I've spoken to the family's medical practice and the practice manager has confirmed they're not aware of Mrs Stanbrook having any illness currently.'

'Really? That's interesting.'

She quickly added, 'Dawson and I are free to go down there this afternoon.'

Roscoe nodded. 'I'll have a word with Gloucestershire Police and let them know what's going on, just out of courtesy. You'd better notify Dr Ling as well.'

She stood up and moved towards the door, but he called her back.

'It's the old lady's funeral next week, isn't it?' he said.

'Yes, sir. It's next Wednesday at St Michael's Church in Sinton Bank.'

'I'll be coming along with you. I strongly believe that, if you want to get close to a family, go to a funeral,' he said.

She took a step towards the door again. 'When do you think the DI will be in a position to meet visitors?'

'Maybe in a few days if his present progress continues. DS Bains from Summerstoke CID will obviously be one of the first people lined up to see him. They urgently need to get a statement from him about what happened in Sidney Road.'

* * *

When lunchtime arrived, the chief inspector devoured a ham and tomato sandwich he'd bought from the police canteen. Then he called his wife, Helen, on his office phone.

He had become so concerned about Tom Vickers' plight that he couldn't remember whether his son's engagement party was scheduled for that coming Saturday or the following Saturday.

'I can only spare a few minutes,' she informed him. 'The place is heaving.'

'Shall I call back?'

'No, you're fine for the moment. You sound tired.'

He nodded. 'Been a long week.'

'Any news about Tom?'

'He's still critical. Today I decided to put our sergeant in sole charge of the Deeley case while this business with Tom is going on. But I'm already having second thoughts.'

'She'll be fine. She's already cracked two major cases for you.'

He nodded again. 'I know but this case seems so complicated. I'd convinced myself David Harper followed the doctor into the wood and killed him because of what happened to his son. Harper was definitely in the wood but now I'm not sure he attacked the doctor. The DS has pointed out there are flaws in that theory and I'm inclined to agree with her.'

Roscoe often sought his wife's advice when he reached a sticking point in his criminal investigations. He trusted the opinion of his confident wife. He admired her intelligence.

She lowered her voice. 'Everyone in Queensbridge is talking about the murder on the heath. I overheard a middle-aged couple talking about it this morning while sitting at a table in the corner. The woman began talking about Harper. Then her husband – I assume it was her husband – said he was convinced Harper was behind it. He referred to an article by the journalist Susan Ellis-Jones in the *Gazette*, which explained how Jerome Harper's condition had been misdiagnosed by Deeley.'

'He does have a strong motive. But we can't charge a man just because of that. We need evidence. Although Harper was in the wood, he claims the doctor was dead before he arrived on the scene.'

'I think maybe you should let your sergeant get on with the case. She's very capable.'

'I know, but I'm unsure whether she's given sufficient thought to all the evidence pointing towards Harper's guilt. She's been focussing on all the reasons why it couldn't have been him. I'm not sure she's had enough experience of life. She's only in her mid-twenties.'

She smiled. 'Come on, Gavin. I'm surprised at you, considering her age to be a factor. She's had some remarkable success since she joined Heart of England. I think you should let the girl get on with her job.'

Chapter 35

Just after two o'clock that afternoon, Sunita Roy and DC Dawson travelled back to Lower Clavington Farm in Gloucestershire. They were accompanied by four constables and four forensic staff.

As their vehicles swept into the farmyard, Sunita parked her car close to the entrance of the white dormer bungalow. As soon as she set foot on the muddy ground, the Stanbrooks' German shepherd began to bark incessantly, and Rufus Stanbrook came to the door in work overalls.

'Stop it, Major!' he bellowed. Then he scowled at his visitors. 'What? The police again? What do you want now?'

Sunita stepped towards him with her hands on her hips.

'Mr Stanbrook, I'm afraid we've got a warrant here to search your premises.'

'What the hell for? I haven't got any drugs or contraband.'

Dawson hurried forward. 'We're also hoping to speak to your wife, sir,' he explained.

'You can't see her!' he insisted. 'She's too ill.'

The sergeant was in no mood for arguments. 'We need to verify that,' she said. 'So, if you'll just step aside, please, Mr Stanbrook.'

Left with little option, the farmer edged to the side while Sunita, Khalid and other members of the team passed through the door. Mr Stanbrook spent a minute pacifying his dog in the living room before locking the pet in his kitchen.

'Where exactly is Mrs Stanbrook?' the sergeant demanded as she walked towards him.

'That's none of your business,' he snapped as he stepped into the hallway and positioned himself at the foot of the oak staircase.

'Mrs Stanbrook's upstairs, is she, sir?' the sergeant asked.

'I don't like you. You're too overbearing,' he told her as he tried to block them from going upstairs. 'This young guy here, I like him. He's got the right attitude.'

'We're not playing good cop, bad cop,' said Sunita. 'We believe you've been impeding our investigation, Mr Stanbrook. You've got five seconds to show us where your wife is or I'm going to arrest you,' she said.

'Well, she's not here. She's in hospital,' he insisted, stroking his beard.

'I'm very sorry to hear that, if that's true,' said Dawson. 'I'm sure we both are. But, if that's the case, you'll have to give us full details of which hospital and which ward.'

'I'm not sure I believe you, Mr Stanbrook,' said Sunita, ignoring her colleague. 'Before things go any further, we're searching the place. Brett, you check the downstairs. I'm going to look upstairs. And, while you're about it, try and keep an eye on our friend here.'

She beckoned over a young PC, Tracy Miller, and the pair pushed their way past Stanbrook. Sunita reached the top of the stairs first and decided to examine the front bedroom. She directed PC Miller to try the second bedroom, which lay at the back.

Sunita had hardly had time to venture inside the main bedroom when she heard Miller shouting, 'Sarge, I need your assistance. There's a lady in here.'

Sunita calmly crossed the small landing to the doorway where Miller was awaiting her. The bedroom door creaked open and she was immediately overwhelmed by a strong, musty smell. It was a small, dark room with old-fashioned, cream-coloured wallpaper featuring a strong red floral motif. A Victorian mahogany double wardrobe stood in the far corner next to the grimy windowpane. In the centre was a double bed in which a frail, wizened old lady was lying. The old woman, whom Sunita assumed to be Valerie Stanbrook, failed to acknowledge her presence.

For a few seconds, Sunita was shocked by the sight of the old lady, who had straggly white hair and a pale, heavily lined face. Then, without warning, she turned and looked up at the officer's sympathetic face. Her bony fingers slipped out from beneath the white sheet and touched the sergeant's hand. She clasped it, gently pulling the detective towards her.

'You're police, aren't you? I could hear your voices,' the old lady said in a faltering voice. 'You look like a kind person. Take me away from here,' she implored.

The sergeant bent down over Valerie Stanbrook. She asked in a low voice, 'Are you in pain?'

'Yes,' the old lady whispered back. 'I need a doctor. Get me to the Royal.'

'May I?' said Sunita, lifting the sheet back and exposing the woman's arm. It was covered in bruises.

'Did your husband do that?' she asked.

The old lady nodded.

'Don't worry. We'll get you help,' the detective muttered, gently placing the lady's hand back beneath the sheet.

The sergeant was incensed at seeing how sickly Valerie Stanbrook appeared. As she left the room, pulling the door behind her, she told PC Miller, who was waiting on the landing, to call an ambulance.

'She obviously needs immediate medical treatment.'

'Yes, Sarge,' said the constable.

Sunita walked back down the stairs in a determined manner. She may not have been able to resolve the murder case that afternoon, but, by God, she was going to resolve what she regarded as a severe case of cruelty and neglect. She marched into the lounge, where Rufus Stanbrook was sitting on his leather settee, chatting to Dawson.

'Rufus Stanbrook,' she said. 'I'm arresting you under Section 32 of the Police and Criminal Evidence Act. You don't have to say anything but it may harm your defence if you don't mention, when questioned, something which you later rely on in court. Anything you do say may be given in evidence.'

'What's this all about?' he demanded, as she gestured for him to stand up and then handcuffed him. Both he and Dawson looked bewildered.

'It's about your wife,' Sunita said.

Stanbrook shrugged. 'What's the offence you're arresting me for? I've a right to know, haven't I?'

She stared into his eyes. 'Well, we'll start with assault. Then we'll move onto the offence of exercising controlling or coercive behaviour. Then we might have a look at ill-treatment and wilful neglect. And, if your wife is unfortunate enough to die, we might have a think about gross negligence manslaughter.'

She asked Miller and a male constable to escort him outside.

'You must be joking. I've never laid a finger on her,' he protested.

'She's covered in bruises,' said the sergeant, as she followed him and the pair of constables outside. 'It seems you treat your dog better than you do your wife. We also want to question you about the murder of your wife's nephew.'

'Oh, come on. This is some kind of set-up. It looks like someone with a grudge has made up a load of nonsense to give me grief.'

She wrote down his comments in her notebook before he was placed in the back seat of one of the police vehicles and driven away.

* * *

About half an hour later, three paramedics helped the farmer's wife onto a stretcher, placed her in the back of an ambulance and drove her to Gloucestershire Royal Hospital in Gloucester. At the same time, PC Miller arranged for a neighbour to care for the couple's dog.

Before the two detectives drove back to St James Street, Dawson took the sergeant aside.

'Sarge, I thought you ought to know one of the lads found a grey hatchback Mini in the garage,' he told her in a hushed voice.

'Was it anything like the one spotted at Foxwell Heath on the morning of the murder?' she asked.

He nodded. 'Exactly the same. I've made a note of the reg and we'll check it when we get back to the office, but I'm pretty certain it's the same car that we saw on CCTV.'

Chapter 36

Carefully watching the steaming cup of coffee she held in her hand for fear of spilling it, Sunita Roy walked slowly towards her desk just after four o'clock that same afternoon.

As she put it down beside her computer, she noticed Gavin Roscoe walking towards her and smiled at him.

'I hear you've let David Harper go, sir.'

'Yes. Hopefully, we can pull him in again if new evidence emerges. He's on police bail and one of the conditions is he's got to attend Queensbridge police station daily. Anyway, what's the latest on Mrs Stanbrook?'

'As I mentioned, she was in a bad way when she was admitted, but the hospital think she's going to pull through.'

'That's good news. By the way, one of the team found out this morning there was a little confusion at Mrs Stanbrook's doctor's surgery. Despite what we were told, they were aware of her illness, so it isn't as though her husband was keeping her situation a secret from the world. As soon as we hear from the hospital that she's well enough, we need to get a statement from her.'

'I'm surprised about that,' she said. 'I thought her GP was unaware of her health problems. I'm still concerned about the bruises on her arm though. While I'm here, is there any more news about Tom?'

'Yes, it's a little more encouraging. They may try and take him off the ventilator at the weekend and give him a chance to breathe on his own.'

'That's brilliant.'

'Right, well, if you have a word with the custody sergeant, I'll find out what interview room we're in and we can get our little chat under way.'

* * *

Half an hour later, two custody officers brought Rufus Stanbrook up to one of the ground-floor interview rooms. The suspect took a seat at the small wooden table. He remained disgruntled at having been arrested.

His solicitor, Dipak Sharma from Evesham, a plump, middle-aged man in glasses, had spent an hour with him earlier and joined him at the table a few minutes later, followed shortly afterwards by the chief inspector and Sunita Roy.

The sergeant was clasping a sheaf of papers, which she placed down in front of her as she sat down.

The chief inspector turned on the recording equipment before taking his seat beside her. He glanced at the farmer.

'Just to remind you, you're under caution and everything is being audio recorded and video recorded. Now, Mr Stanbrook, I want to ask you first of all about Monday, 8 October. I need a detailed account of your movements.'

'I was at the farm all day,' said Stanbrook, stroking his straggly beard.

'What sort of jobs were you doing?' Roscoe asked.

'Checking the general health of the rams with the support of a vet,' he replied. 'Examining things like their teeth and trotters before putting them in with the ewes. Tiring work. We've got nearly four hundred sheep.'

'Anyone with you apart from the vet?'

'Only my flock manager.'

'What time did you start?'

'Six thirty. Had a bit of a lie-in before we started, you might say.'

'So, it would be strange then if we had a record of your car being seen in Warwickshire between nine and ten that morning?'

'My Mini? That was in the garage most of the day. I only used it at lunchtime for a trip to the post office.'

'I think it would be best for you to tell the truth, Mr Stanbrook. We can check with your flock manager. We can check with the vet. We can check with the staff at the post office.'

'I'm sure they'll all back me up. I'm telling the truth.'

Sunita had been watching him. He had been wriggling like a freshly caught salmon as her boss reeled off his questions.

'There hasn't been much truth in what you've told the police so far,' she declared. 'You claimed two hours ago your wife was in hospital and all the time she was sick in bed upstairs.'

'I was just trying to protect her. When I looked in on her before you came, she was asleep. I didn't want her disturbed.'

The sergeant acquired a look of disgust while her colleague walked to a cabinet at the back of the room and removed a large photograph from a drawer. Resuming his seat, he placed it on the table.

'I'm showing Mr Stanbrook exhibit J, a still from a CCTV camera at Foxwell Heath taken on 8 October. It shows a grey Mini Hatch manufactured in 2016. Is this your car, Mr Stanbrook?'

'It looks very much like it, but I don't think it can be,' he said, stroking his beard.

Roscoe looked at him intently. 'For the purposes of the DIR, Mr Stanbrook is shaking his head.'

Sunita interrupted. 'Mr Stanbrook, your car's registration begins with LC66 just like this one, for God's sake.'

The farmer nodded. 'I agree I've got a grey car like this one, but, if you ask me, the letters on this picture are LG, not LC, and you can't see the last three letters at all.'

'I know,' said Roscoe. 'A photographic specialist at headquarters is working on it. But from what we can tell, this looks like your car, Mr Stanbrook.'

Mr Sharma interrupted them. 'I think you're grasping at straws, Chief Inspector. There's no evidence my client's car was in the area at all.'

Roscoe turned to the solicitor.

'Mr Sharma, your client's told us he was at the farm all day, but I'm afraid we have doubts as to the truth of that. As my colleague here has already pointed out, he hasn't got a brilliant track record when it comes to telling us the truth. Now, turning to other matters, we want to discuss your wife, Mr Stanbrook.'

'How is she?'

'I wondered if you were going to show any interest in her welfare,' said the chief inspector. 'Since you ask, she's doing fairly well in hospital. But it seems that's no thanks to you.'

'I love my wife. I've never touched her. I know she's frail – she's seventy-eight, for heaven's sake, and she's had a hard life.'

'A particularly hard life since meeting you,' Sunita muttered.

'That's nonsense!' Stanbrook exclaimed.

The chief inspector ignored him.

'We're now going to show you pictures of bruises on your wife's arms and upper chest which a police photographer took earlier and DS Roy here is going to question you about your relationship with Mrs Stanbrook. So it's over to you, Sergeant.'

Chapter 37

The chief inspector and his sergeant spoke mainly about the Stanbrooks as they drove to Coventry on Saturday morning.

Rufus Stanbrook had been released on police bail after Sunita had grilled him for more than an hour about his wife's bruises.

'He claims she's been tripping over and falling out of bed a lot, but I don't believe a word of it,' she told him.

He nodded. 'As soon as we can get a statement from her, we're probably going to charge him with ill treatment at the very least. But, anyway, it's encouraging to hear Tom's now breathing on his own, isn't it?'

She smiled. 'And he's off the critical care ward as well.'

When they finally reached the car park on that cold, foggy morning, they were hoping Tom would be well enough to see them. Gavin Roscoe was carrying two bags containing bananas and grapes, while Sunita was clutching a small box wrapped in gold paper. They both looked apprehensive as they followed signs to the first floor and approached a young blonde nurse sitting at reception.

'We're here to see one of your patients, Tom Vickers,' said the chief inspector.

The young woman gazed up from behind the light-oak desk. 'Visiting's not till two o'clock.'

He showed his warrant card. 'Heart of England Police. Dr Ahmed said we could come at ten.'

She shrugged. 'All right. Your colleague's already arrived. He's sitting over there. But you'll have to go in one at a time and we may have to call a halt if Mr Vickers becomes too tired.'

The pair glanced towards the waiting area, which comprised two rows of chairs beside a window. A stocky man with short, brown hair and glasses had buried his head in a newspaper and was paying them no attention. Roscoe thought he recognised him.

Sunita stepped forward and grinned at the receptionist. 'You'll let us know, will you?'

The nurse nodded. 'Yes. You won't have to wait long.'

Roscoe strolled towards the rows of chairs.

'DS Bains, isn't it?' he said.

The man lowered his newspaper.

'Yes.' A glimmer of recognition crept across his solemn face. 'DCI Roscoe, if I'm not mistaken.'

He rose and stretched out a podgy hand for the chief inspector to shake.

'It's been a long time,' said Roscoe, beckoning Sunita over. 'Sergeant, this is DS Bains from North Warwickshire.'

'Pleased to meet you,' she said as she shook his hand briefly. She then sat down nearby.

'Likewise,' said Bains.

Roscoe smiled. 'Been here long?'

'Long enough,' he replied brusquely.

'How's the investigation going?'

'Slowly. We've spoken to several witnesses, but we desperately need input from DI Vickers about how he acquired his injuries.'

Roscoe nodded. 'I've decided our DC Dawson is going to be seconded to your team and I'd like him to keep me up to date with how your investigation is going.'

'We'll fit him in, if we can.'

* * *

Ten minutes later, the receptionist gazed towards the visitors. 'The doctor's finished his rounds and says one of you can go in. It's the second door on the right.'

Bains stood up and glanced at his colleagues' faces.

'I was here first...'

Roscoe shrugged. 'You go ahead,' he said.

Abandoning his newspaper, Bains strode off along the corridor towards the patients' rooms.

Twenty minutes later, he was back in reception where Roscoe and Sunita were sitting.

'Remarkably cogent for a man who stopped two bullets,' he declared. 'Look, I've got a busy morning. I'll fill you in next week, if that's all right.'

'You've got my office and mobile numbers?'

'Yes. Don't worry,' said Bains before he hurried away towards the lift.

Damned disrespectful guy, Roscoe thought.

Sunita frowned. 'Not too impressed with him.'

'No,' said Roscoe. 'I'd have had a quiet word with him if I wasn't so concerned about seeing Tom.'

He peered across at the nurse. 'Is it all right if I go in now?' he asked.

She nodded. 'Second door on the right.'

Roscoe passed along the gloomy corridor until he reached the entrance to the bright room with floor-to-ceiling windows which Vickers was sharing with five other patients. He couldn't find the inspector's bed to begin with. Then he realised there was a blue curtain round the furthest bed on the left and guessed his colleague was lying there.

As he drew back the curtain, he found his colleague sitting up in bed with his brown hair neatly combed and a broad smile on his face.

'How are you, old pal?' the chief inspector asked as he pulled up a chair.

The inspector tapped his injured shoulder, which was heavily bandaged.

'Feeling a lot better now than I did a few days ago. I'm hoping to be back at work in a couple of weeks, guv.'

Roscoe frowned. 'There's no need to hurry. You're missed – of course, you're obviously missed. But we can manage for now. You need to focus on getting better. Here you are. I've brought you some fruit.'

He leaned across to his bedside table and placed his gifts on the top.

'Good view from here,' Roscoe remarked.

'Yes, you can see right across the hospital complex. Old Bruiser Bains has just been into see me. You've just missed him.'

The chief inspector nodded. 'Yes, I met him briefly outside. He hasn't changed much.'

They were interrupted by a dark-haired, middle-aged nurse who tugged back the curtain.

'Are you getting tired, Mr Vickers?' she said. 'We don't want you overexerting yourself with too many visitors.'

The inspector smiled back. 'No, I'm all right, thank you. Just having a chat with my guv'nor.'

Roscoe interrupted. 'He's a tough old cookie, you know.'

'Not so much of the "old", thank you.'

'If you're sure, I'll leave you with your visitor,' she said.

The curtain swished back, and she walked away.

Roscoe grinned. 'They're certainly looking after you.'

'All the staff here are great.'

'Listen, Tom, I don't know how much time I've got with you. Do you want to give me a rundown on what happened in Sedgeworth?'

Vickers explained how he was lured to the house in Sidney Road by the prospect of gaining information on the 'body in the bath' case. He told Roscoe how he overpowered a middle-aged man who held him up with a gun but how he was then shot by an accomplice.

'I didn't recognise the older man. Appeared to be Polish and wore dark glasses, but I think I recognised the younger man from the work I've done on the case. I'm pretty certain it was Tyrone Blake, who's part of the 101 Crew. The older guy warned me he was going to shoot me so I had to take drastic action.'

'What was that?'

'I upended the table and tipped piping hot tea over him. He was screaming – he probably had second-degree burns. I grabbed his gun and ran into the back garden after the younger guy. But, as I called for an ambulance, he must have shot me.'

Roscoe shook his head. 'You really shouldn't have gone on your own. You probably realise that now. If you'd explained the urgency, I could have found at least one other officer to go with you.'

Vickers shrugged. 'I know, guv. The ironic thing is they both fled and the ambulance crew I'd called for the Polish guy ended up attending to me.'

Roscoe moved his chair closer to the inspector's bed and lowered his voice.

'Did you mention Blake's name to Bains?'

'Yes.'

'How did he react?'

'He kept a straight face. There were no signs of surprise. He must have clocked that Blake was involved – heard it from someone else. I should explain that, bearing Sepulchre in mind, I didn't tell Bains everything that happened in Sidney Road.'

'How do you mean?'

'Well. There's something that's been worrying me, guv. Remember my key witness, Mrs Shah? The Polish guy knew I'd been to see her.'

Roscoe frowned. 'That's concerning. I'll send someone round to check on her and we'll have to consider security arrangements. Good that you didn't mention her to Bains.'

As they continued talking, the nurse who had interrupted them before returned, sweeping back the curtain.

'Mr Vickers, you still have one more visitor to see and the lunch trolley is on the way.'

Roscoe stood. 'Sorry, Tom. Should have mentioned Sunita's waiting to see you. I'd better go. Just apply yourself to getting better.'

'Great to see you, guv,' the patient replied. 'And thanks again for the fruit.'

* * *

Sunita Roy started to feel embarrassed when she realised it was her turn to visit the inspector. What if he didn't want to see her? She could understand him turning her away. After all, the last time they'd spoken she'd accused him of cheating on her and she'd ended their relationship in a fit of fury.

'I had good reason to be angry with him,' she reasoned with herself. 'But he didn't deserve this – to be so badly hurt in the line of duty.'

He had been such a good friend and work colleague; she felt an obligation towards him. Clutching her gift, she walked cautiously into his ward and drew back the curtain.

'How are you, Tom?' she asked with a timid smile.

'All the better for seeing you,' he replied, hoisting himself up against his pillow. 'Take a seat.'

She handed him her present. 'I've brought you this.'

Within seconds, he had torn off the glittery paper to reveal an MP3 player.

'I've loaded some of the jazz tracks you like.'

'Oh, Sunita, you shouldn't have gone to so much trouble.'

'I've also taken your hire car back to the company. Don't suppose you'll need it for the moment.'

'My Audi should be fixed by now.'

She settled herself down on the chair beside the window.

'Sorting the music out wasn't that much trouble. By the way, the boss asked me to check on the car in Sidney Road – the one the two guys fled in. Did he mention that to you?'

'No.'

'I'm afraid we've drawn a blank. It was picked up on cameras, but they were using false plates. Do you think it was the same guys who forced you off the road?'

He shrugged. 'I've been thinking about that. Hard to say. Those guys were wearing balaclavas.'

'The boss is determined to catch the men who shot you.'

'Yeah, I know he'll do his best. Me and the guv'nor go back a few years. I was his sergeant like you are, after all, and worked closely with him until I got promoted to inspector.'

They heard footsteps approaching. The curtain swayed before it was swept aside.

'I'm afraid time's up,' said the dark-haired nurse. 'Mr Vickers, the lunch trolley is outside.'

Sunita bent across and kissed his forehead.

'Take care of yourself, Tom. See you when you get back to work.'

'Thanks so much for coming, Sunita. Really appreciate it. Oh, and by the way, if you speak to the next-door neighbour who helped me, be sure to thank him. I'm sure he saved my life.'

'He's been asking after you. I'll make sure he knows of your gratitude.'

As she walked back along the corridor, the same nurse accompanied her.

'He's had a rough time, poor fellow,' she told Sunita.

She gave a weak smile. 'I know.'

'We really weren't sure he was going to make it because he lost so much blood. Bit of a miracle, really. You his girlfriend?'

Sunita's smile faded. 'Used to be.'

'Oh, I see. It's just that I could see how pleased he was to see you.'

'He's not my boyfriend anymore, but that doesn't mean you stop caring for someone, does it?'

Chapter 38

Sunita Roy shivered as she strolled along Queensbridge High Street that evening. She pulled her scarf more tightly round her neck as she made her way along the pavement past the town's police station.

She found the entrance to the Apollo Tearooms festooned with red and blue bunting. The sound of clinking glasses and the steady beat from a music track confirmed the engagement party for George Roscoe and Amanda Wakering was already in full swing.

She was just going to step inside when her phone rang and a number she vaguely recognised emerged on the screen.

'Hello?' she said as she strained to hear the caller's voice.

'Sunita, it's Sam. I'm wondering if there's any news about Tom?'

Her eyes lit up. 'Hi, Sam. Nice to hear from you. Funnily enough, the boss and I went to see him today and he's fine. We don't know when he's going to be fit enough to go home, but he's sitting up in bed and looking a lot better.'

'Oh, my goodness. That's brilliant news.'

'Tom specifically asked me to thank you helping him. He thinks you could well have saved his life.'

'It was nothing, Sunita. Anyone would have done the same.'

'Look, I'm at a party at the moment,' said Sunita. 'If you like, I'll give you a call when we next get an update on Tom. It'll probably be towards the end of next week.'

She faced a vibrant melee of partygoers as she squeezed her way through the doorway and was greeted by the chief inspector, still dressed in the blue suit he'd worn at the hospital.

'Sorry about the din,' he remarked as he led her to an empty table at the back of the premises. 'There's chicken in mushroom sauce, beef Wellington or there's a vegetarian option.'

'What's the vegetarian option, sir?'

'I'll just find out.'

He caught his wife's eye as she passed with a plate of mouth-watering food.

'Helen, you remember my sergeant, don't you?'

Helen stopped abruptly and smiled.

'Of course. How are you, Sunita?'

'We were just wondering what the vegetarian dish is, dear,' Roscoe explained.

'It's a spicy vegetable pizza,' said Helen. 'Good heavens, the poor girl hasn't even got a drink yet.'

Roscoe stood up. 'Apologies. What would you like?'

'Just an orange juice, please, and the vegetable pizza sounds lovely.'

'By the way, good news about Tom, isn't it?' Helen remarked before disappearing into the crowd.

As the pair attended to Sunita's requests, the happy couple, George and Amanda, nudged their way towards her.

'This is Dad's sergeant,' George explained to his fiancée. 'Amanda, I'd like you to meet Sunita.'

Sunita got up and shook Amanda's hand.

'Congratulations, both of you,' she said with a smile. 'Have you named the day yet?'

George shook his head. 'Not yet.'

With his arm planted firmly round Amanda's waist, he explained how they'd met at the training college in Ryton.

Amanda grinned. 'It happened so fast. We met on the first day of the course–'

'And I swept you off your feet, didn't I?' said George as a tall, young man with dark hair emerged from the melee behind them.

'Oh, Sunita, let me introduce Sean,' said George. 'He's our best man.'

'I know they're going to try and blame me for everything,' said the newcomer, as he stretched out his hand to greet the sergeant. 'Sean Munro. I'm attached to the police at Shipston-on-Stour.'

'For the moment,' said George.

'Yes. For the moment.'

'Pleased to meet you, Sean. You were on the course with George and Amanda?' Sunita asked.

'That's right. Can you tell by looking at me? We're all betraying signs of having suffered at Ryton, I expect.'

She smiled. 'I've heard it's a very good course.'

'They taught a lot about some things and very little about others,' he complained.

Sunita broke into a smile and they moved on to meet another guest. She found her orange juice and pizza and sat down.

The chief inspector stepped over to her table. 'Just wondered where you were,' he said.

'Sir, I was going to tell you I received an email this afternoon from Diamond Buses. Their main CCTV guy is now back at work.'

Roscoe frowned. 'Remind me. Is this to do with the bus ticket you found in Scott Deeley's bedroom?'

She nodded. 'That's right. The reconstruction's on Monday, so I'm planning to go over to their office in Redditch the following day and see if there's any footage of the doctor getting on and off the bus.'

'Good luck with that,' he said, taking a sip from a glass of beer. 'You'll need a lot of patience, I expect.'

As he spoke to her, Roscoe's phone sprang into life.

'Oh, God. I hope this isn't anything too important. I haven't given my speech yet. Hello, Roscoe … Sorry, I can't hear you. Hold on a moment.'

She watched him weave his way to the door through the press of bodies. He returned minutes later with a shocked expression.

'That was Khalid,' he announced. 'He's just seen on the news that a house in Sedgeworth's been firebombed.'

He quickly turned on the nearby television and switched to the BBC's twenty-four-hour news channel. After hearing how protesters blocked traffic on London bridges and details of a shooting in North London, the BBC reported the firebombing as 'breaking news'. Pictures were shown of an end-of-terrace house in Albion Road. They listened as a news reader reported on the events.

'Fire crews rescued a woman and two children from a blazing house in the Warwickshire town of Sedgeworth this afternoon. Heart of England Police say a fire investigation team have confirmed the cause was arson. The family were rushed to Coventry's University Hospital where they were treated for the effects of smoke inhalation.

'The blaze broke out just after 4 p.m. The woman and her children, aged eight and ten, managed to escape from the back of the terraced house and fire fighters were able to bring the flames under control shortly afterwards. It is understood the woman's husband was away visiting friends at the time. Detectives from Heart of England CID are investigating along with an officer from Warwickshire Fire and Rescue Service.'

'My God, sir,' said Sunita. 'Doesn't Tom's witness live in that street?'

He nodded. 'It looks like her house,' he said.

The news report ended with a camera shot of plants in colourful ceramic pots and troughs near the front door.

Chapter 39

A veil of fog enveloped the hamlet of Loman's Green the following morning as a red Vauxhall Corsa drew up outside a secluded nineteenth-century cottage.

Two women climbed out to the sound of dogs barking in an enclosed area behind the former gamekeeper's home.

'This is the place, Mother,' said Alisha Hamid. 'Can you see the sign outside?'

Her mother glanced at the board beneath one of the front windows with its peeling green paint which bore the name 'J.H. Cooper' in black lettering. Alisha joined her mother on the pavement beside the low hedge.

'Oh, this is so exciting, isn't it?'

'Yes, I can't wait to see the beautiful little faces of the newborn puppies,' Fariza Hussain said.

Alisha lifted the latch on the gate and made her way up the short path, followed by her mother. But, before the pair could reach the door, Howard Cooper had opened it. He smiled at his two visitors and immediately made them feel welcome.

'It was so nice to receive your phone call,' he told them. 'All the paperwork's ready and the puppies are all set for you to see.'

He took the visitors into a small back parlour where he made them comfortable on a green, two-seater sofa.

He shook his head as he hovered over them. 'Have you got over that awful experience on the heath?'

'I'm not sure we'll ever get over it,' said Fariza. 'It was a terrible shock for us both.'

'Both me and my wife have been devastated over the whole thing. We're trying not to think about it. Anyway, I'd better show you the little rascals.'

He disappeared through the back door. A few moments later, he returned with three adorable puppies, who were squealing and howling as they were placed on the carpet.

'Oh, look at this one,' said Alisha, picking up a male puppy which seemed whiter in colour.

He wagged his tail and then sprayed her dress with a small amount of urine, causing both visitors to laugh. Fariza watched the remaining two bitches romping on the carpet – taking it in turns to bite each other and nip the women's toes.

'Two are girls and one's a boy,' Howard explained. 'Do you have any preference?'

'I think a bitch,' said Alisha. 'I like this one here.'

'The one that's a little plumper than the other female?'

'Yes,' said Alisha. 'She's a real character and I notice her colouring is more golden.'

She bent down, picked up the puppy and held it in front of her eyes, peering into the animal's face.

Howard nodded. 'That's right. Our daughter's named that one Jasmine.' He paused before saying, 'So, you two don't live together then?'

'Oh no,' said Alisha. 'I'm married and we've got our own place, but I don't live far from Mum and Dad. We've got a terraced house and medium-sized garden.'

'A garden's so important,' said Howard.

Alisha smiled. 'I like this one very much. How much would it cost?'

Howard stroked his chin. 'Jessica was saying we couldn't let her go for less than two thousand pounds.'

Their faces fell, so he quickly added, 'She's registered with the Kennel Club, of course. We've got all the paperwork. She's just been fully vaccinated, and she's had the flea and worming treatment. She's only got to be microchipped.'

'What do you think, Mum?' Alisha asked.

'She's beautiful.'

'Right, Howard. I'd very much like to have her, if that's all right,' said Alisha.

'Yes, of course. If you give me your address in Redditch, I could bring her over to you next week. That'll give us time to get her microchipped.'

'That'll be great,' said Alisha. 'They're such lovely puppies.'

'Yes, their mother's done well, hasn't she?' said Howard, as he scooped up the puppies and headed out of the back door with them. 'All her litter have turned out beautifully. You won't have any trouble with Jasmine.'

'I think we might change the name slightly,' Alisha called out. 'I'm thinking we'll call her Yasmine with a "Y". It's more suitable for us.'

'Look, I tell you what. I can see that you'll make wonderful owners and that's something that's important to us. I'm sure Jessica would support me in this. We can offer you a small discount on the fee. How about we call it one thousand nine hundred pounds?'

'Well, if you're sure,' said Fariza. 'Looks like we've got a deal.'

'Ladies, it's important to our reputation that we find good homes for our litters.'

'Alisha really needs the company that a puppy can bring. She can't have children, you see.'

'Mum, don't go on about it,' said Alisha.

'I don't want to embarrass her, but having a dog is a great comfort when you've got no children.'

'Of course,' said Howard. 'So there won't be any problem with your other dog. What's he called – Harley?'

'That's right,' said Fariza. 'No, there won't be any problem. He gets on well with other dogs. I suppose we'll be seeing you tomorrow when the cops try to restage events on the heath?'

'Yes, I'll be there with Bella. And you two?'

She lowered her voice. 'Yes, we'll be there with Harley, as the police have instructed. But to be honest, I'm not relishing the prospect of going back there. The whole idea gives me the creeps.'

As the women prepared to leave, they hugged Howard and thanked him for assisting them with the purchase of the puppy.

Fariza touched his arm as they passed through the hallway and approached the front door.

'Take care of yourself,' she whispered.

'I'll do my best,' he replied with a smile. 'I'll call you in a few days.'

Chapter 40

The chief inspector marvelled at the rich autumn tones of the trees and foliage as he drove past Foxwell Heath early on Monday. How beautiful the Warwickshire countryside could be at this time of year, he thought to himself as he admired the kaleidoscope of colours – red, brown, green, yellow and gold.

How ironic that this enchanting place had been the setting for such a brutal killing, he concluded.

As he drew up outside the Deeleys' thatched cottage in Sinton Bank, he realised most of the floral tributes that had once cloaked the ground beside the white picket fence had gone. A few fresh bouquets remained.

His sergeant was standing by the gate, studying a large sketch-plan as he turned off the ignition and climbed out of his car.

'Good morning, sir,' she said cheerily.

'I don't know why you're so good-humoured this morning,' he moaned. 'We've really got our work cut out. There's meant to be twenty-five witnesses and dozens of officers and civil staff. It'll be a devil of a job to keep everyone in order. On top of it all, there's been that firebomb attack.'

She nodded and looked solemn. 'What's happening about that, sir?'

'I've managed to reach Mrs Shah. I'm due to visit her tomorrow morning at her house.'

'Surely she's not still living there with her husband and two children?'

'No, they've been rehoused, but I want to see the damage and she's agreed to show me.'

'Getting back to today's exercise, sir, are we both going to be shadowing the actor as he retraces the last steps of Dr Deeley?'

'No,' he replied. 'I've decided I want you to go to the Yeoman's Lane car park and take charge there, along with PC Kaur. I'm going to tag along behind the actor and the film crew.'

Sunita sighed. 'It's very different weather from 8 October. Today it's mild with fairly good vision but, back then, the whole heath was enveloped in mist.'

Her boss didn't seem to be listening.

'I don't know,' he said. 'I'm beginning to wish I'd never agreed to this.'

'I'd have thought we should get some positive results out of it, sir. If it stirs memories of the day, that can only be good.'

'Well, this is your first experience of a re-enactment, isn't it?' he said. 'It's my fourteenth and this is by far the biggest and most unwieldy.'

'The publicity might bring in new witnesses,' she suggested.

'That reminds me. We'll have to keep the press well away from witnesses. Hold on a minute. If I'm not mistaken, here's the actor who's playing the doctor.'

A solemn man in his mid-fifties wearing blue sportswear was strolling down the narrow lane towards them. He grinned broadly as he reached the cottage.

'DCI Roscoe? I'm Gordon Jones from the agency.'

Roscoe nodded. 'Thank you so much for coming. You really look the part.'

'They said it's a pity my hair's a bit dark. Apparently, the doctor had grey hair.'

'Yes. Never mind. A first-class effort. You know you're going to be walking and jogging slowly, not running, don't you?'

'Yes, sir.'

'And you'll be following the exact route the doctor took, past the farmer's field, alongside Heath Road, round Foxwell village green and back?'

'Yes, sir. I've got a map of the route in the pocket of my shorts.'

'Our colleague, DC Khalid, will be keeping close to you and I'll be somewhere at the back with the video team. Khalid will be here in a minute. He's just picking up some posters. Sergeant, could you link up with PC Kaur? And I'll see you at the briefing later on.'

* * *

The clamour of conversation was almost deafening in the CID office four hours later as members of the team relaxed together after their challenging morning. Most of the discussion related to the re-enactment.

Roscoe was in his office speaking to two of the videographers who had been filming the proceedings. He wanted a clip of the actor playing Dr Deeley in the wood to be released to the press as quickly as possible.

Five minutes later, the video staff left. Roscoe stepped into the main CID room and the office conversations petered out.

'Sorry to keep you all waiting,' said the smiling chief inspector, taking up his stance in front of the whiteboard. 'It's been a very interesting morning. I held a short press conference on the heath earlier and I was very pleased by the interest shown by members of the press. Now, perhaps DS Roy here can fill us in on some of the main points to emerge from this morning.'

'Yes, sir,' she said as she joined him. 'Unfortunately two witnesses failed to appear today. Robert Bowcott said he'd come, but no one's seen hide nor hair of him. He only lives a mile away, so it'll be interesting to hear his excuse. The other notable absentee was Christopher Edwards, the hospital porter from Queensbridge.'

DC Wendy Hopkirk's hand shot up. 'Is that the guy with a Staffie who owned the black Volkswagen Golf?'

Sunita nodded. 'Yes, that's the guy. We're going to knock him up as well and find out why he wasn't there, and we've still got to trace the man on the Honda motorbike.'

'It's sometimes hard to see the value of these exercises,' Roscoe continued. 'But, if you think about it, there are several benefits. We need to check that everyone's in the right place. If someone says they were on the main path and someone else says they weren't, we need to question it.

'Did anyone take an unusual interest in proceedings? Was there anyone that a witness remembers being on the heath that day that wasn't present for the reconstruction, apart from the two men already mentioned? And are there fresh witnesses out there who could come forward as a result of the publicity? These are the kind of outcomes that could emerge from today's operation.'

Sunita nodded. 'We're quietly confident that some of the information gleaned today will lead us forward.'

'Quite right,' he said. 'So I want as many of you as possible to keep in touch with witnesses. Re-interview them, if necessary, and carefully question any members of the public that come forward. Hopefully something will come out of it.'

He continued, 'We may never know precisely who was in the wood at the time of the murder and, of course, we may never learn the killer's true identity. But, in decades to come, I don't want anyone to be in a position to say we failed because we didn't all give this investigation our best efforts.'

Chapter 41

A convoy of police cars wound its way through the suburban streets of Coventry at daybreak that same Monday morning. The vehicles finally drew to a halt outside a shabby corner house with faded curtains drawn across the front windows.

DS Philip Bains glanced at the fresh-faced detective constable in the light-brown suit beside him, Vince Clarke.

'Are you ready, Clarkie? After the entry team have gone through the door, we'll give them a couple of minutes and then follow them in.'

The sergeant stared across Badminton Road at the two-bed terraced house. Although it was surrounded by a wall, topped by a hawthorn hedge, he could see a yard with gates at the rear with vehicle access to and from a side street.

Adopting a stern expression, he grabbed his phone from the dashboard and called the lead officer from the tactical support team.

'Stand by,' he ordered.

The sergeant kept the phone line open. Seconds passed. Six burly officers in full body armour – some wielding Heckler and Koch rifles and ballistic shields – slipped out of their carrier and waited in the street. Suddenly Bains decided the operation should start.

'Strike, strike, strike!' he bellowed.

'Who are we looking for exactly?' asked Clarke.

'Well, we're interested in talking to a black guy and a Polish guy. They're linked to an OCG linked to drugs. They're suspected to be behind a spate of violent incidents involving rival gangs, assaults and stabbings.'

'Someone told me they might be linked to the shooting of that copper and the firebomb attack we're investigating in Sedgeworth.'

'Rumour has it.'

'What do we know about the two guys? No descriptions, like?'

'The information's only available on a need-to-know basis and you don't need to know. What does your watch say?'

'Seven minutes past six,' replied the constable.

They peered across the street as an officer with a manual enforcer broke through the half-glazed wooden front door and charged in, followed closely by his colleagues.

'All right,' said Bains. 'We'll give it till just before ten past.'

'I'm glad I brought my overcoat this morning, Sarge. It's freezing.'

'Stop moaning, Clarkie. We'll be back in the office before you know it.'

A dog could be heard barking constantly from within the house. Officers were shouting, 'Police!'. Curtains in neighbouring houses twitched as residents woke to the sound of the raid.

'Come on. Let's go.'

The pair crossed the street, marched up the short garden path and passed through the doorway into the dingy hallway. The lead officer was just coming down the stairs.

'No sign of anyone, sir,' he remarked. 'Looks like they've done a bunk.'

Bains put his hands to his head. 'Do you mean all this has been a waste of time?'

'Looks like it. But they've left their dog behind. Doesn't look like it's been fed for a day or two.'

Bains shook his head. 'Cruel bastards.'

'Yeah, it looks like an American pitbull.'

They were disturbed by the sound of voices at the garden gate. Bains and Clarke turned round. A uniformed constable was speaking to a man – assumed to be a neighbour – who was wearing an unbuttoned shirt and crumpled trousers.

'Clarkie, go and see what he wants,' Bains demanded before resuming his conversation. 'Sorry, you were saying?'

'Looks like the two men you were after might've had a tip-off, sir. They seem to have left in a hurry. There's a load of white powder in plastic bags in the main bedroom, along with scales and other drug gear. There's a couple of burner phones too.'

'Good. Might be able to do something with them,' said Bains as Clarke hurried back into the house.

Clarke appeared breathless. 'Just one of the neighbours, sir, wanting to know what's going on. He said there's been lots of complaints about the dog. It's been left here a lot on its own and it bit one of the kids a few weeks ago.'

The sergeant groaned as some of the entry team members trooped down the stairs.

'Don't suppose the neighbour knows what's happened to our two chums, does he?'

'Says he's seen two tall men. One's a black guy. He's got close-cropped hair and a dagger tattoo. Doesn't have a description of the second man. One of them drives a silver Porsche.'

'He hasn't seen a black Touareg at any time, I suppose?'

'No, sir.'

'No, that would have been too much to expect. All right, well, we'd better have a quick look round before we start doing some house-to-house.'

Bains led his colleague upstairs where one of the entry team was leaning over the banisters. The sergeant stepped towards the back bedroom and grasped the doorknob.

'I wouldn't go in there if I were you,' the man by the banister told Bains. 'The dog's in there and he's not in the best mood.'

'Has anyone had a good look in there?'

'Someone just had a quick look before they locked the dog in.'

Bains sighed. 'Are the dog team still around? Maybe one of them could help us.'

'They've been sent back.'

'Bloody hell. Is there anything we can use to tackle the dog and keep it at bay? I know. Get your taser out.'

The officer looked blank. 'Are you sure about this, Sarge?'

'Yes.'

The officer unclasped his electroshock weapon as Bains opened the door. The dog sprang out of the room barking aggressively and snarling. Before the taser could be deployed, the animal had darted forward and clamped his teeth round DC Clarke's left leg.

'Get the bastard off me! Get him off me!'

'Taser the bloody animal!' Bains shouted as Clarke continued to holler in pain.

The dog refused to release his grip. Blood spurted down his trouser leg and dripped onto the landing carpet. The officer fired his taser but the animal initially seemed unaffected by the barbs. Two police colleagues rushed upstairs on hearing the pandemonium. They tried to free the man's leg from the dog's jaws by striking the hound with batons and firing CS spray directly into its face.

Finally, the dog released its grip and Clarke collapsed onto the floor in agony. As the dog was forced with a police shield back into the rear bedroom, the young detective was helped downstairs to await an ambulance.

* * *

Twenty minutes later, at ten minutes to seven, as paramedics were attending to the patient, DC Dawson from headquarters CID arrived in the street. He parked a few doors away and hurried over to speak to Bains, who was helping his colleague into the ambulance.

'Oh, I wondered when we were going to see you,' Bains remarked with disdain. 'You're bloody late.'

Dawson scowled. 'I was told the operation was timed to start at seven o'clock.'

'The time we gave you was six. We were quite clear about it. Now, if you'll excuse me, I've got more important matters to deal with. Our DC's been savagely bitten and we need to get him to hospital as soon as possible.'

Chapter 42

The chief inspector was shocked when he drove into Sedgeworth's Albion Road early on Tuesday and witnessed for himself the damage to the Shahs' house.

The front window downstairs was boarded up. The surrounding brickwork and the wall above had been blackened by soot.

He parked his car a short distance away and then ventured along the garden path, deeply concerned that an honest married couple with two children should have been targeted by a firebomber. And possibly as a direct result of Tom Vickers' visit three weeks earlier.

Mrs Shah took a few minutes to respond after he rang the bell. She demanded to know who it was, and Roscoe had to pass his warrant card through the letterbox to reassure her.

'Mrs Shah, I'm DCI Roscoe,' he told her as she unbolted the door and drew it back. 'I'm so sorry to bother you at a time like this.'

'Don't worry. Please come in,' she said with a frown. 'You'd best come through to the kitchen. The living room's uninhabitable.'

As he passed into the hall, he saw the devastating effects of the blaze. The living room walls were blackened. Part of the ceiling had collapsed. The family's television had melted. Soot clung to every surface.

He followed her into the kitchen, where he made himself comfortable at the table. She made them both a cup of tea and smiled at him as they sipped their hot drinks.

'We had some people from Summerstoke Police here over the weekend. But you're from police headquarters, you say?'

Roscoe nodded.

'So you're Tom Vickers' boss then?'

'Yes. Did you hear what happened to him?'

She nodded and her smile faded. 'It's been in the papers. He was shot. Will he be all right?'

'He'll be fine. He's a tough old bird – one of life's survivors. What concerns me right now is how *you* are, Mrs Shah, and your family.'

'We're fine,' she said. 'We were all here on Saturday afternoon, apart from Asad, who was round a friend's. It was really frightening. We were watching cartoons on television when I heard a noise outside and a brick smashed through the window. It nearly hit my daughter, who's eight. She and her brother ran screaming from the room. There was glass all over the carpet. Then something else came flying through the window and suddenly the curtains, the chair, the cushions and the carpet were all on fire.

'I ran out of the room and dialled 999. Then I grabbed a bucket from the kitchen and threw as much water as I could on the flames. I'd probably have been better off keeping the door closed. The house was filling with smoke, and I was finding it hard to breathe. I was choking so much but felt I had to do something. In the end, I shut the door and took the children into the back garden. Then we waited for the fire brigade. To be fair, they came fairly quickly. The damage could have been a lot worse.'

Roscoe sipped his tea. 'You and your children were taken to hospital?' he asked.

'Yes, just as a precaution really. They only came with me because there was no one to look after them. Suppose you know about the message?'

'What message?'

'Just before the bottle of petrol was thrown, like I said, the window was smashed with a brick that landed on the living room table. There was a message tied to it, saying, "Talking costs lives".'

'That wasn't in the police report from Summerstoke CID.'

'I think they might be keeping it confidential for some reason.'

The chief inspector shook his head. 'That doesn't make sense.'

'The point is someone wants me to keep quiet about what I saw across the road last year.'

'Looks that way,' he agreed. 'What's your reaction to that?'

'We're an honest, hard-working family. My father brought us up to believe in justice – in true British justice. I've discussed it with Asad and we won't be browbeaten.'

Roscoe nodded. 'The defence team representing the two jailed men are campaigning hard to get the original convictions overturned. You might be called to give evidence at a retrial. How do you feel about that?'

'I'd be happy to give evidence if the police wanted me to.'

He continued, 'I will discuss with my superior about arranging extra security measures for you and your family.'

'Thank you, Mr Roscoe. We're obviously concerned about our safety.'

Roscoe stood up and prepared to leave.

'There's a long way to go,' he said. 'Inspector Vickers has only just completed his initial re-investigation into the trial and the circumstances surrounding it. There's no guarantee the evidence will be examined again. The wheels of justice grind slowly.'

'We're aware of that, Mr Roscoe. Let's see what happens. But please don't think we're the kind of people who are easily intimidated. We know prosecutions sometimes go astray and we believe people should be prepared to fight injustices when they occur.'

* * *

The chief inspector smiled to himself as he unlocked the door to his office and sat down at his desk. After the petrol-bomb attack on her home, he'd fully expected Mrs Shah to withdraw from giving evidence. To hold her ground in defiance of the brutal threat against her and her family told him a great deal about her strength of character.

A few minutes later, there was a knock on his door. Sunita Roy stepped into the room, clutching some computer printouts.

'You look as if you've been busy, Sergeant.'

She smiled. 'Yes, sir. Could I have a word? I've been trying to track down Mark Smith, the Kent man who supposedly has a grudge against Scott Deeley. We've had a breakthrough, but it's not good news.'

'How do you mean?'

'We finally found the right guy – a Mark Smith, aged thirty-four, from Dover. But he's in prison.'

'Oh, I see.'

'He got sent down in July at Maidstone Crown Court for possessing heroin and crack cocaine with intent to supply.'

'So there's no way he could have been at Foxwell Heath on 8 October?'

'Exactly.'

'Oh, God. You're not having much luck.'

'I've really made an effort, but we seem to be getting nowhere, sir. This is one of the first murder cases where you've virtually given me carte blanche to run the show and I feel I've let you down.'

'Don't be so downbeat, Sergeant. You've worked hard and pursued all the leads. No one could accuse you of not giving your best. Sometimes even the most skilful angler fails to land the big fish.'

'I feel I've sailed back with an empty net.'

'Listen, Sergeant, I'm still suspicious of Stanbrook. We had to let him go on police bail, but he had a lot to gain from the doctor's death.'

She frowned. 'But, sir, none of the evidence stacks up,' she said. 'We just can't prove that the car on the CCTV at the heath was Stanbrook's. The numbers at the end of the plate appear to be different. Not only that – his solicitor thinks the colour of the car spotted on camera is what the manufacturers call Moonwalk Grey, while the car in Stanbrook's garage in Gloucestershire is described as Melting Silver.'

'Maybe that's a sign for us. Maybe the case against Stanbrook is melting away.'

Sunita rose from her chair. 'Dr Ling says she knows an expert on car colours. She's going to have words with him.'

'Look, Sergeant, Stanbrook could still be our man. After all, if he was involved in killing the doctor, he could well have got some false plates and put them on his car when he travelled to Foxwell Heath.'

Chapter 43

The secluded car park behind St Michael's Church was riddled with puddles after a night of rain. The chief inspector carefully managed to avoid stepping into a pool of muddy water as he hauled himself out of his car.

'Good morning, Sergeant!' he yelled to Sunita Roy who was waiting beside a clump of trees a few metres away.

'Good morning, sir,' she responded.

DC Khalid, who had driven her there for the funeral, remained inside his vehicle. There was a problem with his radio, which he was determined to fix. She stepped round the potholes as she approached her boss's BMW.

The vicar of St Michael's, Revd Martin Childs, was still hoping sufficient funds would eventually be found to have the surface of the car park properly asphalted. Until that blessed day, parishioners and visitors to the church were obliged to play a form of hopscotch to avoid getting their feet wet. Sunita nearly slipped over before she finally reached Roscoe.

'You're starting to know this village quite well now, aren't you?' he said while tightening the black tie he was wearing with his grey suit.

She nodded. 'Yes, sir. I was here yesterday afternoon, talking to residents. I walked round the first part of the route Scott Deeley took on 8 October. Then I spent twenty minutes examining the ornate bed, the treatment couch, the rowing machine and all the medical equipment in the cottage. I searched again through the drawers in the antique bureau and had another look at the contents of the dressing table. I'm convinced the handmade gold necklace with the pink flamingo pendant was by far the most significant object we found, along with the bus ticket.'

'You've got a strong feeling about them, haven't you?'

The sergeant, who had chosen a formal black dress to wear beneath her fawn coat, shrugged.

'I'm not really sure, sir, but I think it possibly points to a woman being at the heart of the case. I'm trying to track down the jeweller who took the order for the necklace.'

'Wasn't it some outfit in Birmingham?' said Roscoe. 'You made an attempt to speak to them last month, didn't you?'

'Yes, sir. I had problems tracing them. Then I had to go and visit David Harper and the whole thing was put on the back burner. The necklace cost a lot of money, sir.'

'I know. Nine hundred and fifty pounds, wasn't it?'

'Yes, sir. Should we–?'

'Go into the church? Yes, I suppose we should,' said Roscoe as Khalid slipped out of his car and locked it.

'Sorry, sir. I was just sorting the radio out,' said the constable as he joined them.

The three detectives passed through a small wooden gate that led to the twelfth-century church with its semi-octagonal tower. Its steeple dominated the skyline for miles around. Then they stepped through the wrought iron gates, which had been installed in Victorian times to keep sheep out of the churchyard.

As they approached the Norman arch above the main door, they became aware of the faint warbling sound of the pipe organ emanating from the church. Roscoe, who was walking in front, stopped in his tracks.

'While I think of it, Khalid, could you stand here and take the names of the mourners? You never know. Something useful might come out of it.'

The constable nodded and positioned himself by the entrance steps while his two colleagues entered the church.

Sunita found them both a pew twelve rows from the front. As the chief inspector knelt on a cushion for a few moments to say some silent prayers, she glanced round. She was pleased to see Pam Listers, the welfare officer who had spent more than a week at Sarah Deeley's cottage, was sitting in the row in front of them.

A few minutes after the pair had taken their places, six broad-shouldered undertakers arrived outside the church door, preparing to bring the coffin in.

'I'm disappointed,' Sunita whispered. 'I think this may be a waste of time in terms of the investigation. No one's standing out as being of much interest. This is just the normal mix of friends and relatives you get at a family funeral.'

'I'm afraid you're wrong, Sergeant,' Roscoe assured her. 'It was definitely worth our while coming. If nothing else, it gives us a chance to put faces to names. By the way, do you know who that lady with the large black hat is in the front row?'

'Yes, sir, that's Valerie Stanbrook. Next to her are her daughters, Isabelle and Sophie, and their partners. Mrs Stanbrook's nurse is there along with Bob and Barbara Jones, lifelong friends of Mrs Deeley. They run the Sinton Bank Guesthouse. Sir, I seem to recognise the lady who's just this moment sat down on the other side of the aisle but I can't quite place her.'

Roscoe smiled. 'Yes, be careful what you say to her. That's Susan Ellis-Jones from the *Queensbridge Gazette*.'

'Oh yes. In front of her is Mrs Deeley's carer, Colette Hayward, and Mike Griffin who runs the cafe.'

The chief inspector stroked his chin.

'Who's that lady in the green hat about five rows in front of us who keeps turning round? She looks very suspicious.'

Sunita lowered her voice. 'That's the vicar's wife, sir, Margaret Childs. She's sitting with the Kent contingent – Michelle Goodrich, Dr Hashemi and Dan Deverell, who was Mr Deeley's property manager.'

'Sergeant, is Michelle Goodrich the doctor's receptionist with a fad for anything pink?'

'That's right, sir.'

He frowned. 'Who are those two people by the side door?'

'I'm fairly certain that's Dr Gill Collingwood, from the Solihull medical practice where Dr Deeley used to work, and Connor Doyle, the writer who created the TV programme.'

DC Khalid stepped quietly through the church door and approached them. He bent down and whispered to Roscoe.

'Sir, Rufus Stanbrook's wife is here but he himself is missing.'

'Perhaps he was frightened of meeting up with us again,' Sunita remarked.

At that point, the booming voice of Revd Childs echoed around the nave and Khalid took a seat in the pew behind.

'I am the resurrection and the life, saith the Lord. He that believeth in me, though he were dead, yet shall he live. And whosoever liveth and believeth in me shall never die.'

He led the six pallbearers holding the coffin up the aisle. They placed it on a wooden trestle and bowed before stepping to the rear of the church.

'Let us pray,' said the minister.

Later in the service, Revd Childs, a tall, gaunt man in glasses, told the mourners a little of Mrs Deeley's history. She was born in Coventry in 1934. As a child, she was twice evacuated during the Second World War to

Leamington Spa. She eventually moved with her husband, Derrick, to Sinton Bank. Before retirement, she had a variety of jobs – including working as a nurse and as an animal carer.

'She was known for her love of music and sport as a younger woman,' the vicar went on. 'In her later years, until she became ill, she was a keen churchgoer who regularly visited the vicarage for tea with Margaret and me. We'll all remember her for her intelligence, creativity, and her kindness towards everyone she met.

'I don't need to remind you of the terrible death of her only child, Dr Scott Deeley, who was a well-known member of this parish, although not a regular churchgoer like his mother. This loss obviously affected her deeply and her death came exactly one week after his. She was just thirteen days away from her eighty-fourth birthday.'

As the vicar continued with his eulogy, Roscoe glanced at his sergeant.

'Who are those three women in the second row – behind the nieces?' he asked in a hushed voice.

'I haven't found out yet,' she told him. 'They were among the first here. Maybe I'll have a word with them after the service.'

He nodded. 'Yes, I think you should do that. Khalid may have got their names.'

During the service, the congregation sang the hymns *Praise My Soul The King of Heaven* and Psalm 23, *The Lord Is My Shepherd*. Roscoe sang both with gusto, causing Pam Listers and Dr Collingwood to glance across at him.

At the end of the service, the vicar invited all the mourners to join him at the graveside for the committal. Valerie Stanbrook, who walked slowly with a stick and was assisted by her nurse, led the way to her sister's grave. The detectives hung back to let relatives and friends assemble before they gathered at the back.

Roscoe was watching Michelle Goodrich and Dr Hashemi, who seemed to be having an argument. He turned to Sunita.

'Is the wake being held at the cottage?'

'No, sir. It's being held at the Cricketers Arms at Foxwell Green. I suppose we ought to go. It'll give us a chance to chat to some of the bereaved.'

As the committal ended and mourners began to disperse, Roscoe heard a voice behind him.

'Hello, sir. We always seem to meet when something bad's just happened.'

Susan Ellis-Jones, dressed in a long black coat, was smiling. The chief inspector shook hands with her.

'Haven't seen you in weeks.'

'I know.'

'You're more likely to find me at a funeral these days,' he told her. 'People don't tend to invite me to celebrations. Maybe it's my gloomy face. You're a long way from Queensbridge High Street, aren't you?'

'Only twelve miles. We've written a lot about the Deeley case and, of course, the Harpers live in Queensbridge.'

'You remember DS Roy, don't you?'

The two women smiled and shook hands.

Roscoe continued, 'Harper's just one of a number of people we've been speaking to. By the way, thank you for your tip-off about the Hossett murder last year. Your sighting of the man's car was one of the key pointers in finding the killer.'

'I'd no idea of its importance at the time, but I was glad to help. Great to meet you again, both of you, although on a sad day.'

'Likewise, Susan. See you next in happier times, hopefully.'

The newspaper's senior reporter strolled off towards the car park.

Over the next ten minutes, as Roscoe struck up conversations with guesthouse owner Bob Jones and lettings manager Dan Deverell, all the other grieving relatives and friends began to drift away. Eventually, only Roscoe, Sunita, Khalid and Mr Deverell remained at the graveside.

'Her health declined steeply after Scott was killed,' Mr Deverell was saying. 'Such a shame. She was a lovely old girl.'

'Sir, do you think we should be going?' Sunita asked. 'We'll miss the start of the wake.'

'Yes, you're right,' Roscoe said. 'Sorry, Mr Deverell. My sergeant's reminded me of the time.'

'I've got to get back to Kent. I might see you at Scott's funeral. Do you know when that might be?'

Roscoe shrugged. 'That's all down to the coroner,' he said.

Just as they returned to the church door, Sunita noticed a garment of clothing lying on the grass next to the path. She stooped to pick it up. It was a green headscarf with a pink flamingo design.

Chapter 44

After more than a year spent living in Warwick, Sunita Roy had forgotten how hectic life in Birmingham could be. From the moment she stepped off a train at New Street Station on Thursday, 22 November, she was unprepared for the hustle and bustle of the Midlands city.

The air was filled with loud-speaker announcements, train noise, hurried footsteps, and the buzz of conversation as she passed through the station. Then she entered the Bull Ring shopping centre with its brightly lit stores, showing their tantalising ranges of fashion, jewellery and electronics goods. Many were now heralding the arrival of the Christmas shopping season with festive decorations.

Within minutes, she had left the centre and was walking past redbrick commercial premises built in the 1960s and past Grade II-listed Digbeth Police Station, where she had been based for a short time as a young constable with the West Midlands force before joining Heart of England Police.

As a light rain began to fall, she proceeded along Digbeth High Street. Memories of her time in the area came streaming back. The Kerryman pub and The Big Bulls Head, a pub and restaurant, were still trading along this dusty, noisy, urban thoroughfare.

Sunita cast her eyes around and eventually found Rochester Street, a turning on the left. But the numbering system seemed jumbled and she wandered down the street several times in her search for the firm Mayfair Bespoke Jewellery.

She had tried the week before to make contact by phone but she'd found their number unobtainable and suspected the business may have closed down. Now she believed her fears were justified. But then, in the centre of a parade of shops, to her relief, she found a jewellery business and wondered if that could be the place.

Sunita pushed the door and a bell sounded, summoning an assistant, a lady in her thirties. She was a short, amiable woman in a pink floral top with a long-flowing black skirt.

'Can I help you?' asked the woman.

Sunita showed her warrant card.

'I was looking for Mayfair Bespoke Jewellery.'

The woman smiled. 'I'm sorry. They closed down about seven years ago. We've taken them over.'

The sergeant frowned. 'I'm making inquiries into an order for some handmade jewellery that would have been placed with them in July 2007.'

'I don't think you've got much hope of getting anywhere with that. That's – what? – eleven years ago. I don't think we'd have any records that far back. Staff have changed several times.'

Sunita sighed. 'Can I speak to the manager, please?'

The woman shook her head. 'We don't have a manager. There's an owner.'

'Can I speak to him?'

'I'll see if he's available.'

She disappeared into the back of the shop. Shortly afterwards, a tall, elderly man with receding grey hair appeared behind the counter.

'Can I help?'

'Sorry to trouble you,' said Sunita, presenting her warrant card again. 'Heart of England Police. Just making some inquiries about a piece of hand-crafted jewellery that I believe Mayfair Bespoke Jewellery would have made back in July 2007.'

He screwed up his face. 'That's a long time ago, young lady. Tell me a little more about this. I'll see if I can help.'

She removed a small box from her pocket and placed it on the glass counter. Removing the lid, she picked up the gold necklace that was inside and passed it to the shop owner. He placed a magnifying glass in his eye and studied the necklace and its rose-gold pendant. Then he tore a blank page from a book of receipts and made some notes on the back.

'That's a fine piece of work,' he remarked. 'Do you have some paperwork?'

She pulled the receipt from her pocket and handed it to him. He nodded.

'Yes, this definitely was made by the company which we took over. What did you want to know exactly?'

'We just need to know anything at all about the order and purchase. It's cropped up in a murder investigation. We believe the murdered man, a family doctor called Dr Scott Deeley, ordered it and intended it as a gift for someone. So, any information – no matter how trivial – could be helpful. And I can't stress how important this might prove to be for our investigation.'

'Look, I can see how important this is to you. I'll see what I can do. My name's Leeman Morris, by the way.'

She reached out and shook his hand. 'DS Roy.'

'You say he was a family doctor?'

'Yes, he had a practice in Solihull at the time he placed the order.'

He stroked his chin.

'There's a woman called Jenny who used to work for Mayfair. I've got her number somewhere. I'll give her a call and see if she can remember anything. That's the best I can do. But don't get your hopes up too high. We're going to be relying on the memory of a woman who took orders back then. So, I can't promise anything. We'll just do the best we can.'

* * *

Sunita Roy recognised a stylish house when she saw one. Connor Doyle's Edwardian home, which she visited later that day in a quiet row of houses, half a mile from Queensbridge railway station, was such a house.

Once she had been invited through the imposing black front door, she was led into a magnificent hallway with high ceilings, and a sweeping cantilevered staircase.

She spotted a Tracey Emin collage on the hall wall as she followed the American-born writer into his drawing room. Two small white sofas sat facing each other beside the neo-classical marble fireplace, and a crystal chandelier sparkled overhead. A pair of floor-to-ceiling windows offered the view of a garden which, in summer months, she was convinced would prove an exotic haven of flowers and shrubs.

'Would you like a coffee, Sergeant Roy?' asked Connor, as he studied her warrant card. 'It's freshly made.'

'That would be very nice. White, two sugars, please,' she replied, sitting on the nearest sofa.

'Just one minute,' he said.

While he made coffee in his kitchen, she admired a sketch of a naked man by British artist Duncan Grant which stood above the fireplace.

'Do you like it?' asked Connor a few minutes later, as he returned with a silver tray containing two large coffee cups and a sugar bowl.

'It wouldn't be my choice but Grant's very popular at the moment, isn't he?' she said.

'Even more so since his death, I think. Anyway, Sergeant. You're privileged. I've stubbornly refused to speak to anyone about my friendship with Dr Deeley, but since meeting you at Sarah's funeral, I couldn't turn down your request on the phone to meet.'

'Very kind of you,' said Sunita as she removed her notebook from the pocket of her jacket.

'Don't mention it,' he replied, sitting down on the sofa opposite. 'I just hope my information in some way helps the police to find whoever took poor Scotty from our lives.'

As she picked up her cup for a sip of her drink, a coffee-stained scrap of paper that had been stuck to the bottom fluttered to the floor.

'Is this yours?' she asked, handing it to him.

For a moment, Connor looked bemused. Then it crossed his mind what it was.

'Sorry. That threw me for a moment. That's Dr Collingwood's phone number. She thinks she may've left her scarf in my car and wants me to call her back.'

'I found a scarf outside the church. I wonder if it's hers?'

'You're welcome to take her number and call her. You never know.'

Sunita jotted the number down and smiled.

'Anyway, you were going to tell me about Scott, weren't you?'

'Of course. I'm sorry if I rattle on a bit. My friendship with Scott began when I was signed up to write the script for a drama based on a GP practice. One of the production assistants was a patient at Scott's Solihull practice and couldn't praise him enough. She'd had some medical problem – a miscarriage or something – and he'd been a tower of strength in his support for her.

'She asked him if he was interested in helping the programme makers in an advisory capacity in return for a fee. He was delighted at the idea because he believed other contemporary medical dramas on TV weren't totally realistic. He wanted to make sure the facts were right.

'So, anyway, we met up and hit it off at once. He was straight, of course, but we had much in common. We shared a common purpose in wanting the drama to show the interaction between medical staff and patients in their daily lives. And that's how we came up with Dr Frank Sutton and *Morning Surgery*.

'Scott became a consultant to the programme and was paid a nice little retainer. Dr Sutton was a popular character. At one point, do you know we had nearly two and a half million viewers? Not bad for a Midlands-based lunchtime drama show.'

'It ran for about ten years, didn't it?'

'Yes. From 1996 to 2006, when the bastards at Midlands TV said they needed a fresh concept, and the doors of *Morning Surgery* were closed for the last time.'

'Wasn't it something to do with the freeholder who owned the studio where the programme was made wanting to build flats?'

'That was the excuse they used, yes. But the real reason was the TV bosses thought it had got stale and wanted a quiz show – as if there weren't enough of those around already – or a chat show for aggrieved, menopausal women.'

Sunita felt Connor was drifting away from the subject of Dr Deeley. She decided to steer him back to it.

'So you must have been devastated to hear of Scott's murder,' she said.

'Of course. That should never have been the manner of his death. He was so likeable, so charming, so helpful towards everyone he met. We kept in regular contact even after he moved away. I can't understand why anyone would want to end his life so abruptly. It's unfathomable.

'He realised his mother was moving inexorably towards the final days of her life – she was "heavily into part two", as he described it. He wanted to make her final years as comfortable as possible before her passing. I was staggered when he and his mother died just a week apart.

'I met up with Dr Collingwood from the Solihull practice and we went to the funeral together. We both knew Mrs Deeley through Scott and wanted to pay our last respects.'

Sunita sipped her coffee. 'Did he leave the area because of the Jerome Harper case?'

'No, not at all,' said Connor. 'He was shaken by that experience, of course, and he did his best to make amends. No, the reason he decided to move away was rather unexciting. He was finding his work in Solihull very stressful. Some nights he wasn't getting home until nine or ten o'clock. The chance came of him joining a practice in Kent with a lighter workload and he jumped at it.

'There have been rumours in the press about him moving to Kent because he had a girlfriend there. I can assure you he never mentioned anything like that to me. His part-time consultancy work as an advisor to the programme had finished by then anyway and it didn't look as if Midlands TV would ever make another episode. So there was no reason at that time for him to remain in the Midlands.'

'Can you think of anyone who might have wanted him killed?'

'No one at all. He's the last person you'd have expected to meet a violent end.'

Chapter 45

The streets around Queensbridge were cloaked in fog as the chief inspector set off for work on Tuesday, 27 November.

'Just like the Deeley case – shrouded in haze,' he muttered to himself.

By the time he reached St James Street, the fog had lifted but a light rain was beginning to fall. As he marched past the CID desks, Sunita Roy glanced round and smiled.

'Morning, sir. Good news from the hospital.'

'What's that?'

'They're hoping to allow Tom home next week.'

'That's excellent news. How is he?'

'Getting bored. He's eager to get back into his stride again.'

'I can't understand him. If I'd been nearly killed in the course of duty, I'd expect several weeks off to recover.'

He took his keys from his pocket and unlocked the door to his room.

'Tom shouldn't rush it. The body needs plenty of time to recuperate after an ordeal like that.' While opening the door, he glanced over his shoulder. 'Sergeant, could you come and see me in a few minutes, please?'

After hanging up his coat in his cupboard, he was about to ease himself into his chair when he received an unexpected phone call.

'Chief Inspector, there's a Nisa Shah on the phone, asking for you,' the switchboard operator informed him. 'She says its important.'

'All right. Put her through,' he replied.

Within seconds, he was talking to the woman from Albion Road, Sedgeworth he'd visited the week before.

'Mr Roscoe, I'm really sorry. I've had a change of heart. I don't think I can give evidence after all.'

He stepped round his desk and sat down.

'I'm sorry to hear that.'

'I knew you would be. I've been talking to my husband, Asad. He was angry when I told him what I'd said to you. He says, in view of the fire, we've obviously come up against some very dangerous people. He's banned me from helping the police.'

'Mrs Shah, I have to remind you that you've given a formal statement to my colleague, Tom Vickers, and that he's got a video recording of your account.'

'I don't care. I may have to withdraw my statement. I just have to comply with my husband. He says we've got to think of our future as a family.'

Roscoe sighed. 'I can understand that, Mrs Shah, but as I mentioned to you when we met, we can make additional security arrangements for you. For instance, we can give you a panic alarm, if need be, and a mobile phone which you'd have to carry and keep charged at all times.'

'I realise those kind of arrangements could be made, and I'm very grateful, but I'm afraid my mind is made up. Our family survived last weekend's petrol bomb. We might not be so lucky next time.'

She then ended the call.

As he turned on his computer and began writing a memo to his chief superintendent about Mrs Shah's decision, Sunita Roy tapped on the door.

'Come in, Sergeant,' he yelled. 'Just had some disappointing news.'

'What's that, sir?' she asked. She drew up a chair and sat down.

'That Shah woman's dropped out. She's refusing to give evidence now.'

'Can't say I blame her. That fire and the message on the brick must have been terrifying.'

He nodded. 'Tell me about the reconstruction. How did you get on with our two absentees, Bowcott and Edwards?'

'Robert Bowcott's come out with a tale of how the murder and being arrested caused him to suffer depression. He decided not to attend because it would have added further stress. He went to the pub instead.'

Roscoe leaned forward with his head in his hands. 'Heaven help us. What about Edwards?'

'He claims he forgot it was on Monday and was disappointed to have missed it.'

'Any idea where he actually was on Monday?'

'One of his neighbours told me his car was outside his house all morning.'

Roscoe shook his head. 'That doesn't prove anything. I don't know. The things we have to deal with.'

'We've got people sifting through all the information passed to us during the reconstruction. But nothing major's come to light so far.'

'I'm going to be speaking to the chief superintendent this afternoon to see if we can get some money together and offer a reward – perhaps in conjunction with Crimestoppers. That's sometimes a useful way of raising the profile of a case. Anyway, how are you getting on with your own inquiries?'

She shrugged. 'Slow progress, sir. Do you remember the scarf I found in the churchyard?'

'Yes. You handed it to the vicar while we were at the wake in the Cricketers' Arms, didn't you?'

'That's right. He had no idea whose it was, but he was confident the owner would eventually come forward.'

Roscoe leaned back on his chair. 'I'm sure you're wasting your time with that.'

Sunita shook her head. 'I don't know. It's just a line of inquiry, like so many others. It might take us somewhere or it might not. At one point, I thought the scarf might belong to Dr Collingwood, who lost one, but hers turned up. I called the vicar back this morning. He's asked around but no one's come forward to claim it. It's just lying on a table in the vicar's hallway.'

Roscoe smiled on hearing no one had come forward to inquire about the missing garment.

'I can't see why you're so interested in it,' he observed. 'It's simply a discarded fashion accessory which happens to have a flamingo design like the necklace you discovered. It's a very popular design.'

Sunita looked him in the face. 'I've just got a theory about it – that's all,' she said. 'It's quite possible I'm mistaken.'

'Tell me about the flamingo necklace belonging to Dr Deeley. You went up to Digbeth. Anything come of that?'

'Yes, sir. The firm that took the order closed down, but it's been taken over by another Birmingham firm run by a man named Leeman Morris. They're now called Mercia Bespoke Jewellery. He called me yesterday, saying he'd found a phone number for the female shop assistant who took the order from Dr Deeley in the summer of 2007.'

'Did she remember anything after all this time?'

'He phoned the woman at her home,' said Sunita. 'She didn't remember anything at all at first. But when Mr Morris explained the man placing the order had been a family doctor, this seemed to spark something off in her mind. She recalled that the buyer had wanted the necklace for his sweetheart. The cost to him appeared to be unimportant. He simply wanted to make this woman happy by having a specially crafted piece of jewellery made for her.

'But something must have happened because, despite him having paid for it, he never came to collect it. In the end, the shop assistant had to send it to him by post.'

Chapter 46

Gavin Roscoe admired his reflection in the washroom mirror at St James Street police headquarters on Monday, 3 December. He straightened his blue tie. He combed his hair for a second time.

'Who is this handsome DCI who's barely reached the age of fifty?' he asked himself. 'Only the next detective superintendent with Heart of England Police, that's who.'

An officer with the rank just above Roscoe's had announced his plan to retire in the new year. Roscoe regarded himself as the obvious candidate to replace him. Minutes earlier, Chief Superintendent Nicola Norris had requested to see him. Could this be a pivotal moment in his career?

He climbed the stairs to the second floor two at a time with the confidence of a Texas banker approaching an oilfield. Then he checked himself. Perhaps it would not create the best impression if he were to arrive red-faced and breathless. He should pace himself. He took the final steps to Norris's office door in a sedate manner and knocked.

'Come in!' she yelled.

Roscoe walked in gingerly, greeting his superior with a hearty, 'Good morning, ma'am! You wished to see me, ma'am?'

The chief superintendent was hunched over her laptop.

'Ah, Gavin. I haven't seen you for a few days and wanted to know how things were going. How's Tom Vickers, first of all?'

Perhaps this was simply an introductory approach by her.

'Much improved, ma'am. Apparently, somehow or other, he's managed to get hold of some of his jazz collection and he's been inviting one or two of the nurses to dance round the ward with him.'

She reminded Roscoe of an elderly aunt as she peered over the top of her glasses.

'Sounds like he's a lot better.'

'Yes. He may be allowed home soon. If only to give the nurses a break.'

'Excellent news.'

He took a chair from the back of the room and made himself comfortable in front of her desk.

'I assume you've read Tom's report on Operation Sepulchre?' she asked.

His thoughts about a promotion offer were rapidly fading.

He nodded. 'Tom's worked very hard.'

'Gavin, I've been speaking to legal services. We can't see any grounds for reopening the "murder in the bath" case. Our officers over in Summerstoke worked their butts off on bringing Winston Stevens and Raj Kumar to trial and I feel the convictions were right. So I'm proposing we file the report away, marked "No further action".'

Roscoe drew a quick breath. 'Tom will be gutted. He was planning to update the report as soon as he's back at work.'

'I can't believe details of the shooting incident or any other matter would make a huge difference to my conclusion.'

The chief inspector shifted uneasily in his chair.

'If I could try and speak on his behalf, the descriptions of the two men leaving O'Sullivan's house and given to the jury differ from some of the witness accounts. The defendants' alibi evidence was brushed aside by the prosecution at the trial and a key witness was totally disregarded.'

'I've read the report and most of these issues have been raised. I accept that, for some strange reason, Nisa Shah's evidence doesn't appear to have been heard at the trial. But I understand from you she's no longer willing to testify in any case. Is that correct?'

'Yes, ma'am. She's changed her mind after being the victim of intimidation.'

'The petrol bomb attack on her home?'

'Yes.'

She leaned forward across her desk.

'I'll be straight with you, Gavin. You wouldn't expect any different from me. Even with her evidence, there'd be a struggle to find fault with the original convictions. So that's where we stand at the moment.'

Roscoe shook his head. 'You can see I'm disappointed, ma'am. We know both Stevens and Kumar have police records, but nonetheless we've been spurred on by a feeling that a miscarriage of justice may have occurred.'

He privately suspected one or two senior officers at Summerstoke CID were not beyond acting outside the law and were possibly even in league with criminals, but he had no strong evidence to support this theory. He remained silent about it.

'We've become aware of rumours that police in Summerstoke may have breached professional standards,' he added.

'I've also heard rumours of that nature, but there's nothing about that in Tom's report. That may have been a wild theory dreamed up by that defence lawyer, Giles Farquhar. Listen, Gavin, as you mention the question of irregularities in police conduct, I ought to mention something. I've a close family friend – my goddaughter, actually – who's just started work over there as an information analyst in Summerstoke CID. So, if there were to be any funny business going on, I should get to hear about it fairly quickly.'

Roscoe took a deep breath. He may as well forget about the job vacancy, he thought. She clearly had other priorities.

He decided to raise another issue.

'Ma'am, on a different tack, I'm becoming concerned about the lack of progress being made into Tom's shooting. Have you heard anything from Summerstoke CID about how their inquiries are going?'

'I've received a brief preliminary report on the shooting. They've named a couple of men they wish to interview. I've got the details on my laptop.'

She fumbled on her desk and pressed a few keys on her small silver computer.

'Here we are. Tadeusz Yanis Filipowski, aged fifty-six. Last known address: 69 Badminton Road, Coventry. Second man is Tyrone Blake, aged thirty. No fixed abode. Haven't Summerstoke been liaising with you?'

'No, ma'am. I'm afraid they haven't. In fact, they seem to have been doing everything they can to obstruct us. Our DC Dawson was seconded to their team and they've been keeping him in the dark about their work. They carried out a dawn operation at the Badminton Road address and gave him the wrong time. As a result, he missed the whole event.'

She pulled a face. 'Probably some simple misunderstanding. I can't imagine why they'd want to obstruct him.'

Roscoe knew why that might be. They might be hiding something. She closed her laptop.

'I understand the men who shot our inspector were seen driving off in a black Volkswagen Touareg, which we've had difficulty tracing because it had false number plates.'

'That's right, ma'am. Have you read my latest memo?'

'About the blazing car found in a field outside Summerstoke? Yes. No DNA or dabs found at all.'

'Obviously, the people concerned knew what they were doing. The only clear evidence on the shooting is that the house they used in Sidney Road was the home of a drug addict with links to the gang known as the 101 Crew. Filipowski and Blake are believed to be involved with that gang.'

'Well, Gavin, it's hard to see where we go from here. I think we've got to have patience and let the inquiries being undertaken by Summerstoke CID take their course. You're aware that both Filipowski and Blake have gone on the run?'

'Just the barest details have been made known to me.'

'DS Bains from Summerstoke has evidence they've fled abroad. They've contacted Interpol, but they're obviously in hiding and realistically our hands are tied until they return to the UK.'

'I'm afraid this just isn't good enough, ma'am. These two men lured a good, honest copper into a trap and then shot him. It's a miracle he didn't die. Summerstoke detectives have made a half-hearted effort to track down the suspects, whose identities became known almost immediately afterwards. I can't understand why they haven't taken the hunt for the two men abroad.'

'You mean by sending officers off on the trail of the two men?'

'Yes.'

'Well. We don't know where they are.'

'Poland, surely?'

'That's one possibility, of course. But we've no address for them. On the other hand, we can be confident they'll return to the Midlands eventually because of their strong links to drug trafficking.'

'But when's that going to be? Ma'am, I think we should make inquiries with the suspects' families and send a team of officers abroad with the intention of finding their whereabouts. Then we should mount surveillance outside their bolthole and apprehend them.'

'I'm sorry, Gavin. I can't permit that. There's the issue of resources. Plus they're fugitives on the run with the wherewithal to flit from one address to another on a whim. No, we must bide our time.'

Roscoe shook his head. 'Ma'am, with respect, these men may never return to Britain. They must know they're wanted. Their names are going to be released to the press soon and their pictures are going to be plastered all over the newspapers and on television. We need to set up a team to fly out and apprehend them.'

'No, Gavin. I'm sorry if my decision disappoints you but we're going to leave things to Summerstoke CID. They're keeping me regularly informed of their investigation and we're going to wait and see how things transpire.'

'Is that all you wanted to speak to me about, ma'am?' he asked.

'Yes, that's all, Gavin,' she replied.

He was disappointed. He'd hoped his achievements as a chief inspector were to be rewarded. He'd also hoped to speed up moves to see the men who shot Tom Vickers brought to justice. Both aspirations had been dashed – at least, for the moment. He stood up and walked away.

Chapter 47

The branches of a majestic pine tree close to an orange streetlight cast moving shadows across the rain-sodden ground as Sunita Roy stepped out of her car the following night. She walked beside the stone wall that fronted the vicarage garden, avoiding the occasional puddles. Then, slowly and thoughtfully, she trudged past the open wooden gates and made her way up the gravel drive.

A light drizzle began to fall as she turned on a pocket torch to guide her way.

Many women would baulk at the idea of working by night, she reminded herself. For her, it was not an issue. But that didn't mean she didn't feel daunted by her sombre surroundings.

A gentle wind swished through the fir trees on either side of her. The garden ahead lay cloaked in darkness, but, by the light of her torch, she caught occasional glimpses of white viburnum blooms and yellow, scented japonica flowers which had survived the frosts.

The church bell tolled from the nearby church of St Michael. She stopped for a moment to listen. After a few rings, the sound stopped and all she could hear was water gushing down a waste pipe somewhere on the building that was looming up before her.

Within a couple of minutes, she found herself standing outside the ivy-clad Gothic-style vicarage. She gauged that the building, which had stone mullion windows with leaded lights, was probably eighteenth century. She could just discern the shapes of two giant chimney stacks standing proudly at either end of the roof. The only visible light came from one of the upstairs windows.

Sunita struck the heavy brass knocker in the centre of the white front door and waited. As she did so, the wind blew more fiercely, so she raised her scarf until it fitted more snugly round her neck. After a further few minutes, an exterior light above the door came on. Someone was standing behind the door, listening.

'If you're wanting the vicar, he's gone to the church,' said an anxious female voice.

'Sorry to call late in the day,' said Sunita. 'It's DS Roy from Heart of England Police.'

The oak door creaked open. Margaret, the wife of vicar Martin Childs, was standing in the hallway, which was festooned in red and gold ceiling decorations. She took a step outside in order to see her more clearly under the glow of the light.

'I remember you,' she said in a refined voice. 'You were at Mrs Deeley's funeral a couple of weeks ago.'

'That's right,' said Sunita. 'You say the vicar's not here?'

'Just gone to the church to talk to the organist. Then he was going to tidy the vestry. I'm afraid he won't be back until late.'

'That's a shame. I wanted to ask him about the green and pink scarf that I found in the churchyard. Do you know if anyone came forward to claim it? He was going to ask around among the mourners.'

'You mean the scarf with the flamingos on? Actually, it's mine,' said Mrs Childs, who seemed to be feeling the cold, despite wearing a thick green jersey and matching skirt. 'My husband never pays any attention to what I'm wearing. Typical man!'

'Oh, I see,' said Sunita, who was rather disappointed by the woman's admission. Perhaps this line of inquiry, like so many others in the 'body in the woods' case, had led her down another blind alley. She gazed at the ground. She shook her head.

'You seem disappointed,' said Mrs Childs.

'That wasn't the answer I was expecting to hear,' the sergeant admitted. 'Well, thank you for your time. Obviously, I don't need to bother the vicar now. Please pass on my best wishes to your husband.'

Sunita turned and began walking back towards the front gates, rapt in thought. Mrs Childs went back inside, shut the door and turned off the outside light. Then an idea occurred to Sunita. She retraced her steps and knocked on the door again. This time Mrs Childs drew open the door more promptly.

'Sorry to bother you again, Mrs Childs,' she said. 'I just wondered. Did you buy the scarf from a shop or was it a gift?'

The minister's wife was now beginning to lose her patience. Sunita sensed Mrs Childs felt it was too cold a night to be standing in the doorway discussing such trivialities with callers.

'Why all this interest in a scarf?' she demanded. 'If you must know, my sister gave it to me because she'd got several. I hope you're satisfied now. I really don't see where you're going with this.'

'Forgive me, Mrs Childs. To be honest, I'm not altogether sure myself where this is leading, but I've got a feeling this may help explain a mystery I've been trying to solve.'

Sunita subconsciously tugged on her own scarf again. She rubbed her hands together in the chill air. She sensed that if she could only get inside the vicarage and steer Mrs Childs into a proper conversation, the vicar's wife might have valuable information to impart.

'I fail to see the importance in a scarf that once belonged to my sister,' Mrs Childs continued.

'Can I just ask who your sister is and where she lives?' Sunita asked.

'Look, I'd rather you came inside out of the cold and told me what all this is about. Would you like to come in?'

'If it's not too much trouble,' said the sergeant. 'I'm afraid I won't be able to tell you too much because police obviously need to be discreet in their investigations. Your sister didn't attend the funeral then?'

'No, she didn't attend the funeral. She was too upset. Coming to Sinton Bank revives too many memories.'

'It's very good of you to invite me in,' said Sunita as she followed the lady of the house into the hall.

'Well, as it happens, I was just going up to bed,' said Mrs Childs. 'But, before I do, I was going to make some cocoa. Would you like some?'

'That would be extremely kind of you. It would certainly help to warm me up, Mrs Childs.'

'All right, come inside and I suppose I'd better tell you a little about my sister, if you think it's so important.'

Chapter 48

Early on Wednesday, 5 December, after a night spent sleeping fitfully, Sunita Roy rose from her bed.

She slipped on her white dressing gown and strolled into her living room. She opened the blinds and peered out at the overcast sky. A golden sun could be faintly seen, struggling to break its way through the clouds. The racecourse at the end of the road was shrouded in a silvery mist. From the trees across the street, she could detect the sound of birdsong.

She glanced at her watch. It was nearly half past seven. She was unsure why she was finding it so hard to sleep. Perhaps it was because various aspects of the Scott Deeley case were still swirling around in her mind.

She turned on her laptop and was surprised to find an email from the genealogist in Birmingham who assisted in tracing family members connected with suspects and witnesses. She had written to him just before midnight and was delighted he had responded so swiftly. She had requested information about a Warwickshire family, which he had been able to provide in some detail.

'That's cool,' she murmured to herself before emailing him back with a simple thank-you note.

An hour later, after she'd washed and dressed, she was devouring her breakfast of scrambled eggs and toast when her mobile rang.

'Good morning, sir. Everything all right?' she asked as the chief inspector's name and face appeared on her handset's screen.

'Just wondered how you got on last night, Sergeant?'

'It went very well, sir. Mrs Childs was extremely helpful and I've made a lot of progress on the Deeley case. Will you be in the office in an hour's time?'

'Yes, I will.'

'I think it would be best if I explained everything when I come in. Is Khalid going to be around this morning?'

'He's on the rota for nine thirty.'

'That's good because I think he should hear what I've got to say as well. I've just received the final nugget of information I was waiting for – the last piece of the puzzle. I'm fairly certain now I know who the killer is.'

* * *

Just before eleven o'clock that morning, Sunita found herself a parking space in front of St James Street police headquarters. With a confident air, she locked her car, entered the building and made her way to CID.

The chief inspector was waiting for her in his room with Khalid. They were both eager to hear about the possible breakthrough she had made in the case.

'I'm now certain who killed Scott Deeley,' said Sunita as she and Khalid drew up chairs and sat down. 'But I only reached my conclusions over the past few days. I've been waiting for some final information to come in.'

'So it *is* Harper after all?' Roscoe said.

Sunita shook her head. 'I'm afraid, sir, we're making a mistake if we point the finger at Harper. We can also forget about the man on the Honda motorbike and the men parked in Heath Road at the time of the murder.

'Let me explain. At the heart of the Scott Deeley case, in my mind, has been the flamingo necklace which was clearly intended for someone dear to him. I believe Dr Deeley bought it for his sweetheart but was, for some reason, never able to present it to her. I wondered for a time if this was a matter of unrequited love, but, after speaking to Sandy Perry, I realise that the woman concerned was very much in love with him too.'

'Sorry?' said the chief inspector. 'Am I missing something? Who's this Sandy Perry?'

Khalid glanced across at Roscoe. 'Sir, she was a close friend of the doctor's who called in with information about him seven weeks ago. She was reluctant at first to give me her name and details, but eventually I tracked her down and there's a witness statement on file. She was one of the women in the second pew at the funeral service.'

'Thank you, Omar,' said Roscoe.

'If it's all right for me to continue, sir,' said Sunita, 'Sandy Perry worked at a hospital with Dr Deeley years ago. She knew him very well and revealed he had a secret lover, but claimed she never learned the woman's identity.

'Anyway, when a scarf decorated with flamingos was dropped at the funeral, I thought it was too much of a coincidence for there not to be a connection with the necklace. I ruled out Michelle Goodrich as being the owner of the scarf – despite the pink flamingos on it and her love of pink items – because the necklace had been ordered, as far as we could tell, before he met her at the medical practice in Kent.'

The chief inspector interrupted her. 'Sergeant, you mentioned to me you'd made inquiries with the jewellers about the necklace. They'd been taken over by another firm run by a Mr Morris, hadn't they? In the end, you spoke to the retired shop assistant who knew about the necklace and she'd had to post it to the doctor. Isn't that right?'

She nodded. 'That's right. She remembered the order for the necklace because it came from a doctor and he admitted to her that the necklace was intended for a woman he doted on. It was further embedded in her memory because he'd failed to collect it, despite prompting, and the shop had been obliged to post it to him in the summer of 2007.'

Roscoe interrupted again. 'You were taking a bit of a gamble there, Sergeant, if I may say so. This necklace might've been completely irrelevant. Your pink flamingo might've turned out to be a red herring.'

She and Khalid smiled.

'Good point you make, sir,' she said. 'Anyway, the necklace was sent to Dr Deeley in the summer of 2007. It was around that time that the doctor, rather inexplicably, left the Midlands. It was suspected at the time he might have moved away because of the furore over the death of the eleven-year-old boy, Jerome Harper. It was suggested he was being persecuted by the dead boy's father.

'But this didn't make sense to me. The doctor was a resilient man who'd been supported over his conduct in the case by fellow doctors and he was cleared of any wrongdoing or negligence by the General Medical Council. So that was no reason for him to leave the area.

'The TV programme where he was employed as a part-time script advisor had been taken off air at the time he went to Kent, but the termination of his consultancy work was hardly reason for him to up sticks and move away.

'I began to suspect that matters of the heart were behind his departure and that he couldn't stand to remain living in an area where he was so close to a woman whose love he couldn't have. He seemed to be acting like a man who wanted to create a fresh start for himself. Of course, he told Michelle Goodrich – who was, firstly, his receptionist and later became very close to him – he'd been suffering from stress. But I'm sure that was just an excuse.

'So, getting back to the scarf, I went to the vicarage last night and found it belonged to the vicar's wife, Margaret Childs. She'd received it as a gift from her sister, who had a great many scarves – all with flamingo designs because of her great love of the wading bird.

'You see the mother of the two sisters, Deirdre Matthams, worked with Sarah Deeley at West Midlands

Safari Park in Bewdley in Worcestershire at a time when they had the largest flock of flamingos in Britain. Mrs Matthams was occasionally allowed to take her two girls to work with her and that's how Margaret Childs' sister came to adore the birds.

'Mrs Childs' sister is called Jessica Cooper. She runs a boarding and breeding kennels in Loman's Green, not far from Sinton Bank, and is married to a man named James Cooper. The name meant nothing to me at first, but then I got our family history researcher in Birmingham to find out about Jessica and her family. He's informed me the couple married in June 2007 and the husband's full name is James Howard Cooper, but he's always used Howard as his main Christian name. The only time he's been referred to as James is on his birth and marriage certificates.'

Khalid looked aghast. 'Oh my God!' he exclaimed. 'That's the guy who called the police – the guy who found the body. Brett and I were chatting about it the other day. We were wondering why it is that so many murder victims are found by a man walking a dog.'

Sunita looked solemn. 'It looks as if he might have done more than just find the body. It appears Howard Cooper knew of the close bond between his wife and Dr Deeley. I can't be sure at the moment, but it looks likely that their romance began either before or around the time of the Coopers' marriage. At some point, Jessica Cooper must have decided to honour her vows and end the affair. By then he'd already instructed the jewellers to make the necklace and it was no doubt too late to cancel the order.

'She must have decided to try to make their marriage work, forcing the doctor to opt for fresh pastures in Kent, hoping he'd eventually forget her and find a new love. But it seems that, despite finding some solace with Miss Goodrich, he was unable to commit fully to her because of his lingering feelings for Jessica Cooper. Margaret Childs showed me some photographs. Jessica's quite an attractive woman, I can tell you.'

Her two listeners smiled.

She continued, 'I also spent a few hours the other day with the bus company staff in Redditch going through the CCTV for 1 October. Do you remember we found a bus ticket at Honeysuckle Cottage? Dr Deeley had made an unusual journey by bus, leaving his car at home. I was intrigued by this. Sure enough, my patience with their CCTV people was rewarded. I found images of a grey-haired man in a black coat rising from his seat and getting off the bus at the Loman's Green bus stop.'

Roscoe leaned forward. 'Where the Coopers live.'

'Exactly. We can't know for sure but there's a good chance he'd gone to visit her or at least check out the lay of the land. And maybe Howard Cooper spotted him outside.'

'It's a bit circumstantial.'

'I know. But why else should the doctor find himself in Loman's Green? It's a small hamlet. There's nothing there except the kennels and a pub. Anyway, getting back to the woods at Foxwell Heath, we can only imagine the fear and the fury of Howard Cooper when he saw the doctor – the man his wife was possibly still pining for. There he was, jogging through the very woods where he, Howard Cooper, had chosen to walk one of his dogs.'

The chief inspector nodded.

'We need to arrest this Howard Cooper, speak to his wife and carry out a search of their home. We must start getting a team of people together. Omar, can you apply to the magistrates for a warrant? He's definitely a person of interest to this investigation. What you've just told us seems to have a certain ring of truth about it, Sergeant.'

She stared out of the window at the children playing on swings and slides in the recreation ground on the far side of the road. Then she looked back at Roscoe.

'Very well done, Sergeant. This was, at first glance, a difficult case. The wood covers a vast area and we'd no way of knowing precisely who was on the heath at the time of the murder. You've come up with a solution that appears simple and straightforward. For that, you should be congratulated.'

Sunita smiled. 'I wouldn't say simple, sir. I took a chance. I followed an inkling, and I also applied the rules of logic. On top of that, I got lucky.'

'As I've told you before, you make your own luck in this game, Sergeant,' said the chief inspector. 'I admire the way you've followed your hunch, despite my misgivings. You know, sometimes when you're trying to unravel the circumstances of a crime, you get an inkling about something, and you just have to go with it. That's exactly what you did, although perhaps you should have kept me a little more up to date with the progress you were making before today.'

Sunita nodded in agreement. 'I'm sorry if I kept you in the dark a little, but I was uncertain where my inquiries were taking me and didn't want to waste your time, sir.'

Roscoe smiled. 'You've done an extremely good job in pointing out the probable killer of Scott Deeley and why he might have been killed,' he said. 'However, the task isn't finished. We still have to catch our man.'

Chapter 49

The chief inspector drove away from police headquarters at around four o'clock with his sergeant beside him following her revelations about the couple in Loman's Green.

Many of the houses they passed in West Warwickshire were decked in festive lights. Sunita Roy noticed some residents had gone to the trouble of decorating their front windows with nativity scenes, trees or Santa Claus figures as Christmas was rapidly approaching. But her mind was preoccupied with thoughts about the Coopers and how their lives had come to feature in the case.

DC Khalid, who had spent several hours obtaining a search warrant, followed Roscoe's BMW in a patrol car with two uniformed officers. Scenes of crime officers, including senior forensic investigator Dr Alice Ling, had been alerted and were due to set off from headquarters shortly afterwards.

The chief inspector was eager to question Howard and Jessica Cooper and carry out a full search of their cottage.

He estimated the journey to the hamlet would take around twenty minutes if traffic was light, but as he followed the A34 road towards Henley-in-Arden, he realised their trip coincided with the start of the evening rush hour and it was nearly a quarter to five and getting dark by the time they reached the secluded stone cottage where the Coopers ran their kennels.

Sunita noticed a light shining from behind closed curtains in an upstairs room while colourful Christmas lights twinkled from a small tree in a hallway window. Dogs began barking the moment the two detectives stepped out of Roscoe's BMW. The noise came from behind high wooden fencing to the left of the cottage.

As she unfastened the gate latch, a woman's face appeared briefly at the window beside the glittering tree. It was an anxious face, concerned at seeing two vehicles arrive in the fading light. The sergeant could hear the sound of bolts being drawn behind the front door and a security light glared down as she slowly walked up the stone path, past a bird table in the centre of the lawn.

Within seconds she had reached a clump of rhododendron bushes, their paddle-shaped leaves rustling in the gentle evening breeze.

'Who is it?' the woman's voice cried out while opening the door a fraction.

'Police!' yelled Sunita as the woman peered round the door at her.

The chief inspector, who was just a few steps behind, produced his warrant card.

'We're from Heart of England,' said Sunita. 'Are you Mrs Cooper?'

'Yes,' the woman replied cautiously.

Jessica, who was holding a golden retriever bitch by the collar, opened the door fully. The sergeant was briefly mesmerised by this attractive woman with blue eyes and long blonde hair.

'What's this about?' the woman demanded. 'Has one of our puppies died? Has someone been bitten?'

The sergeant shook her head as she and Roscoe stood side by side outside the door.

'No. It's nothing to do with your dogs. We're investigating a man's death. Scott Deeley.'

'You'd better come in,' said Jessica, after examining Roscoe's warrant card and returning it to him.

For some reason, the dogs at the far end of the building stopped barking. Sunita noticed a man had walked down the stairs and was hovering in the dimly lit hallway behind Jessica. She faintly remembered seeing him on the day of the crime reconstruction.

All the while, Jessica maintained her grip on the dog's collar.

'There's no need for this!' insisted the man, who pushed past Jessica and tried to block the detectives' way.

'Who are you, sir?' said Roscoe. 'Are you Mr Cooper?'

'I am Mr Cooper, but you must have been directed here by mistake,' he said. 'We've got nothing to do with the death of Deeley.'

'This is a murder inquiry, sir,' Roscoe continued. 'We've every right to question you and, if need be, we're going to search your house.'

'Have you got a warrant?' Cooper demanded.

'We *have* got a warrant and it's in your interests to cooperate, sir,' said the chief inspector, as he produced the document from his jacket pocket and handed it to the kennel owner.

Sunita gazed into the man's eyes. 'Who knows? This may only take a few minutes.'

Jessica touched the man's arm.

'Come on, Howard,' she said. 'I'm sure we can sort this out quickly, dear. They must be at the wrong house. What have we got to do with the death of poor Scott?'

She hurried through to the back of the house, calling the golden retriever after her. Sunita watched her lock the animal in one of the outside kennels before returning.

The two detectives accompanied Howard Cooper into the small back parlour. DC Khalid had also ventured inside and Roscoe instructed him to commence a search of the downstairs rooms.

'Now what's this about?' Jessica demanded.

'As I said, we're investigating the murder of Dr Deeley,' said Sunita. 'Mrs Cooper, you were in a relationship with the doctor at one time?'

Jessica slumped down onto the green settee. She looked shocked.

'Yes,' she said. 'But it wasn't for long.' She looked up at her husband. 'I was married. It wasn't fair on Howard. We ended it.'

Turning to the husband, the sergeant asked, 'You're James Howard Cooper?'

'That's right,' he admitted.

Sunita continued, 'Mr Cooper, it was reported to us you were walking one of your dogs on Foxwell Heath on Monday, 8 October when by chance you spotted the body of Dr Deeley.'

'Yes. I found him dead. I was first to call the police about it. I made a full statement.'

Jessica stared across the room at her husband.

'It was you that found Scott's body?'

He nodded.

'I heard it was a dog walker who found it,' she continued. 'But you never told me it was you, Howard. You swore you hadn't been anywhere near Foxwell Heath at the time.'

'I didn't want to upset you about it. You were distressed enough, reading all the reports about the death.'

Jessica turned to Sunita, who was standing by the doorway. She said indignantly, 'Howard's name wasn't in the papers.'

'We didn't release details to the press of the dog walkers who found the body,' the sergeant replied. 'The fact of the matter is you didn't find him dead, did you, Mr Cooper? He was very much alive when you first saw him, I suggest.'

Cooper sneered. 'He was very much dead.'

'You must have been delighted when, eleven years ago, he moved out of the area and you and Jessica were able to get on with your lives,' the sergeant went on. 'But then everything changed. You became aware that he was back and it gave you the shock of your life. You first saw him at the start of October when he travelled over here to Loman's Green. I strongly suspect he was looking for Jessica.'

He raised an eyebrow. 'How the hell–?'

'Then you caught sight of him for a second time on that cold, misty, autumn morning of 8 October and you were overcome by anger. The man who'd so nearly cost you your marriage was back. Here he was, taking a leisurely run in the woods that were just a short distance from your home.

'Your whole life and happiness seemed under threat again. In a moment of desperation, you attacked him, causing him to fall and strike his head on a tree branch. You took advantage of his plight and attempted to strangle him. When that failed to kill him, you chanced upon a metal carving fork that had been discarded at the site of an abandoned campfire. You plunged it into his chest until he was dead.'

Jessica let out a scream, which set the dogs in the kennels barking again.

'Oh my God! Tell me this isn't happening!' she yelled.

As she sobbed into a paper handkerchief, Sunita resumed her account of the dramatic events in the woods as she visualised them taking place.

'You dragged the body into the bushes and then began walking back towards the car park,' she said. 'The trouble was that your golden retriever, Bella, wouldn't leave the body alone. She wandered back to the corpse, no doubt sniffing around it and clawing away at the leaves that were hiding it from the world. At the same time, you encountered two women, Fariza Hussain and her daughter Alisha.

'Their dog also noticed the body and you had to think fast. So, you offered to investigate what the dog had found in the bushes and were then forced to join them in making a 999 call. You must have been the most reluctant 999 caller in Britain. You were forced to summon police to the scene of your own crime.'

'A load of nonsense!' Cooper insisted. 'I didn't know the guy. How could I have recognised him? It's just pure coincidence that Jessica knew him for a few months a long time ago. I didn't kill him. I just did my bit as a good citizen and reported the discovery of a man's body in the wood. I wish I hadn't bothered now.'

Just then there was a knock on the door. Jessica opened it, still clutching her paper tissue, to find Dr Alice Ling and three forensic officers standing outside.

'There's a Dr Ling to see you,' she informed the chief inspector.

'Mrs Cooper, would you mind if they came in?' said Roscoe. 'They're part of our team.'

She nodded in agreement. The new arrivals brought in some equipment and began examining the rooms upstairs. The chief inspector returned to the matter in hand.

'Sergeant, I think we should take Mr Cooper to St James Street for further questioning.' Then, turning towards the suspect, he said, 'James Howard Cooper, I'm arresting you for the murder of Scott Deeley. You don't have to say anything. But it may harm your defence if you don't mention when questioned something which you later rely on in court. Anything you do say may be given in evidence.'

As Roscoe called Khalid into the room, Cooper sneered.

'This is absolutely ridiculous!'

Khalid and one of the uniformed constables then handcuffed Cooper. Jessica rose from the settee. Weeping, she hugged her husband, who was then led away.

'You had nothing to do with Scott's death, did you?' she shouted after him.

'Of course not,' he assured her. 'He was dead when I found him.'

'Take him away!' said Roscoe. 'After a couple of hours in the cells, he might have a different story to tell.'

'You're making a big mistake, Chief Inspector,' Jessica insisted. 'I trust my husband implicitly. I can't imagine him hurting anyone.'

* * *

Sunita had been watching Howard Cooper's arrest. Then, without saying a word to her boss, she slipped out of the back room and made her way upstairs. She found Dr Ling in one of the bedrooms.

'Ah, DS Roy,' said Ling. 'I've got something that'll be of interest to you.'

She walked over to the other side of the room. All the time, Cooper's heartbroken wife, Jessica, was continuing downstairs with a loud tirade in support of her husband.

'Howard never really knew Scott,' she was saying. 'After eleven years, Scott must have changed. I'm not sure my husband would have recognised him in the woods.'

Dr Ling walked back towards the sergeant clutching two transparent bags. One contained a crumpled, cream-coloured tie with a blue diamond design. The other held a red, short-sleeved shirt.

'I found these at the back of the top drawer over there,' said Ling, as she pointed to an old-fashioned dresser in the corner. 'Looks like blood on the shirt.'

Sunita thanked her. 'Can I borrow these?' she asked.

The doctor nodded. 'Be sure to let me have them back so we can test them in the lab.'

Sunita returned downstairs to find Roscoe was still talking to Jessica.

'Sir, these were found at the back of one of the bedroom drawers.'

The chief inspector had a whispered conversation with his sergeant in the hall.

'We've been looking for the ligature used to try to throttle Dr Deeley on Foxwell Heath,' Sunita told him. 'I think this might fit the bill. This cream tie is wrinkled and twisted. It's been stretched and pulled through some rough use. There's at least one grey hair on it. If we get it tested in the lab, we may find other hairs, as well as human skin cells. The shirt's got some dried patches on it. Could be blood.'

Jessica was sitting on the settee, weeping into her hands.

'Are you all right, Mrs Cooper?' asked Roscoe, returning to the back room and briefly placing his hand on her shoulder in reassurance.

'I overheard you. I found that tie while cleaning the room,' she sobbed. 'I asked him why it was screwed up. He claimed he'd mislaid one of the leads and he'd used it to restrain a dog.'

'I'm sorry,' said Roscoe, who had watched her break down. 'It looks like he may have tried to strangle the doctor with it.'

'Poor Scott,' she cried. 'He was the kindest, sweetest man.'

'We'll have to take a statement from you later – when you've recovered from the shock of all this,' said Roscoe.

'Scott was so good to me,' she went on. 'He was generous, intelligent, talented, caring and a hard-working medical man. Everyone he met was inspired by him. He was a shining star and I'll never get over his death. To think that my dear husband might be responsible – it doesn't bear thinking about.'

She paused to wipe her eyes.

'Do you know, I first knew Scott when we were teenagers. Our mothers both worked at the safari park.'

'You're a fan of flamingos?' Sunita suggested.

'Yes. How did you know?' said Jessica as she opened a drawer and removed another paper tissue.

'I've been making inquiries,' said Sunita. 'Dr Deeley bought you a beautiful necklace with a flamingo pendant which we found in his room at the cottage. He may have intended it as a present.'

'Did he? Oh my God!'

'He was obviously holding a torch for you,' the sergeant went on. 'He could never settle into another relationship after knowing you.'

'Our love for each other was special, but it seemed it just wasn't meant to be,' she said. 'Our true feelings for each other only came to light after I'd married Howard, and I didn't think it fair on him to continue my relationship with Scott.

'Of course, Scott took it very badly. After a few weeks, I discovered he'd moved away to Kent. In a sense, he was thinking of me as well as himself. He was allowing me space to get over him and get on with my life. I had no idea he'd come back to this area to care for his mother.

That is so typical of him. He was always thinking of others.'

'It seems that your husband certainly did recognise the doctor in the wood and reacted in a brutal manner,' said Sunita. 'Perhaps it was a desperate move by him – an action taken on the spur of the moment, which he may one day come to regret.'

Jessica shook her head. 'I don't know. I personally had no idea that Scott was back in Sinton Bank until after his death. You mentioned Scott had been to Loman's Green. I never saw him, but I suppose Howard might've done. That might explain why Howard was behaving a little oddly at the start of October.'

'Your husband must have known what he looked like. He must have seen him at some time in the past,' Sunita said.

'Howard had met him a few times in the past. He was our doctor for a while, when we lived near Solihull.'

The sergeant nodded her head knowingly.

'It looks as though he lied when he claimed he couldn't have recognised him in the wood,' Roscoe noted. 'Even after eleven years, he almost certainly knew who the man was and, acting in a blind panic induced by jealousy or rage, he snuffed out his life.'

Jessica wiped her eyes again.

'I've just been thinking. The last time I ever saw Scott was on 11 October 2007. He mentioned something about remembering my birthday but that was the day I chose to end our affair. Oh my God! He'd gone to all that trouble to find me a precious necklace.'

'It was a beautiful one as well,' said Sunita. 'It was specially crafted in rose gold by bespoke jewellers.'

Jessica was sobbing. 'He went to all that bother and, in the end, how was he rewarded? I broke his heart.'

Chapter 50

The ground-floor interview room at police headquarters was a cold, gloomy office with plain cream walls and a solitary window overlooking the car park. In the centre was a plain mahogany desk with two chairs either side. Digital video recording equipment was stacked on the top of a dark grey cabinet at the back of the room.

Howard Cooper was brought in by two uniformed constables just after seven o'clock that evening.

Tall, bespectacled duty solicitor Roger Sims, who had already had a long discussion with his client in the cells below, arrived shortly afterwards, along with the chief inspector and his sergeant.

Roscoe reminded Cooper of the caution that had been given to him prior to his arrest at Loman's Green and was about to begin questioning the suspect when Mr Sims interrupted.

'Chief Inspector, my client has had the opportunity to reflect on his situation over the past couple of hours and he wishes to help the police as much as he can.'

Roscoe tutted. 'He wasn't so bloody helpful earlier this afternoon.'

'I think it's fair to say he's had a change of heart. He realises you're dealing with a serious matter. He feels it may help both the police and himself if he gives an honest account of what he knows. So we've drafted a short statement, which I propose to read on his behalf.'

'Very well,' said the chief inspector. 'Let's hear what he's got to say.'

Mr Sims cleared his throat and began.

This is a statement given by me, James Howard Cooper, on 5 December at Heart of England Police Headquarters. On 1 October, I was at home at Gamekeeper's Cottage in Loman's Green when I heard the rattle of the letterbox. Someone had hand-delivered a letter. I opened the door and saw a man in a dark coat who was walking away down the path. When he reached the gate, he turned round. That moment sent a chill through me. I recognised him immediately, although something like eleven years had passed since I'd last seen him. It was Scott Deeley.

'How could you be so sure it was the doctor?' Sunita asked.

Cooper glanced at his lawyer before replying, 'I've asked myself that question a few times. I don't know if it was his facial expression, the way he moved his hands, the way he walked. I just knew it was him.'

Mr Sims frowned. 'Could I be allowed to continue with my client's statement?'

She nodded and Sims began reading again.

Once he'd gone, I picked up the letter which was handwritten and simply had the name 'Jessica' on it. Of course, I was desperate to know what it said. I'm not accustomed to reading other people's mail but my curiosity and my concern about its possible contents were overwhelming.

So I put the kettle on and used the steam to unseal it. I suppose you could describe it as a love letter. He said how much he'd missed her and hoped she still felt the same about him. He thought about her every day since they parted and wondered if he could meet up with her.

I was extremely upset to find he still held strong feelings for my wife. I decided to destroy the letter. I went out into the yard and set fire to it. Then I put the ashes in a dustpan and tried to forget all about it.

The following Monday, 8 October, I was walking on Foxwell Heath with Bella when I spotted Deeley again. He was in his tracksuit, heading towards Sinton Bank. He must have recognised me. Perhaps he guessed I'd destroyed his letter. Anyway, for no reason, he left the footpath he was following and ran towards me, hurling abuse at me like a madman. He hit me extremely hard on the face, causing the dog to bark.

I was scared for my life, so although I'm not a man of violence, I knew I had to defend myself. I struck him on the head. I suppose it was just a lucky blow. He fell backwards and struck his head on a tree branch.

He was completely dazed for a moment, and I became worried that I might be accused of causing him serious harm, so I tried to help him up. Then he must have noticed the site of an old campfire a few metres away. He staggered to his feet, grabbed some kind of cooking utensil and charged at me with it. Again, I had no choice but to defend myself. We wrestled on the ground and somehow he managed to stab himself with it.

I didn't know what to do. I realised almost at once he was dying. I knew I was in serious trouble. Although I'd acted properly in trying to deal with a man who seemed out of control, I knew it would be hard for people like you to believe me. So, when he was no longer breathing, I hid the body in the bracken and tried to pretend the fight between us had never happened.

Of course, when the two ladies arrived on the scene, I had to act as though I'd no knowledge of the body and together we reported its discovery to the police. That's the end of my statement.

Roscoe leaned back on his seat. 'Thank you for giving us such a lengthy statement. However, I, for one, don't believe much of it.'

'It's extremely hard to believe that the doctor fell onto the carving fork,' said Sunita. 'The pathologist told us it would have been impossible for him to stab himself with the fork and said it must have been thrust into the doctor's chest with great force. I also have to tell you that our senior forensic officer is testing the microscopic traces of blood found on the shoes and trousers you were seen wearing on the heath. She is confident it will turn out to be Dr Deeley's blood. I can believe some of what you told us

– details of the letter, for example. But most of your account appears to be a pack of lies.'

Roscoe nodded. 'I agree. There's no evidence of cuts and bruises on the doctor's hands. So the possibility that he put up a fight is extremely unlikely. I'm now going to formally charge you with murder and you're going to be appearing before the magistrates in the morning. I believe that your statement, when it's finally put before a jury, will be torn to shreds by the prosecution.'

Chapter 51

Tadeusz Filipowki stepped down from the train clutching his blue suitcase just before midday on Thursday. Then he walked slowly along the platform towards the barrier, glancing over his shoulder from time to time.

He now wished he'd heeded Tyrone Blake's advice and taken the first plane out of Britain three weeks ago.

Instead, he'd spent his time sofa-surfing, staying with friends as he tried to continue running his various operations. Then he had gone on his business trip to Manchester. All the while, he knew the police were looking for him and might confront him at any time.

A public announcement about suspicious packages – inconsequential as far as he was concerned – blared out from a nearby loudspeaker as he approached the concourse at Birmingham's New Street Station.

He made his way up the escalator to the bustling Grand Central shopping centre above, with its iconic atrium roof. It housed around sixty outlets – mainly fashion and homeware shops, restaurants, and cafes.

Every time he noticed a CCTV camera, he wondered if his face was being scrutinised. His friend in the police had warned him all ports and airports had been issued with his photograph and description.

He had noticed two officers in uniform wandering through crowds earlier on. He'd twice heard a siren – possibly a police siren.

Now perspiring profusely, he craved a cold drink. After a few minutes, he found a cafe which was not too crowded and approached the serving area. A young, fair-haired male assistant's eyes peered at him across the glass counter.

'Just a fizzy drink – cola's fine,' said Filipowski, as he wiped his brow with a handkerchief.

The assistant was doing it again – staring at him, thought Filipowski as he paid and his change was placed on the counter. He had to stop himself from giving the impudent man a mouthful of abuse.

He felt like saying, if he kept gawping, someone would put their fist in his mouth. But he decided against it. He had to keep a low profile.

He snatched his change, stomped off to a table in the corner and sat down, sipping from his glass while the man began chatting on his mobile.

During the next forty-five minutes, Filipowski occasionally cast his eyes towards the barista, who was now flitting about, making coffees and filling baguettes.

Suddenly Filipowski felt a strong hand grip his shoulder. He spun round. A detective in a brown jacket and blue jeans was standing beside him, displaying a warrant card. Three burly uniformed police colleagues were standing a few metres away on the public walkway.

'DC Khalid, Heart of England CID,' announced the young detective. 'The game's up, mate. You'd best come quietly.'

'What am I meant to have done?'

'There's a long list, but right now you're being arrested on suspicion of conspiracy to commit damage to a house in Sedgeworth,' said Khalid. He recited the police caution.

Filipowski didn't react for a moment. He simply glanced towards the cafe counter, where the assistant who'd served him was grinning in his direction. It was then that he knew for certain. The bastard had tipped off the cops.

At first, he gave the impression he would cooperate with the detective constable, rising from his seat, grabbing his case and mumbling, 'OK.'

Then, as Khalid stepped back to allow him room, he took to his heels and sprinted out of the cafe.

* * *

Khalid beckoned to his police colleagues, and they raced after the businessman as he wove his way through the crowds towards the escalators.

The constable didn't believe he would get far. The mall was bustling with shoppers, which made it hard for someone to run. On the other hand, a fugitive could get lost in a crowd, Khalid realised.

He remembered exactly what Filipowski looked like. He was tall and slim with closely cropped dark hair. He was wearing a short, dark coat and grey trousers and clutching a small blue suitcase.

Filipowski rushed down the escalator and headed across the station concourse. Then he raced out of the building like a fox with its tail on fire.

After fleeing through the glass doors of the Hill Street exit, he collided with a male shopper, knocking him to the ground, before manoeuvring his way down the wide steps.

As the stranger hurled abuse at him, he kept running, aware his pursuers were gaining on him slightly. The incident with the shopper had given Khalid a chance to gain ground.

The detective watched as Filipowski turned left into Station Street, passing two Chinese restaurants, a snooker club, and the Electric Cinema, before turning right into

Dudley Street and passing under the bridge beneath Queensway.

Khalid was much physically fitter and younger than his colleagues. They were now slipping behind. Catching the boss of 101 Crew would from now on be his responsibility.

The fugitive turned left again into the mainly pedestrianised Edgbaston Street, passing the old Debenhams building, until he reached Moat Lane. He bolted across the busy street – dashing in front of a bus – and glanced over his shoulder. Khalid was closer. He was waiting for a break in the traffic.

One moment he saw the businessman outside the Old Bull pub at the junction of Digbeth and Moat Lane, the next moment he'd vanished.

'Must have gone into the bloody pub,' he muttered.

Khalid darted across the street and entered the traditional-style pub, which seemed dark inside despite a profusion of windows. Filipowski was nowhere to be seen.

He tapped on the shoulder of a man in glasses sitting at the bar.

'Excuse me, mate,' he said, breathless after his half-mile run. 'Seen a guy with a blue case?'

'No, sorry, mate,' the customer replied, apparently annoyed to have been disturbed while drinking his pint.

Khalid took out his warrant card and waved it towards the blonde barmaid. 'Excuse me,' he said. 'Man with a blue case?'

'I think he might be in the gents,' she said. 'It's just round the corner.'

'Thanks,' he mumbled and made his way past the tables of midday drinkers until he reached the end of the bar counter.

The men's toilets seemed empty as Khalid stepped inside. No one was standing at the urinals. One of the cubicles was in use.

'Come on. I know you're in there,' he yelled, banging on the door. Then, to his embarrassment, a young man just a few years older than himself emerged.

'What's up, mate?' asked the bewildered stranger.

'Sorry. I thought you were someone else,' said Khalid as he hurried into the bar and then ran back into the street. By then, his three colleagues had turned up.

'You've lost him, yeah?' asked one of the officers.

'He can't be far away,' Khalid insisted. 'Let's split up. I'm sure it was him I saw going into the pub just a minute ago.'

As he glanced around, Khalid noticed a few metres of Moat Lane had been coned off for some roadworks. A light-blue portable container unit was in the centre of the sectioned-off area on the far side of the street with workmen's signs lying beside it.

At that moment, he observed a head with short dark hair peering round the side of it.

'Come on, lads,' he shouted, springing down the street as the pursuit entered a fresh stage.

Filipowski, now panting and perspiring heavily, set off as though a pack of hounds was on his tail. But he was flagging now.

Khalid had played rugby until he was twenty-three and he often trained at the gym. He had also been a cross-country finalist for Warwickshire three years in a row. He eventually caught up with Filipowski, grabbing the back of his coat and stopping him in his tracks.

The man struck Khalid on the jaw and struggled to get away, but it was no use and after a minute conceded himself to his fate. His short-lived bid for freedom had come to an end.

The detective's colleagues caught up with them. Filipowski was handcuffed and led away.

Khalid punched the air with delight. Then he phoned the control room at St James Street to advise them the wanted man had finally been caught.

Chapter 52

Four hours later, Filipowski found himself in the same ground-floor interview room in which Howard Cooper had been questioned the day before.

The agitated man stared out of the barred window. He seemed unable to believe the bad luck that had befallen him.

Sitting beside him was his solicitor friend, Salman Siddiqui, a short, corpulent man who had already advised him to say as little as possible in response to questions.

Within a few minutes, the chief inspector and DC Khalid arrived and, after Khalid had switched on the video recording equipment, the pair settled into chairs across the table. Khalid had a cardboard box with him containing an evidence bag.

'You've been arrested for possession of cocaine and conspiracy to commit criminal damage,' Roscoe told him. 'Do you understand?'

'I understand,' mumbled Filipowski.

'Chief Inspector, I was under the impression the charges might relate to a different matter,' said Mr Siddiqui. 'Could you explain a little?'

'Yes, of course,' Roscoe replied. 'There are other extremely serious matters police would like to explore with your client, but those matters are currently being handled by a different team, who are based in Summerstoke. So I'm afraid, after we've done with Mr Filipowski, he'll face further questioning.'

Mr Siddiqui whispered a few words in Filipowski's ear. The client nodded.

'Very well,' said Mr Siddiqui, 'if that's how it's got to be. It's all very unfortunate because my client is an honest businessman, trying to run his various activities and he tells me he has faced constant harassment from police since he first came to this country.'

Roscoe sneered. 'Perhaps if he restricted his activities to legitimate businesses and followed the laws of the land, he wouldn't attract the attention of the police as much as he does.'

'That is an outrageous slur,' said the solicitor. 'My client has at all times happily obeyed the law.'

Roscoe shrugged. 'All right, we'll say no more about that for the moment. Well, Mr Filipowski, as you know, police have been searching for you after raiding your house in Coventry. You left in rather a hurry in the middle of last month.'

He noticed for the first time how Filipowski had dry, reddish skin on his face and hands – no doubt caused by the hot tea Vickers had splashed over him while fleeing the gangster's gun.

'I had urgent business affairs to see to,' the suspect announced tersely.

'All right,' said Roscoe. 'Let's turn to Saturday, 17 November. This was the day a family's home was firebombed in a street in Sedgeworth. Where were you that afternoon?'

'Staying with a friend,' he declared, staring directly into the chief inspector's eyes.

'What's the name of this friend?'

'No comment.'

'Are you familiar with Albion Road?'

Filipowski shook his head.

'Do you remember meeting my colleague, DI Vickers, in that same town on 13 November?"

'No.'

'He has a clear recollection of meeting you in Sedgeworth four days before the arson attack and he has a recording of you asking about a resident in that very street, Albion Road,' he said.

'No comment,' said Filipowski.

'As you are no doubt aware, on that Saturday afternoon, a couple and their two young children were forced to run for their lives out of their living room as a petrol bomb hurtled through their front window and started an inferno.'

Filipowski sneered. 'Nothing to do with me.'

'Do you know a man called Tyrone Blake?'

The suspect glanced at his solicitor. Then he replied, 'He works for me.'

'Do you know where we can find him?'

'No comment.'

'A car being driven by him was seen on CCTV in the vicinity at the time of this criminal damage.'

Filipowski shrugged. 'Like I say, it was nothing to do with me.'

'Now DC Khalid arrested you at half past twelve today near to New Street Station. While searching your case, he discovered some cocaine, and I want to ask you about this.'

Khalid removed some small transparent bags containing white powder from his box and placed them on the table in front of the chief inspector.

'We found eighteen bags of the class A drug with a street value of nine hundred pounds,' Roscoe remarked. 'You realise it's an extremely serious offence to be in possession of cocaine, don't you? You've been in prison over it before, haven't you?'

Filipowski again glanced at Mr Siddiqui before saying in a low voice, 'No comment.'

'How do you account for it being there?'

'No comment.'

'This is your opportunity to give your explanation of how it got into your case?'

'No comment.'

'All right,' said Roscoe, as he stood up and stopped the recording. 'I think that's as far as I want to go this afternoon.'

The solicitor interrupted to say, 'Chief Inspector, may I ask if you plan to charge my client with any offence or release him today?'

The chief inspector nodded. 'As I mentioned just now, colleagues from Summerstoke Police are waiting to see Mr Filipowski in a few minutes. So he will be placed back in his cell to await questioning by them. I'm afraid, in view of the serious nature of the various offences involved, it's extremely unlikely he will be granted bail.'

* * *

Tom Vickers was sitting in a wheelchair flanked by two nurses as the chief inspector drew up outside University Hospital on Friday, 7 December. Vickers had a broad smile on his face as the DCI jumped out and went round to open the passenger door for his friend and colleague.

'Sorry to have to drag you away from your fan club,' he joked as he smiled at the two women and helped the inspector into the passenger seat.

Vickers ignored him. 'Thanks so much for all your kindness,' he told the pair. 'Don't forget to share the chocolates with the night staff.'

'Why should they get a look-in?' said one with a laugh.

Then, as the inspector waved to the pair, Roscoe's car swept out of the hospital car park.

'All the staff have been fantastic,' Vickers explained

'You have the look of a man who was reluctant to leave.'

'Oh, they were great, but I've been so bored. I can't wait to get home. I was half-hoping to see the sergeant.'

'She asked me to pass on her best wishes. But she's tied up at the office.'

'Why doesn't that surprise me?' he grumbled.

'Yesterday afternoon I was having a chat with Tadeusz Filipowski, the guy you doused in tea,' Roscoe remarked.

'Bloody hell, guv,' said Vickers with a sharp intake of breath. 'How did that happen?'

'We got a tip-off he was at New Street Station. Omar was in the area. He liaised with the transport police and arrested him.'

'Did he put up much of a fight?'

'Bit of a chase, but Omar was too quick for him. Of course, back at St James Street, we couldn't ask him much about what happened in Sidney Road because that's Bains' investigation. He denied all knowledge of the firebombing.'

Vickers shrugged. 'He would do, guv. God, I'm so glad he's been caught. No news about Blake?'

'Looks like he's abroad,' said Roscoe. 'Norris won't let us send anyone after him for budgetary reasons.'

'As soon as I'm fit again, I'll throw myself back into the Sepulchre investigation,' Vickers said.

'Anyway,' said Roscoe, 'did you know that, on Wednesday, we also made an arrest in the Deeley case?'

'Yes, I saw something on the Midlands news last night. It just said someone was assisting.'

'Howard Cooper from Loman's Green.'

'Wasn't that the guy who found the body?'

'Yes. The doctor had a fling years ago with Cooper's wife and he was extremely upset when he discovered the doctor had moved back to the Midlands.'

'Good God. How did we find that out?'

'DS Roy. She's worked night and day on the case for weeks and her efforts finally paid off. Cooper feared for his marriage, so when he saw the doctor in the woods by chance, they got into a fight and the doctor got killed.'

'So it wasn't that guy Harper after all?' he said.

'No. He's in the clear,' Roscoe admitted. 'With some good teamwork, we caught the right guy.'

'It's all been happening while I've been flat on my back.'

'Being waited upon by those young ladies,' said the chief inspector with a smile.

'All I can say is, well done, Sunita,' Vickers said quietly.

Their car left Hinckley Road and they began travelling towards Birmingham on the M6 motorway.

Roscoe glanced across at his passenger. 'Tom, I must be honest – in your smart grey coat and blue jeans, you don't look like a man who's been on the wrong end of a gun.'

'Looks can be deceiving, guv. The doctors reckon I could probably go back to light duties in a month or so. But full recovery can take much longer. It's not just the visible injuries. The doctors say there's all my shock and anger to deal with – you know, the psychological effects.'

'You don't sound angry.'

'Sometimes, at night, I lie awake, unable to sleep. That's when my mind turns to the bastards who tried to blow me away, guv. The doctors have warned me I'll probably feel anxious, think about that afternoon in Sidney Road over and over, and become irritable from time to time.'

'It might be hard for us to notice any difference,' Roscoe mumbled to himself.

THE END

If you enjoyed this book, please let others know by leaving a quick review on Amazon. Also, if you spot anything untoward in the paperback, get in touch. We strive for the best quality and appreciate reader feedback.

editor@thebookfolks.com

www.thebookfolks.com

More fiction in this series

MURDER ON OXFORD LANE (Book 1)

A budding chorister doesn't return home from practice but his wife doesn't appear concerned. DS Sunita Roy becomes convinced he has been murdered but she has her own problems in the form of an ex-boyfriend who won't take no for an answer. Will she keep her eye on the ball when all expect her to fail?

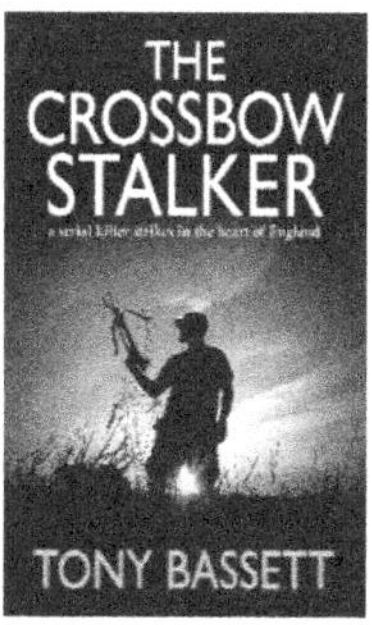

THE CROSSBOW STALKER (Book 2)

When a serial killer armed with a crossbow terrorises the West Midlands, Chief Inspector Gavin Roscoe suspects a motive of jealousy and revenge. But as the number of victims increases, the connection initially established between them wears thin. DS Sunita Roy has a different theory and resolves to pursue her own instincts, come what may.

OUT FOR REVENGE (Book 4)

There's a noticeable change of atmosphere in the city when a dangerous prisoner is released. He has plans to up his drugs business. But someone will quickly put an end to that. Detective Sunita Roy has the unenviable task of hunting down the gangsters who were likely responsible. But when the cops close in, they'll have an even bigger problem than they first imagined.

Other titles of interest

RISE TO THE FLY by Cheryl Rees-Price

When the bodies of a retired couple are found by a reservoir, the police are concerned to discover fishing flies have been impaled on their tongues. After they find nothing in the couple's past to indicate a reason for the murder, they begin to look local. What will they turn up in this dark and secluded corner of Wales?

GONE TO THE DOGS by Nicola Clifford

Reporter Stacey Logan is looking into the case of a missing teenager, but she can't help but put her nose into Detective Ben James' murder investigation. Tensions within the community reach fever pitch as events come to a head.

All FREE *with Kindle Unlimited and available in paperback.*

www.thebookfolks.com

Made in United States
Orlando, FL
06 August 2023

35812028R00168